The Last
Voyage of
Mrs Henry
Parker

Also by Joanna Nell

The Single Ladies of Jacaranda Retirement Village

The Last Voyage of Mrs Henry Parker

JOANNA NELL

HODDER &
STOUGHTON

First published in Australia and New Zealand in 2019
By Hachette Australia
An imprint of Hachette Australia Pty Ltd

First published in Great Britain in 2019 by Hodder & Stoughton
An Hachette UK company

1

A CIP catalogue record for this title is available from the British Library

Hardback ISBN 978 1 473 68588 8
Trade Paperback ISBN 978 1 473 68591 8
eBook ISBN 978 1 473 68592 5

Printed and bound in Great Britain by Clays Ltd, Elcograf S.p.A.

Hodder & Stoughton policy is to use papers that are natural, renewable
and recyclable products and made from wood grown in sustainable
forests. The logging and manufacturing processes are expected to
conform to the environmental regulations of the country of origin.

Hodder & Stoughton Ltd
Carmelite House
50 Victoria Embankment
London EC4Y 0DZ

www.hodder.co.uk

For Stretch

The sea, once it casts its spell, holds one in its net of wonder forever.

JACQUES-YVES COUSTEAU (1910–1997)

No one should be alone in their old age, he thought.

ERNEST HEMINGWAY, *THE OLD MAN AND THE SEA* (1952)

1

Tea, Biscuits and Toucans

She wasn't in bad shape for her age. Although her classic lines might be considered old-fashioned compared to the faster, newer vessels that adorned the glossy brochures, the old girl was indifferent. She floated imperiously at the dockside in her bright, white splendour, her years revealed only in the layers of flaking paint that could be counted like the annual rings of a mature tree, or in the rust leaching from the anchor box. There was an uncommon wisdom about her, an inner stillness, as though she was simply content to be.

The white-uniformed security officer greeted the passengers as they trailed miniature cases up the shallow incline of the gangway. Evelyn waited patiently behind a trio of little girls whose pink cases each bore a different cartoon character she didn't recognise. The girls fizzled with excitement, pointing to this and that. Like princesses crossing a drawbridge into a fairytale castle. Far below, a thin moat of dark green water divided ship from shore, and one world from another. For

Evelyn, the magic of embarking the ship at the beginning of every cruise never staled, each voyage unfolding with the anticipation of an empty page in a well-thumbed travel journal.

'Welcome home, Mrs Parker,' said the young security officer as Evelyn stepped aboard with her right foot. 'Six hundred and sixty-two cruises already.'

Evelyn smiled, squinting at his name badge. 'Thank you, Ruben.'

Six hundred and sixty-two voyages since she and Henry had stepped aboard the brand-new Sunset Cruises flagship. Six hundred and sixty-two cruises since a fading opera singer agreed to be godmother to the ship, naming her *Golden Sunset*, and releasing a bottle of champagne that made a ding in the fresh white paint at the prow. There was a framed photograph in the atrium marking the moment the champagne bottle exploded with good luck. The opera singer was long dead, but Evelyn remembered the day like it was yesterday, she with a new handbag over her arm and Henry in his finery, both seated in the VIP section at the naming ceremony. Ahead of them, their twilight years and a never-ending voyage in the lap of luxury.

Golden Sunset had plenty of life left in her, taking passengers away from their everydays and returning them seven or ten or twenty-one days later, fatter and happier. Her engines were sound, marking her progress in hours rather than miles, each turn of the prop like a heartbeat.

'Is Dr Henry Parker on board yet? I seem to have mislaid him,' said Evelyn. She was grateful that she had someone like Ruben. He was one of her special people, her not-for-worrying people. With Ruben to keep tally of her voyages, there was one less thing to worry about. But then some things were easier to keep track of. Husbands were a different matter.

She scanned the faces climbing the gangway behind her. None of them was Henry's.

'Don't you worry, ma'am,' said the security officer. 'I'm sure he will turn up.'

'Most troubling,' mumbled Evelyn.

Ruben looked anything but troubled. 'May I see your cruise card, please?'

Evelyn stiffened at what looked like a gun in his hand. A young couple stepped impatiently in front of her and handed over the blue and white plastic cards that hung from their necks on gaudy woven tapes bearing the Sunset Cruises logo. Many passengers wore them. They had a name. Lanterns? Halyards? *Lanyards*.

Evelyn reached into her handbag and fumbled for the familiar tangle attached to her own cruise card. Instead, she found the loose foil at one end of a packet of mints, and a wad of letters in sealed envelopes, secured by a rubber band. She thrust each item back down into the cavity of the bag, her rummaging eventually producing a white plastic card attached to a lantern-halyard-*lanyard*.

'Is all this rigmarole really necessary?' said Evelyn. 'I've only been ashore for a few hours.'

If the security officer knew her by name, knew exactly how many cruises she'd been aboard already, why did he need to repeat the whole tedious process every turnaround day? With a head of pure white hair, and a stoop as if she were permanently walking into an invisible wind, Evelyn was hardly terrorist material. She'd passed some shifty-looking types in the terminal building. But her feet hurt and she needed a cup of tea. Now wasn't the time to voice her suspicions.

The security officer shot Evelyn's card with his gun. By some technological magic, her image appeared on the television screen. The startled expression on the old lady's crumpled face was apparently sufficient likeness for her to be allowed back on board.

Evelyn knew that she and Henry, like the ship that was their home, were approaching the end of their lives. Yet the older she got, the less she worried about getting old. It was as inevitable as the weather, and just as unpredictable. Like the weather, it could be forecast but not controlled. Best to be prepared, Evelyn maintained, but go ahead with the picnic regardless. When it came to ageing, the best you could do was to carry an umbrella. And a life jacket.

Stepping over the threshold onto the ship with her right foot – always right foot first – Evelyn tripped, her toe catching on something she didn't see. Hands and arms appeared, reaching from all directions towards her like spokes on a bicycle wheel.

'Are you all right?'

'Steady now, Mrs Parker.'

'Shall I fetch a wheelchair?'

Irritated by the uninvited grasps, she shook off the ministrations. Crew members appeared from nowhere, crowding her with their hands and their uniforms. All nationalities, from every corner of the world, one big happy family. Her only family, apart from Henry, and yet Evelyn struggled to put a name to any of their faces. She imagined it was how the Queen must feel, meeting all these people and forgetting them again almost immediately. And like Her Majesty, Evelyn carried a handbag wherever she went, but never anything as vulgar as money. By some miracle, her finances took care of themselves. Or rather her solicitor, Dobbs, took care of things.

She had a feeling young Dobbs was more than a solicitor. He was another one of her people, but to her embarrassment, Evelyn couldn't recall his first name. It began with H. Horace? Humphrey? He showed her where to sign her name on forms and had a wonderful biscuit selection. Heath? Herbert? Harvey? It would come to her.

Tripping had taken her by surprise. She was normally so good on her feet, for a woman of her age, attributing her steadiness to a lifetime of counteracting the perpetual movements of the ocean. A human gimbal.

'That's enough,' said Evelyn, brushing away any lingering assistance as if she were removing lint from her sleeves. She pulled the monogrammed handkerchief from beneath the elasticated wristband of her watch and sniffed into it. The air conditioning always made her nose drip.

The cool atrium was an oasis after the humidity and chaos of the terminal building and the city beyond. The tasteful lighting and sanitised luxury of the interior was always welcome after a busy day ashore, and Evelyn breathed a sigh of relief when she reached the quiet comfort of her cabin. Inside, the bed was neatly made and the floors still wore the tramlines of the vacuum cleaner. Through the closed balcony windows she could still see the tops of the cranes, like freakish rides in a dockside theme park.

When Evelyn placed her handbag on the bed, it tilted and lost its balance, spilling the bundle of unopened letters out onto the pale blue bedspread. Unlike the standard company issue, the bed covering had been Evelyn's choice, and it had been perfectly to her taste, right up until Sunset Cruises changed all the floor coverings during the last refit. Wanting the cabin to feel like home rather than a hotel, she'd insisted on keeping it. The new gold and burgundy carpet now clashed horribly with the bed.

Evelyn removed the rubber band from the bundle and balanced the letters on top of the already teetering pile on the dressing-table-desk. As one of her not-for-worrying people, she trusted young Dobbs would take care of anything important. These were most likely circulars or advertising material. Several were from the Dreadnought Home for Retired Seafarers, who sent her endless brochures and information. She'd stopped opening them. Neither she nor Henry had the slightest intention of ending up in an aged care facility.

There was a parcel on the dressing-table-desk. It was wrapped in brown paper and addressed to *Mrs Henry Parker, Passenger on MV Golden Sunset*. She couldn't think what it could be or who might have sent it. It wasn't her birthday yet. *Was it?*

Flopping into the armchair, Evelyn unwrapped the parcel on her lap. She released the edges of the brown paper with a bony finger to reveal a white shoebox. It wasn't a brand she recognised, and on removing the lid, Evelyn assumed the shoes must belong to someone else. She baulked at the sight of the ugly lace-ups. They were made from white canvas fabric with a flat rubber sole. The kind people wore when they were in a hurry.

'Good heavens,' she said out loud, examining one of the pair at close quarters.

She'd often eyed other women in similar shoes, searching their faces for the same agonising pinch that she experienced with each step. But they all looked as if their minds were anywhere but on what was happening at the end of their legs.

Kicking off her signature navy court shoes, Evelyn circled her ankles and splayed her toes in an effort to revive the squashed digits. They were good feet for her age apparently, the girl in the spa complimenting her impressive arches as she filed her toenails. The spa girls weren't very good with hard skin as a rule, but this particular one had been exceptionally diligent with her paring-back tools, and Evelyn had graciously accepted the compliment on her taut metatarsals, rewarding her with a mint.

Evelyn untangled the laces and slipped her right foot into the corresponding shoe. To her surprise, it fit. She did the same with the left foot and tied the laces. Like Cinderella, although she was more suitably shod for a gymnasium than a ball. For the first time in who knew how long, Evelyn's feet didn't hurt. She'd been suffering the most terrible discomfort in her soles of late. A prickling, burning numbness that made it impossible to feel the ground. She hadn't mentioned it to Henry, in case he started to worry, but she was sure it was the beginning of something. It had a name. Two words. Several syllables. Medical charades. What was the name of the condition? It would come to her.

Evelyn hooked a small footstool with one big toe and pulled it towards her, admiring her new feet. They were just the thing for her daily laps of the boat deck. Four times around was a mile. She had no idea where they'd come from, but Evelyn couldn't wait to show Henry her new walk-a-mile shoes.

With her feet taken care of, Evelyn decided there was just time before the muster drill to fit in her daily brain training. It was as important to exercise one's mind as one's body, she always maintained. And while ever she could recite her poetry, she could rest assured she wasn't going ga-ga. Half-a-dozen verses were usually enough before her brain needed a lie-down.

Evelyn yawned, a fog of weariness descending, bringing her old friend Samuel Taylor Coleridge and the irresistible urge to rest her eyes.

There passed a weary time. Each throat
Was parched, and glazed each eye.
A weary time! a weary time!
How glazed each weary eye,

Some days were more challenging than others, not least turnaround day – which in itself was the cognitive equivalent of conquering Mount Everest. Luckily she had her trusty chauffeur who, like a Sherpa, knew the way, navigating effortlessly to Dobbs's office in the city and chatting about everything from his family to his childhood. He was friendly, whatever his name was, bordering on overfamiliar, but they always arrived on time, and more importantly, he always delivered her back to the ship before it sailed.

Today the chauffeur had hovered whilst Dobbs discussed her circumstances. There'd been a pot of tea – strong as she preferred it – and a shortbread finger. She'd lost the thread of what he was saying when her hearing aid died. Miraculously, the chauffeur had spare batteries at the ready but by the time she'd caught up, Dobbs had moved on. The incomprehensible legal speak washed over her. For some reason, all she remembered were his socks. They were covered with toucans. Which was odd. Dobbs had never struck her as the toucan type.

2

On the Tip of Her Tongue

SHE WOKE TO A TINNY ANNOUNCEMENT JUST AS SHE HAD begun to nod off in the chair. It took Evelyn a moment to get her bearings and work out what was going on. It was the captain, whose name was on the tip of her tongue. By the time her brain had tuned in, he was already warning the passengers – and probably half the city given that the PA broadcast on the outside decks too – to prepare for the compulsory muster drill.

Evelyn sank further into her chair, disinclined to leave it for something as trivial as a compulsory safety drill.

She'd heard the whole tedious thing enough times she could recite it word for word. If the circumstances required. That's what came of being blessed with a rather superior memory: the ability to remember verbatim things of little consequence. Things like safety briefings along with more important matters such as the details of obscure seafaring legends and traditions, nineteenth-century poetry or, her particular favourite, entire passages of Florence Nightingale's pioneering book, *Notes on*

Nursing. Such things were handy to have at her fingertips, in the right situation.

She wondered if her cabin steward Virgilio might turn a blind eye if she eschewed the compulsory drill in favour of a nice cup of tea. Tea or no tea, however, she wouldn't go until Henry returned. It was something they always did together. In the unlikely event that the ship sank, she imagined the two of them, side by side, helping each other on with their life jackets. Her husband was usually so big on safety, and yet today he was showing scant regard both for safety and the itinerary. Once the drill was over, *Golden Sunset* would depart almost straight away. And still there was no sign of Henry.

Expecting to find either her tardy husband, or Virgilio with a tea tray, Evelyn hauled herself out of the armchair to answer a knock on her door. It was neither. Instead of Henry or refreshments, she found a stairway guide wearing a fluorescent yellow hat and matching life jacket. Without so much as a by-your-leave, he instructed her to proceed immediately to her muster station.

Muttering, Evelyn went in search of her life jacket. It shouldn't be hard to find – bright orange and the size of a double mattress. She scanned the cabin, her brain failing to register an obvious life-preserving device of any colour. It didn't bode well. This was different to losing her key or magnifying glass. If the ship was drowning, there was no time to try to visualise the last time she used it or implement any of her other handy remembering techniques.

Every horizontal surface in the cramped cabin was crowded with books and framed photographs, piles of papers and unopened envelopes, plus the trinkets and souvenirs she'd collected from their travels. There was no sign of her life jacket.

Leaning precariously past her centre of gravity to look under the bed, she found nothing but more of the hideous carpet that clashed with the bedspread.

Having searched the main cabin, she stuck her head into the tiny bathroom. Admittedly it was an unlikely storage place, given there was barely room to comb her thinning hair without bruising her elbows. Her eye registered the clinical white surfaces, finding nothing but her usual pot of cold cream beside the sink, a tiny bottle of complimentary shampoo and a new soap still wrapped in paper. Virgilio's trademark towel monkey dangled from the shower rose, and Henry's razor, a few grey bristles trapped between the blades, was resting on the mirrored shelf above the sink, waiting patiently for his next shave. Beside it was his precious aftershave bottle. Henry had a particular favourite, Acqua di Parma – her father's too as it happened – and the tiny bathroom in the cabin was always filled with the citrus, spice, wood and leather of his little extravagance.

Only the wardrobe was left. Evelyn was running out of options. To her relief, on the shelf above the clothes rail were two identical life jackets lying side by side like a canoodling couple. She made a mental note to remember their hiding place, in the event of an emergency. Or to allow more time for tea before the next muster drill.

Evelyn's fingers reached the black webbing straps and she prised the life jackets from their cosy embrace between an old cardboard box and the bulkhead. She couldn't think what was in the box, or why it was taking up valuable room in their cramped closet. With space at such a premium, they'd whittled down their belongings to essentials when they moved on board. The cabin was overdue for a sort-out, but there was no time now. The drill was about to begin and Henry was cutting it very fine.

She was used to him being late, either busy with his patients or, since he'd retired, equally pressing business such as a visit to his favourite bookshop in the city when the ship docked on turnaround day. Evelyn wished Henry had come to see Dobbs, today of all days. She'd left with a sense of deep unease and the feeling that life was about to change.

Evelyn tried not to be irritated. She was worried about Henry. He hadn't been himself recently, wandering off without her. Secretly, Evelyn feared he was going if not fully ga-ga, then at least ga. Not a surprise at his age, but a man of Henry's intellect could potentially hide his dwindling faculties until his decline was quite advanced, especially in familiar surroundings. She had made the decision to simply go along with it rather than challenge him. She didn't want to hurt his feelings. Humour him and maintain a strict routine. After so many years together, Evelyn knew how to handle her husband. And that included taking his life jacket along to the drill in preparation for his usual last-minute arrival.

She paused at the door, a life jacket wedged in each armpit, reaching for her handbag. Peeking inside to make sure she had her mints, she slipped the handle over her wrist and studied the diagram on the back of the cabin door.

Your muster station is Lifeboat 10.

There was a helpful red dot to indicate the position of her cabin and a green arrow demonstrating the quickest route to her gathering-in-an-emergency place.

Evelyn stepped out into the alleyway and straight into a stampede of passengers, each carrying an identical orange life jacket. Swept along by the press of bodies, Evelyn had to half jog to keep up. To her surprise she found the ground unusually springy beneath her new rubber-soled feet. At the stairwell, however, she had to hold the chrome handrail to descend the single flight following the green floor lights that illuminated the route like a runway. It was tricky with the two life jackets, a handbag and all those people, but she managed to avoid the indignity of a stumble or, worse, well-meaning strangers.

The crowd spilled out onto the open deck where more smiling yellow-hatted people directed the human traffic into efficient rows. It was hot on the west side of the ship, the humidity only intensifying the smell of diesel and fresh paint. Evelyn blinked in the sun and took refuge in the shade of a V-shaped man near the end of the back row. Passengers of every shape and size filled the deck in orderly lines.

At the beginning of each cruise, Evelyn liked to appraise the new arrivals, their fashions and habits, and to eavesdrop on their conversations. They were after all, apart from her visits to Dobbs in his office, her only link to the outside world. Long ago she'd given up reading shore-side newspapers or watching the endless loop of terrible happenings on the news channel of the ship's TV. Instead, everything she needed to know was written in the ship's newsletter, delivered under her cabin door each day by her steward.

Evelyn dropped her handbag and both life jackets onto the deck and tried to remove her light woollen cardigan to relieve her prickling skin. Her heart fluttered for a few beats before finding its rhythm again. She swooned in the heat and only just managed to stay upright, but not before she had elbowed a lady beside her in the cramped space.

Evelyn mumbled an apology and shook off several offers to summon medical assistance.

'I'm perfectly fine, thank you,' she said. 'Besides, I am a nurse and my husband is a doctor.'

This seemed to appease the onlookers, who turned their attention back to the life-jacket-donning demonstration. Naturally Evelyn could do this with her eyes closed, should the need ever arise. But today for some reason she found herself trussed up in an embarrassing tangle of straps. Had they changed the whole not-for-drowning jacket design since last time?

Nearby, a grey-haired couple were trying to wrangle the three princesses who'd been behind her on the gangway. She smiled. She loved children. As long as they behaved.

Evelyn startled at a shrill sound. She turned to see one of the youngsters blowing into the orange plastic whistle dangling from her not-for-drowning jacket. When a meaningful stare didn't work, Evelyn spoke up. For the sake of her fellow hearing-aid wearers.

'You should never whistle on a ship, my dear,' said Evelyn. She saw the little girl's face drop.

'Why not?' said the little girl warily.

Evelyn softened her voice. 'It's bad luck.'

'Who says?'

'It's an old seafaring superstition.'

'Why?'

Evelyn's patience was beginning to ebb. It was most frustrating. She was usually so good with children. 'Well, it is said that whistling annoys Saint Anthony, the patron saint of wind. He might send us the wrong kind of wind. We don't want a storm, do we?'

The little girl narrowed her eyes at Evelyn. 'I'm not scared,' she said. 'I like thunderstorms.'

Evelyn changed tack. 'Germs then. That whistle is covered in germs. Nasty little things, bugs.'

'But I like bugs too.' The girl jutted one hip. Evelyn did the same. 'Spiders are my favourite.'

Once upon a time, children had been seen and not heard. Nowadays, they were far more obvious. Quite impossible to ignore, in fact. 'I'm talking about the kind of bugs that can make you sick. Very sick.' Evelyn wagged a finger to indicate just how sick. She considered herself something of an authority on the subject, having come top in hygiene. Admittedly that was in 1950, but the world was still a filthy place. 'The human mouth contains billions of bacteria. *Streptococcus, staphylococcus.* Not to mention the anaerobes like *Bacteroides.* Don't they teach you anything at kindergarten?'

'I know "The Wheels on the Bus",' said the girl.

This was a ship, not a bus, thought Evelyn. Honestly, no wonder children were so ignorant nowadays. Someone had to prepare the younger generation for the real world, and it might as well be her. She cleared her throat and began. '*The causes of the enormous child mortality are perfectly well known; they are chiefly want of cleanliness, want of ventilation, want of whitewashing; in one word, defective household hygiene.*' She wondered if Florence Nightingale had had a similar affinity with children. Evelyn waited for the girl to process the information. Holiday or no holiday, she wanted to add, there would be a test at the end.

The girl was thinking, running her tongue around the inside of her cheeks. 'I don't understand,' she said, 'if there are billions of bugs that can make me sick already living in my mouth . . . then how come I'm not sick?'

She might be a little slow on the uptake, but she had a point. Evelyn could have talked about commensals and how the bacteria were simply hitching a ride, living side by side in harmony with their human host. As long as nothing upset the delicate balance between them, no harm would come to either. Instead, she smiled, defeated by the child's irrefutable logic. With his hankering for a good philosophical debate, Henry would like her. Evelyn couldn't wait to introduce him to the insightful little girl who liked spiders and thunderstorms.

Henry.

Now, where was that husband of hers?

3

Port Out, Starboard Home

EVELYN WOKE TO THE GENTLE CREAK OF THE BULKHEADS AS if the ship was stretching and cracking her joints. Not usually one for an afternoon nap, Evelyn was annoyed that she'd dropped off. She felt unusually refreshed, however, and swinging her legs off the bed she was relieved to see her feet looking more feet-like again.

It was still light. She opened the balcony door a fraction and listened, straining to hear the pop of champagne corks and the band playing their jaunty sail-away set on the deck above. But there was only the sound of the water breaking against the ship's hull. No Rod Stewart. No Bobby Darin.

Gone was the giant Meccano skyline, the smell of paint and exhaust fumes. The ship was way out at sea, not a dot of land on the vast horizon. The cerulean-blue sky almost hurt her eyes. Breezes and currents marbled the waveless ocean.

According to the illuminated numbers on the bedside clock, it was past eight. The sunset was curiously late today. Evelyn checked her watch. It was a useless thing; the tiny numbers on the dial had shrunk over the years and were now as good as invisible. It had worked perfectly when Henry had presented it as a wedding present. Back when her eyeballs were the right shape. She still wore it every day, although more as a device for anchoring her handkerchief than for telling the time.

Henry must have been and gone again while she was napping. How thoughtful of him, leaving her to enjoy a siesta when he could so easily have joined her. But her husband was nothing if not a considerate man. He always sought permission before disappearing into his own thoughts in case she assumed he was ignoring her. In fact, Henry was inclined to spend so much time inside his head, it was as though his body was redundant, merely a vessel to transport and nourish his colossal brain. Perhaps that's where he was now, tucked away in some quiet corner, contemplating. He would come back eventually, when he was bored with his thoughts.

Ten past eight now, and neither of them ready. It was one thing to make a fashionably late entrance to dinner, and quite another to miss the entrée entirely. She would have to say something. Ships weren't like restaurants where diners could turn up at their leisure and have their meals cooked to order. This was catering on a grand scale, and though each meal was delicious, there were hundreds of steaks grilling at any one time, a thousand soufflés rising side by side.

There was nothing for it but to choose her own outfit and hope that Henry was already dressed and ready for dinner. Without her husband on hand, she would have to fall back once again on Virgilio's styling advice. As luck would have it, the young steward had demonstrated quite an eye when it came to selecting a suitable dress for dinner. He'd been blessed with a certain knack for accessories too, she'd discovered, his talents clearly wasted in making beds and folding towels into animals. Evelyn had found him wearing her pearls once, admiring himself in the long mirror on the wardrobe door when she'd returned to her cabin unexpectedly. They'd had an agreement ever since.

Irritated to be kept waiting, Evelyn surveyed the rack of dresses in the tiny closet. With such limited hanging space, it was a case of quality over quantity, each piece carefully curated for a life spent aboard a luxurious ship. Every decade a different neckline, waistline or hemline; a museum of fashion eras, each chronicled in the various framed photographs dotted around the cabin.

There was more space between the wooden coat hangers than usual, drawing Evelyn's eye to Henry's side of the wardrobe. He must have had a clear-out while she was visiting Dobbs. The only items still hanging were his old mess jacket yellowing in the corner, a couple of shirts, and his favourite dark woollen bridge coat from Miller Rayner in Oxford Street. He'd invested in the coat early in his career. It was an expensive item, even back then, but the dense weave had kept out the chilliest of Arctic and Antarctic winds.

With time running out, Evelyn settled on a floor-length satin gown in gunmetal grey. She'd had it custom made in Hong Kong on her first world cruise. She remembered it well, the brown paper package bearing the finished dress already waiting for her when the ship docked in Singapore. Nowadays it didn't fit quite as well as it had then, the fabric billowing in the bodice as she struggled to fasten the zip at the back. On seeing her reflection in the long mirror on the inside of the bathroom door, however, she still considered it a good colour against her pale skin. If anything, with her head of white hair, it now suited her even better than it had when she'd been a youthful mousy brown.

Next Evelyn selected a pair of silver shoes from the bottom shelf of the wardrobe. To her surprise, they were too small for her feet. Perhaps they'd shrunk in the sea air. She looked around for an alternative. Tucked away at the back of the shelf was a pair of white towelling slippers bearing the company logo. Fine if she was off for her weekly callus filing, but not really suitable for formal night. Her frustrated gaze came to rest on the mysterious flat white shoes with laces. They were the kind worn by sweaty people. Uncouth individuals who puffed and panted and made loud running noises with their feet. The shoes might be comfortable enough to run in, but at her age Evelyn preferred the security of at least one foot in contact with the ground at any given moment.

With no time to waste, she squashed her cottonwool feet into the not-for-running shoes and pulled her evening gloves over her veiny wrists until they hung like loose washing at her elbows. She delved into her jewellery box and vowed to wear the first item that came to hand. Her mother's tiara. Adjusting it on her head, she fetched her handbag and headed for the door.

The alleyway was remarkably quiet and there was no sign of Virgilio in the pantry. Usually at this time of night the stewards were busy turning down beds, and the public areas crammed with passengers heading for the second sitting of dinner. Evelyn's relief at finding an empty elevator was sprinkled with apprehension. She must be very, very late.

Inside the elevator, she noticed a clear Perspex box containing a stack of pocket-sized maps of the ship. It was a new thing. The front desk must be getting fed up with giving directions every cruise. Not that she really needed a map, having success-fully navigated her way around the ship since the day it was launched. Evelyn took one anyway and slipped it into her handbag. It might come in handy, and with so many hidden extras nowadays, it was unusual to find the company giving anything away for free.

At deck eight, the doors opened. Far from the last passenger to arrive, to her great surprise Evelyn found herself in a bottle-neck outside the restaurant. It was not unusual for the first night of the cruise when the new passengers waited to be shown to their allotted tables. Naturally, when the maître d' Olivier – her not-for-starving person – spotted her, he would wave her straight through to where Henry was no doubt waiting impatiently. For all the times he'd been late, she knew he was never at his best when that colossal brain of his needed feeding.

The dining room was currently decorated in the Art Deco style. It was a definite step up from the previous Romanesque era but she still had fond memories of the trompe l'oeil frescos of the Rococo period. Adjacent to the largest picture window on the starboard side, with an uninterrupted view of the ocean, their chosen table had been the one constant over the architectural centuries.

'Port out, starboard home,' Henry had tried to explain when she'd asked why, when they'd first boarded the ship years ago, they'd changed tables depending on the direction the ship was sailing: port heading north, starboard heading south.

'What are you on about?' Evelyn had replied, mildly irrit-ated that their supposedly relaxing retirement was proving so complicated.

'POSH.'

'POSH?'

'When the old P&O steamships sailed to India, the upper classes used to request a cabin on the port side of the ship on the way out, and the starboard side on the journey home, to avoid the harsh sun that would tan their delicate pale skins. It was a sign of importance to have a ticket stamped with "POSH".'

Naturally, she'd heard him tell this story numerous times. He was barely into old age and already getting repetitive.

'It's not even true,' she'd reminded him. 'Don't you remember me telling you about that naval historian who'd researched it for a book? He couldn't find any evidence whatsoever. It's a myth, Henry.'

She'd watched his face crumple like a small boy's. He was only trying to be romantic, to eat dinner at a west-facing table every night. In the end, it had become exhausting, not least for the poor maître d'.

'What's the point of living aboard a ship if you can't watch the sun set over the horizon every night?' Henry had said. 'I just wanted it to be perfect.'

'It's already perfect, Henry. At least fifty percent of the time. The other fifty percent is also perfect, because we're together.' She'd tried not to sigh as she'd said it.

Eventually, he'd let it go and, after sulking for a whole cruise, had settled for a regular table. In the exact same spot. Every night for twenty years.

She caught the eye of a passenger standing next to her in the queue. Evelyn leaned closer:

'The western wave was all a-flame.
The day was well nigh done!
Almost upon the western wave
Rested the broad bright Sun;'

The passenger, a nervous-looking young man, half smiled, no doubt impressed by her recitation. 'Excuse me?'

People were so ignorant these days, thought Evelyn to herself. Half the time they made no sense at all. 'Samuel Taylor Coleridge. *The Rime of the Ancient Mariner.*'

During their courting days, Henry had tried to impress her with Coleridge or Kipling, but when Evelyn started reading the same poetry herself through sheer boredom, she'd begun to correct him or prompt him when he stumbled over a phrase. At first, Henry had seen her unique capacity for recall as a novelty, an amusing party piece in the same way one might knot a cherry stalk with one's tongue. She knew it was something more, a superpower of sorts.

Evelyn shuffled forward in the line of casually dressed passengers. Shorts, peaked caps and rubber shoes gripped between toes seemed to be the rig of the day. There were so many football shirts in the crowd that she wondered if this was a themed cruise. But judging by the less-than-athletic physiques of the wearers, she soon gathered it was merely an ironic fashion statement. Accepted, the golden age of luxury liners like the *Queen Mary* and *Mauretania* were long gone, but surely there should be a minimum dress standard for dinner?

Behind her, Evelyn heard sniggers. She turned quickly to offer her disapproval but the sudden movement released a rush of blood to the back of her head and she almost lost the floor. Regaining her composure, she came face to face with a young couple sporting matching tattoos on their arms. She inspected the inked limbs as though they were hanging in the Tate.

'May I suggest a swallow next?' she said, tapping a vacant plot of skin on the man's forearm. 'They migrate long distances and return to the same areas to breed every year, symbolising a safe return home. Yes, swallows are very popular. And anchors, of course.'

There wasn't much Evelyn didn't know about sailors. It was only fair that she educate the less well informed. And do her bit to keep seafaring traditions alive. She walked away before the couple could thank her.

The waiting passengers parted as Evelyn made her way to the front of the queue. In her satin dress, each stride sounded like the snap of a luffing sail as it caught the wind. 'Stand up straight, girl, shoulders back!' she heard her mother say.

'Ma'am?' It was a waiter Evelyn didn't recognise. He looked up from his clipboard and did a double-take. This was more like it. At last someone was paying attention.

Evelyn summoned her most imperial look. 'Where is Olivier?'

'May I have your name please, signora?' The man's name badge told her this was Bruno, one of the head waiters. There was an Italian flag next to his name. He wasn't one of her usual people.

Evelyn snorted and adjusted her tiara. 'Mrs Henry Parker.' If there was one thing worse than everyone knowing who she was, it was someone who didn't.

'Cabin number?'

She'd had enough of this nonsense. Evelyn tapped her finger on the lectern. 'Where is the Frenchman?'

Then the Italian-who-wasn't-the-Frenchman took her by the arm and tried to lead her aside. 'Please wait here.'

The impudence! She pulled away from his clutches. 'Take your hands off me. I want to see Olivier.'

Momentarily, the chatter inside the restaurant hushed at the sound of Evelyn's raised voice. The waiter stood back, holding his hands up as if in surrender.

'But signora—'

There was someone else beside her now. 'Henry, there you are. Now tell this man . . .' She turned, expecting to see her husband, but instead found a stranger, albeit a vaguely familiar stranger.

'*Bonjour*, Mrs Parker.' The almost-stranger's name badge said *Olivier. Maître d'*. Had he done something different with his hair? she wondered.

'This is all terribly inconvenient,' said Evelyn, adjusting her evening gloves where they'd fallen down like wrinkled stockings around her wrists. 'Take me to my table right away. We'll miss dinner at this rate.'

'I was trying to explain—' said the Italian. He had a moustache that made his words more difficult to follow. He'd begun to wave his arms around, adding to her distress. 'That she has already missed *dinner*.' He turned to face Evelyn, his flapping arms now thankfully reined in. 'Signora, this is the line for *breakfast*.'

Evelyn felt as if her mooring ropes had snapped, the sensation that she couldn't quite name creeping up from her feet until her whole body felt like cottonwool. The Frenchman caught her as she toppled, her tiara rolling across the carpet like a diamond-encrusted tumbleweed. She yielded to his rescue and allowed herself to be led away from the crowd.

'I don't understand it,' said Evelyn. 'Why are you serving breakfast in the evening?'

Olivier tilted his head to one side and waited as the truth sank in. Evelyn's hand rushed to cover her mouth.

'Try not to worry. It happens all the time.'

'Not to Mrs Henry Parker, it doesn't.'

The Frenchman tried to placate her. 'Let's get you back and I'll organise for breakfast to be delivered to your stateroom.'

'Are you sure you haven't changed the clocks?' Evelyn was suspicious.

He smiled and gently shook his head. 'The usual, kippers and a poached egg with lightly browned toast?'

'The eggs, you know how I like them. Not too runny,' said Evelyn. 'And a pot of tea, but make it strong.'

The restorative power of tea. In these uncertain times, it was the one thing she could trust.

'Would you like me to see you back to your cabin?'

'That won't be necessary,' replied Evelyn, tightening her lips into a smile.

The man who was not Italian cleared his throat. 'May I assist you with one more thing, Mrs Parker?' He gestured to the back of her dress before pulling the zip all the way to the top.

'I think it best that we keep this strictly entre nous, don't you?' Evelyn tapped the side of her nose. Everyone made mistakes. And in his present state, she certainly wouldn't want Henry to worry. Hiding the tiara in her handbag, she pressed the button to summon the elevator.

4

A Way with Mangoes

THIS TIME EVELYN WAS RELIEVED TO FIND HER CABIN EMPTY.
There was still time to get changed and pretend to be a normal
person before Henry returned. She would have to hurry. He
might walk in at any moment, and the last thing she wanted was
for him to see her all dressed to the nines at the wrong nine.

The bed was immaculately made, the sheets and bedspread
shrink-wrapped around the mattress. It was reassuring to see
Virgilio making an effort with his hospital corners. The hours
spent perfecting her own technique under Matron's watchful
gaze clearly hadn't been in vain, and Virgilio had been a quick
learner under Evelyn's tutelage.

The smell of a fresh mango drew her attention to the fruit
bowl. He'd refilled it while she was out. *Good chap.* There was
an orange and a couple of apples, although her peeling knife
wasn't where she'd left it. The same went for her magnifying
glass. If she didn't know better, she might think Virgilio was
deliberately moving things to confuse her.

Evelyn's mouth watered at the sight of the golden-skinned fruit. Virgilio was by far their best steward aboard *Golden Sunset*. His predecessors had all been willing and keen to please, but Virgilio stood out. He had valuable contacts, friends in all the right places, especially the galley, and with her sweet tooth in mind he always managed to find something special for her fruit bowl. When she grew tired of strawberries and began to leave them untouched, he found her juicy red grapes or a peach. Never bananas. Not on a ship. Naturally, Evelyn rewarded him for his inventiveness and for accommodating her exacting standards. The right tip kept him sweet and the mangoes even sweeter.

There was someone at the door. *Henry.* At last. There'd be a piece of her mind for all the worry he'd caused her.

'Just a moment,' she shouted, fingers fumbling at the back of her dress for the metal zipper.

A second knock sounded, louder this time. The zip moved an inch, then snagged on a piece of fabric and stalled. She was trapped, a prisoner in her own formal dress. Evelyn had no choice but to own up to the whole breakfast debacle and have Henry release her from her satin straitjacket. Another option came to her in the space between knocks.

Evelyn reached for the white towelling bathrobe hanging on the back of the bathroom door and slipped it over the top of her evening dress. She cinched in the waist and tied a bow. There were several inches of grey silk peeping out at the bottom, above her not-for-running shoes. It would have to do.

To her surprise, when she opened the door it wasn't Henry standing there but a young woman. They were all young. Everyone looked twelve years old these days. This one was wearing a white uniform.

She had three stripes on her epaulettes, each separated by a strip of red braid. *Red for blood.*

'I hope I'm not disturbing you, Mrs Parker,' said the woman with the blood-red stripes.

Evelyn glanced at the woman's name badge as nonchalantly as possible. 'Good morning, Dr Hannah King, Ship's Doctor Golden Sunset. What can I do for you?'

'I was passing and I just thought I'd pop in. To see how you were.'

Pop in? Evelyn narrowed her eyes, suspicious. 'I do hope you're not going to charge me for a cabin visit.'

'Of course not,' laughed Dr Hannah King. 'I was just passing.'

'As you can see, I am perfectly well,' Evelyn said, wriggling to hitch up her evening dress under the bathrobe.

The young doctor cleared her throat. 'Are you sure? Only the maître d' was concerned about the,' she lowered her voice, 'incident at breakfast.'

Evelyn's heart dropped a couple of beats. 'Oh, that? A minor misunderstanding. More of a miscalculation really. Apparently it happens all the time.'

'How have you been feeling?'

'Never better.'

'Any palpitations?'

Evelyn felt her heart stutter like a cold engine trying to start. She took a deep breath in and held it until her pulse returned to normal. 'None. Whatsoever.'

'Only, I was hoping you might make an appointment at the medical centre. For a check-up.'

'Whatever for? I am a nurse. My husband is a doctor.' Evelyn straightened, revealing more of her hem. She slumped forward again, quickly.

Dr Hannah King seemed to weigh her next words. 'Even nurses and doctors' wives need their own doctor, Mrs Parker.'

Evelyn sniffed. 'In that case, I'd like to book an appointment with Dr Johansson.' Such a capable young man. With his perpetually furrowed brow and thick spectacles, he looked reassuringly like a doctor. Like Henry had, at that age.

Dr Hannah King puffed out her small bosom and said, 'That won't be possible, I'm afraid. Dr Johansson has gone home. I am the ship's doctor now.'

Gone home? She wondered if Henry knew. The two men had struck up rather a friendship despite their age difference. Henry had seen it as his role to mentor the sporty young man, offering snippets of advice, trying inexpertly to discuss cricket, and regaling him with tales from the good old days. In the end Evelyn had had to have a quiet word with her husband, suggesting he let the doctor get on with his work without the constant interruptions. His frequent social visits to the ship's medical centre must have been a distraction to the hard-working staff. But Evelyn could also see it from her husband's point of view. It must have been difficult for Henry. A retired ship's doctor was still a doctor.

'Are you sure there isn't anything health related you want to discuss while I'm here?' Dr Hannah King was surprisingly persistent. Evelyn thought for a moment. She debated mentioning the problem with her feet, but didn't want to draw attention to her new shoes in case they weren't actually hers. She tilted forward, hoping that parallax might conceal them beneath the hem of her dressing-gown.

'Not a single one,' she said with a beatific smile.

'It's just that I've been receiving reports of some unusual behaviour.'

'Not me. You must be mixing me up with someone else. We all get a little muddled from time to time.' She desperately wanted to forget the whole unfortunate incident at breakfast, but it refused to go away, hanging around like day-old fish in the rubbish.

'Please, Mrs Parker.' Dr Hannah King Ship's Doctor Golden Sunset took a step forward. She had one foot over the threshold. 'May I come in?'

Evelyn tried to close the door. 'I mustn't hold you up, Doctor. I know how busy you must be.'

'Not at all.' The doctor matched her pressure for pressure on the door, and forced smile for forced smile. 'I have plenty of time for a chat.'

'Well, you'll have to excuse me, I'm afraid I'm late for . . .' Still leaning into the door, Evelyn looked down and noticed today's copy of the ship's newsletter on the floor, where it had been poked under the door. She could just about read the larger font headings, her standing height apparently the perfect focal length. 'Mindful Colouring. In the library. Ten o'clock.'

Dr King followed her gaze to the floor, her eyes widening as she took in the bottom of Evelyn's evening dress and her not-for-running shoes.

'I see,' she said. 'In that case, why don't you head down to the medical centre when it's finished? There's something important we need to discuss.'

Business must be slow. Passengers were far too healthy these days, and judging by the force Dr Hannah King was exerting on the door, she was obviously keen to turn this into a professional consultation. Without warning, Evelyn removed her hand and stood swiftly aside. The young doctor catapulted over the threshold and into the door itself, banging her head.

'Are you all right, dear?' asked Evelyn.

Dr Hannah King rubbed her forehead. 'Yes . . . no . . . I mean, are you taking your tablets?'

'Do you mean the little white ones?'

'Yes,' said Dr Hannah King Ship's Doctor Golden Sunset, breaking into an eager smile. 'The little white ones.'

'No.'

'But Mrs Parker . . .'

Evelyn shooed the doctor from the cabin with a little clap of her hands. 'Now if you'll excuse me, I don't want to be late for Mindful Colouring. Goodbye. Thank you for coming.'

5

An Unlucky Seagull

EVELYN COULDN'T THINK WHY SHE WAS OUTSIDE THE LIBRARY. Nowadays she rarely completed a book. Novels were particularly hard to follow. She'd tried everything she could think of not to lose the plot, including tracing the words across the page with her finger, but she still ended up reading the same paragraph over and over again. Sex scenes were the exception. They played havoc with her heart rhythm, but at least with her anatomy training, she could work out what was going on.

It hadn't always been this way. She'd been a voracious reader in her youth, a voracious everything. These days she had less appetite for escapism and adventure, preferring the certainty of everything she already knew.

'Are you here for Mindful Colouring?' said a woman, looking up as Evelyn walked through the glass doors into the library.

Mindful what? Her hearing aid must be playing tricks again. Evelyn double-checked the ship's newsletter in her hand.

Focusing on the typed letters made her feel queasy. Perhaps it was time to invest in a pair of prescription eyeballs.

'That's what it says here,' she replied, not quite believing it herself. It was circled in blue-black Quink ink.

'Come and sit over here next to me,' said the woman, smiling to reveal a set of large teeth. 'I won't bite.'

The woman was of indeterminate age, younger than Evelyn – most people were nowadays – though not yet old. She had more width than height, but she looked like a happy person, her features naturally defaulting to a smile when she stopped talking.

It was chilly under the air-conditioning vents and Evelyn considered going back to her cabin for a cardigan, but it was a lot of trouble to go to when shivering would work just as well.

Half-a-dozen upholstered chairs surrounded the polished circular wooden table in the centre of the library. With padded armrests and decent high backs, each looked perfectly designed to accommodate an afternoon nap. Evelyn rarely slept during the day. In fact she prided herself on her ability to stay awake after lunch. At her age, it was an achievement. Afternoon naps were strictly for people in nursing homes, and bull-necked men with sleep apnoea.

'Thank you,' said Evelyn. She lowered herself with a sigh, glad to relieve her knees of even her modest body weight. Had she taken the stairs or the elevator? It felt like the stairs.

The woman began to talk, chomping through the words as if she were starving. 'One of the entertainment staff was here a moment ago, but he had to leave again, said he had to set up for trivia too because apparently the trivia person has a migraine, not that I'd wish that on anyone, I should know, I used to get the most terrible migraines, absolute humdingers, but that was before the menopause.'

Evelyn waited for an opening in the verbal traffic to join the conversation. Just when she'd given up hope, the woman paused and said, 'I'm Nola, by the way.'

'Mrs Henry Parker.' They shook hands. 'How do you do.' The woman's palm was warm and fleshy, reminding her of the ripe mango in the fruit bowl.

'Pleased to meet you,' said the woman, whose name Evelyn had already forgotten.

She inclined her head towards a slim, sparsely thatched man in the far corner of the library. For a split second it could have been a younger Henry sitting there with a book open in his lap.

Shielding her mouth like a preschooler with a secret, the woman added with a roll of her eyes, 'That's Frank. He's my current husband.' Evelyn supposed it must be a joke, because the woman was laughing. This woman whose name she couldn't remember. But then she'd always been hopeless with names. 'Aren't you, Frank?'

'Frank,' said Evelyn out loud. As in 'frank and earnest'. Frank looked up and nodded in acknowledgement before returning to his book. Frank. *Frank.*

'Comes with me everywhere, don't you, luv?' Another eye roll. 'We're joined at the hip.'

'How delightfully whimsical,' said Evelyn, secretly wondering if having Henry surgically attached would have been a better way to keep tabs on him.

The woman barely paused. 'Childhood sweethearts. Been together forty years.'

'Forty?' Evelyn tried to calculate how long she and Henry had been married. She knew the year of their wedding, but her maths wasn't up to the task of working out what year it was now. She let it go.

'Yes, you get less for murder these days.' The woman rolled her eyes again and Evelyn began to worry she had nystagmus or a rare disorder of her central nervous system. She'd read about it once in a textbook. *Cassell's Modern Dictionary of Nursing and Medical Terms*. A fascinating read. But before Evelyn could enquire about her cerebellar function, the woman thrust a pile of drawings in front of her. 'Here. Choose a picture and start colouring.'

Evelyn sifted through the sheets of paper, each bearing a different black and white line drawing. Some were simple geographic patterns, others animals or birds with feathers and details drawn in. There were pots of pencils in the centre of the table, coloured pens too. Every colour imaginable. The rolling-eyed woman had a picture of a peacock in front of her and had already filled in several sections of the fanned-out tail feathers in blue.

The penny spun and wobbled before it eventually dropped. 'Oh, colouring, as in colouring-in,' said Evelyn.

'I know,' replied the woman. 'It's a bit daft really, isn't it? It's supposed to be relaxing. A bit like yoga with coloured pencils.' She chuckled. 'I did yoga once upon a time. Never again, I can tell you. I went for six months and still couldn't touch my knees. It was so confusing. I didn't know if I was meant to be up dog, down dog or dead dog.'

Evelyn didn't like dogs and passed over a picture of one. Finally, she chose a bird from the pile. She preferred birds. This one was a large seabird of some kind, in full flight. There were clouds behind and above its large pointed wings, and a peaked wave breaking towards the bottom of the paper. There was a special significance attached to this bird and its big webbed feet. An omen or superstition of some sort. It was a bad-luck bird. She racked her brains for its name. Was it an owl? An eagle? Seagull?

Sneaking a sideways glance at the woman's picture, she chose a pencil from the pot and tried to work out where to put the colour blue. The sky seemed a safe bet, as did the ocean. Pushing the drawing to the full stretch of her arms and squinting a fraction, she set to work filling in the space around the clouds, noting the potential for confusion ahead when she came to the horizon.

It was tricky, gripping the pencil between her stiff fingers, but as they began to limber up, so did Evelyn's thoughts, transporting her back to a blank page in a sketchbook, and a vast ocean that stretched in all directions. The image lapped at the shore of her memory and prickled her skin with goose bumps before vanishing once more.

Back in the present, the woman was talking again, a conveyor belt of words and sentences that Evelyn could barely keep up with. In the time it took to colour in the sky, Evelyn had travelled from an early childhood in Ireland to a remote cattle property miles away, a place she had never heard of. She'd endured flood and drought, exorbitant feed prices and greedy supermarkets. There were two daughters, one son and so many grandchildren Evelyn lost count. Something about an unscrupulous financial adviser, and Vera. Frank's mother.

'She's the reason we're here,' said the woman, pausing to indicate this was of significance.

'I see,' said Evelyn, who didn't quite. *Vera*. Was she supposed to know Vera?

'She died.'

'Vera did?' Evelyn was shocked to find her already dead. Before she'd even got to know her properly.

'It was hard to be sad. She was ninety-nine. Lived that long just to prove the doctors wrong.'

Evelyn nodded thoughtfully. It seemed an awful lot of trouble to go to simply to make a point. She barely knew Frank's mother, but already Evelyn liked the woman, and was disappointed on her behalf. 'What a shame she didn't make a hundred.'

The woman continued. 'It's a hell of a lot of hearing-aid batteries, I can tell you. And don't get me started on . . .'

The woman started on the thing she hadn't intended to get started on. The harder Evelyn tried to follow what she was saying, the further behind she found herself in the flow of words. It was like trying to dam a stream, only to have the water break through each time. After a while, however, she found all she needed to do was smile and nod. This time there was more about the pessimistic geriatrician, somebody's knee and finally, to her relief, retirement. The words were soothing, washing over Evelyn as the blue pencil bled colour onto the paper. It was like tinnitus, a noise in her ears that she could either tune in to or ignore but was always there in the background.

Eventually, the man in the corner stood and closed his book.

'Nola,' he said with a sigh, 'I don't think poor Mrs Parker needs to know our entire life story.' He opened the glass bookcase behind the table and began to run his finger along the shelf, spectacles perched on the tip of his nose.

Nola. Evelyn exhaled with relief. Contagious. Rhymes with ebola. Bubbling over. Fizzy as cola. Nola.

'I'm so sorry, Mrs Parker.' Nola was all smiling teeth. 'My family is from County Limerick,' she said, as if this explained things. With barely a breath's pause, she was off again.

To Evelyn's relief, Frank seized a narrow gap between his wife's words and provided some helpful information about Vera.

'This is our first holiday in many years, Mrs Parker. My mother always wanted to travel by ship, but as a farmer's wife she never had the opportunity. She bequeathed us this cruise in her will.'

Nola made a sound through her nose. 'Knowing full well that I get seasick even looking at a ship,' she grumbled, turning a strange colour at the mere mention of the word.

'Now, now Nola,' said Frank. 'It's not like she did it out of spite. She simply forgot about you and that episode on the ferry.'

'The vomit comet, the locals called it. Now there's a story . . .' Nola did the eye-rolling thing again. Evelyn wondered if it was the seasickness. Her vestibular apparatus playing up.

'I can sympathise, I used to suffer the most awful seasickness,' said Evelyn, remembering the inescapable nausea that would buzz around her head like an annoying fly. 'Until I met Henry, that is. My husband's a doctor, you know. A ship's doctor in fact.'

'Well, well. How fascinating. Isn't that fascinating, Frank?'

'Yes, dear. Fascinating.'

'Is he any good with seasickness?'

'Indeed,' replied Evelyn. 'He knows a thing or two, but after more than sixty years at sea, I think I know just as much as he does. Perhaps more. I was a nurse, you know.'

'Did you say sixty years? That's a long cruise.'

'The ship is our home, mine and Henry's.' The ship and the sea.

Evelyn manoeuvred the tip of the pencil carefully inside the black lines, her fingers, usually so stiff and unobliging, now moving with ease. She watched the colour fill the paper in a series of overlapping strokes. She wasn't normally one for small talk except in awkward situations, relieved when the other passengers went ashore and the ship was hers for a few peaceful hours. But this talk felt anything but small. Colouring in an unlucky seagull with a couple she'd only just met, Evelyn sensed a story building inside her, the words waiting patiently below the surface to be told.

'Did you hear that, Frank? Mrs Parker *lives aboard Golden Sunset*. Well, well,' said Fizzy Nola.

'Well, well,' said Earnest Frank.

'I'll bet you have a few stories to tell, Mrs P, from all those years at sea. How did you come to be married to a ship's doctor of all people? I want the full story, all the details. There's plenty of time. Migraines can last hours,' said Nola.

'That's the thing about headaches,' added Frank. 'They can go on and on.'

6

A Splendid-looking Spleen

TO INTRODUCE YOU TO HENRY, I FIRST NEED TO INTRODUCE you to my father. It won't take long. He's about to die.

Father had been a French diplomat before the war, at the embassy in London. He'd stayed on after his posting finished, becoming a successful businessman, and moving to a mews in Chelsea while my mother returned to Paris. They were both miserable; my mother, at least, felt she'd be happier in her native tongue.

I was coming to the end of my preliminary training at St Thomas' in London. I'd wanted to be a nurse ever since Father had taken me to a Florence Nightingale exhibition at the hospital as a little girl. I was so taken by the Lady with the Lamp that I never considered anything else but nursing. My mother declared it a passing phase, which only made me more determined.

On 4 December 1952 I met my father outside Selfridges at quarter to three. It was a typical winter's day but by the time we'd finished our sandwiches and scones at four, London was unrecognisable. A thick yellow blanket of smog had sunk over the city, making it difficult to see even a few feet ahead. There was an acrid, sulphuric smell to the air that clung to the back of my throat and made my eyes water. It was suffocating, a real 'pea-souper' as they used to call them. Everywhere, people were stumbling into each other and coughing. Everyone was coughing.

Father set off towards the underground while I searched for my bus. By then the traffic had ground to a halt. Even with headlights on, neither cars nor buses could see where they were going.

I gave up and walked back to the nurses' home, following the trail of gas lamps over Westminster Bridge. It was worse than the blackout during the war and it took me hours to get home. By the time the news reached me, my father was already dead. Respiratory complications. Along with four thousand other Londoners over the next few days.

~

The cold, conditioned library air made Evelyn shiver. It was as though she had fallen asleep for a moment, dipping her toe into a familiar dream. She wasn't sure why she was talking about her father, the sharp tip of a mustard-coloured pencil balanced between her knotty fingers, hovering over a line drawing of a bird.

A rosy-cheeked woman was sitting next to her, chin resting on the heel of her hand and lips parted around her smiling teeth. She seemed to hang on every detail, the words flowing from Evelyn as easily as breathing. Surrounded by shelves of books that no longer made sense, there was one plot that Evelyn could follow, remembering it as clearly as if it had happened yesterday.

'Do go on,' said the woman. 'Pull up a chair, Frank, dear, and come and listen to Mrs Henry Parker tell her story.'

Evelyn closed her eyes and watched the pictures dance on the inside of her lids, of places and people she hadn't thought about for a long, long time. She took a deep breath and exhaled another memory.

~

I came top of my class at St Thomas' in anatomy, physiology and hygiene. My mother said it was merely a knack for remembering things. From an early age she used to wheel me out to entertain foreign dignitaries with word-perfect poetry recitals. When I told her about the results she looked at me as if I'd done little more than tie my shoelaces for the first time.

Father, on seeing my disappointment, told me, 'You're no slouch, Evelyn. Don't ever let anyone convince you that you are anything less than a bright young woman who can do whatever she puts her mind to.' With those words he'd given me a small package wrapped in brown paper. *Notes on Nursing: What It Is, and What It Is Not.*

I'd never been under the illusion that I was a beauty. Bright was all I needed. With my father's prominent nose and my mother's pale colouring, I had the kind of looks that led people to assume I was exceptionally intelligent or well-bred. Mother was obviously hoping for that bloom of beauty girls experience as they become women. But in my case, there was no ugly duckling moment.

My father, somewhat of an authority on the subject, it transpired, always maintained that there was no such thing as an ugly woman.

'All women are beautiful,' he told me, then went on to assure me that in my case beauty was more than skin deep.

I was delighted. It was the finest compliment I could imagine. Owning an attractive pancreas or a good-looking spleen was far more important to me than the fullness of my lips or the silkiness of my hair, which would undoubtedly fade in time.

There was a small inheritance from my father but I knew it wouldn't last forever. It certainly wouldn't keep me in the luxury that, through no fault of my own, I'd grown accustomed to as the daughter of a diplomat. Father had given me a safety net. At the very least it brought me independence from my mother.

I'd met him at Selfridges the day of the London smog to break the news that I was moving to Australia. I showed him the list of 'desired occupations for migrants without personal nominations'. It was there in black and white. *Single women: Nurses SRN & Mental.* In fact, I had my sights set on midwifery training and had already lined up an interview at King George V Memorial Hospital for Mothers and Babies.

'That's a long way to go, Evelyn,' my father had said, pushing away his empty teacup. He'd raised me to be a strong, independent young woman. The problem, from his point of view at least, was that I'd become exactly that. And now I was about to leave him and move to the other side of the world.

'I know, but it's such an exciting opportunity. Australia. Just think, such a young and vibrant country. I'll miss you but it's something I have to do. I can't explain why.'

It was hard to ignore the echoes of war in London, in the scarred buildings and rationed food. And although there was a sense of optimism growing, I was impatient for adventure, and a self-sufficient life free from the shackles of my privileged upbringing.

It was as though I was trying to rebalance some unjust social equation, break out of my gilded cage. Exactly as Florence Nightingale had when she was born into a rich, upper-class family in 1820. Sydney wasn't the battlefields of Crimea, but it was a start, and once I had my midwifery certificate, I planned to travel to wherever my services were needed; to the outback or remote islands in the Pacific.

To be fair, Father didn't try to stop me. I knew he would have given his blessing eventually, no doubt on the proviso that he pay for me to travel first class. In honour of my father, I used part of the inheritance to ease my crossing, and a few weeks after his death, I boarded the *Orcades* at Tilbury docks, alone.

My mother had remarried by then, and she and her scandalously young husband were too wrapped up in each other to make the journey from Paris. He ran off with another woman a few months later, shattering her brief happiness, ironically leaving her crushed and heartbroken in a way she never was with my father.

Stepping out from the Riverside Station at the docks onto the quay, I tried to take it all in, relieved to be free of the weeping relatives the other passengers had brought with them in addition to their baggage. I couldn't abide tears.

The docks were busy, crowded and dirty, with tall cranes everywhere that reminded me of the fighting machines from *The War of the Worlds*. Overhead, a crane hoisted the luggage of fifteen hundred passengers from the dockside into the ship's hold, carried in what looked like giant rope bags.

I'd seen pictures, black and white newsreel footage of *Orcades*, but the sheer scale and majesty of the ship quite took my breath away. Twenty-eight thousand tons and over seven hundred feet long. It's easy to read the numbers without truly appreciating what they mean in real life. She was a mansion on the water, seven decks of sumptuous lounges and restaurants, dance floors, shops, swimming pools, all topped by that giant corn-coloured funnel decorated at its stem with her badge – the symbolic harp of the Orcadian sagas. And here was I, a twenty-year-old, newly minted nurse, setting out on a saga of my own.

While the other passengers waved tearful farewells to friends, family and lovers on the quayside, I watched the churning green water behind the tug's engine as she pulled us away from the mooring and out into the Thames. The dark smoke belched from the funnel and thinned into the pale spring clouds, taking with it any lingering doubts about what I was doing.

The ship's horn sounded with a loud thump that I felt through my whole body. It was as though that sound had woken me up from a long sleep and I was alive for the first time. The hawsers fell away from the moorings like a mother's apron strings and the weight lifted from my shoulders. I inhaled the diesel fumes and the tidal stench of the riverbank, my lungs growing with each breath. To me it was the smell of freedom. The beginning of a journey to the rest of my life.

On the cusp of my twenty-first birthday, I had the world at my feet. But no one had warned me about the perils of the sea. It was a dangerous place where storms and shipwrecks, sea monsters and scurvy had claimed the lives of countless sailors. For many an ancient seafarer, it was only their superstitions and good luck charms that kept them alive. But I had no need to be superstitious for I was blissfully unaware of what lay ahead.

~

Evelyn's mouth was parched from talking, the words as dry and dusty as the old memories. She was barely a day into her voyage on *Orcades* and so was somewhat peeved when the colouring-in officer returned to the library. With the trivia officer now lying in a darkened room with a cool washcloth over his forehead, it was apparently time to pack away the mindful things ready for bingo. And all before Evelyn had introduced Henry to her new friends whose names had slipped her mind. She'd never thought of herself as a storyteller before, yet they were hanging on her every word. And the more Evelyn touched those memories, the more vividly they returned. She hadn't thought about that journey on *Orcades* for many years and yet she could swear she saw the soot from the corn-coloured funnel dusting her skin and feel the vibrations of the old ship's propellers beneath her feet.

'What a pity, Mrs P,' said the woman whose name escaped Evelyn. 'It looks like our time's up. Just as we were reaching the Bay of Biscay.'

'What a pity,' echoed the husband.

Evelyn examined the drawing of the flying seabird. Osprey?

'You must excuse me,' she said, folding her bird into four. Penguin? No silly, penguins couldn't fly. It would come to her. She stowed the folded bird away inside her handbag next to the packet of mints, the pocket map and her mother's tiara.

'Would you care to join us at the buffet, Mrs P?'

'I'm meeting Henry for morning tea. In our usual place, at our usual time.'

Routine should have brought certainty and comfort, but Evelyn felt only a deep unease. Something was wrong, like an ornament out of place or an itch that she couldn't scratch.

Her mind had popped out, visited elsewhere for a while. It had returned home to find Henry gone.

7

The Tincture of Time

'IN THAT CASE, FRANK AND I WILL JOIN YOU FOR MORNING tea. You can introduce us to your husband.' It didn't sound like a question. The fizzy woman and her earnest husband were already matching Evelyn step for step towards the elevator.

'Of course,' Evelyn replied. 'The more the merrier. We can discuss seasickness over a nice cup of tea and a scone.' She could hardly object, given the bond they'd recently formed over colouring-in, and losing Vera. What's more, Evelyn felt as if she was limbering up her small-talk skills after a long rest. If she relied solely on Henry for conversation, her words would have seized up altogether by now.

Evelyn practised chatting all the way to the elevator. She was worried how Henry might react to two strangers joining them for tea. For a doctor, he could be rather awkward with people. It was as though he could cope with company in small doses, but beyond that he was inclined to a people hangover that would see him holed up in their cabin for hours on end conducting the

Royal Philharmonic Orchestra out on the balcony. It was best to leave him alone to *pomp, pomp-pomp, pomp, pomp* to Wagner, and once he'd ridden the Valkyries, Evelyn would drag him away for a cup of Earl Grey and turn him into a husband once more.

Approaching the elevator, Evelyn's uneasy feeling grew. She would have to introduce her companions and she hadn't the foggiest who either of them were. She could hardly start with, 'Henry, meet this passenger whose name I don't know. She loves peacocks and suffers from seasickness. And this is her husband, whose name I don't know either. His mother Vera died recently but no one was upset, apart from the doctors.'

As they waited for the elevator, the woman laughed, lost in another anecdote about this Vera woman.

Think. *Think,* thought Evelyn. Sometimes she wished they would make name badges compulsory for all the passengers as well as the crew. There was nothing for it but to tap into her skills as an exceptional rememberer.

Chatty woman, infectious laugh. Contagious. Rhymes with Ebola. Fizzy as cola. Nola.

The woman's name returned with a sigh of relief. One down, one to go. Evelyn turned her attention to the husband, who was listening intently to a story he had no doubt heard a dozen times before. Laughing when his wife laughed, pinching his brows at the appropriate moments, as if he was following a set of matrimonial stage directions. He really did look quite serious at times. Quite *earnest* in fact.

As in frank and earnest. *Frank.*

Almost weightless with relief, Evelyn repeated the names under her breath all the way up to deck twelve. The real secret with names, she'd found, was to say them out loud as often as possible.

'After you, *Nola*. Why thank you, *Frank*.'

When they arrived, the buffet area was abuzz with hungry passengers who, their breakfast barely digested, were clearly terrified of missing out on an all-inclusive calorie.

Evelyn tried to recall what she'd had for breakfast, indeed whether she'd actually eaten breakfast. She breathed into her palm. Kippers, as she suspected. Something about breakfast had left a bad taste in her mouth, however, and it was more than the smoked fish.

They joined the cake queue, Nola entertaining the other waiting passengers with an anecdote about running Vera's false teeth through the dishwasher each night. For all her dizzying eye-rolls on the subject, Evelyn noticed, her new friend seemed rather fond of her elderly mother-in-law. True, she must have had the patience of a saint to cope with the old lady's capricious moods and endless complaints, not to mention all the cups of tea she left to go cold. From hearing-aid batteries to dentures, however, Nola hadn't stopped talking about her.

At the front of the queue, Evelyn watched Nola fill her plate with an assortment of calorific treats and tried not to pass judgement.

'I was a size eight before breakfast,' joked Nola. At least Evelyn assumed she was joking. Either that or she'd been back for more than seconds. 'Seriously though,' continued Nola, 'I want to make sure I get my money's worth before the seasickness kicks in. Once we get out of the calm water, I'll be chucking my guts up.'

On hearing this, the woman in front thought twice about the strawberry tart on the end of the serving tongs and walked away with a couple of plain biscuits instead. Oblivious, Nola removed a chocolate brownie from the middle of the display, leaving a precarious Jenga puzzle arrangement for the next person. Evelyn noticed for the first time the grey elasticated anti-nausea bands around Nola's wrists.

'You may as well place a horse chestnut in your left pocket when it comes to seasickness, my dear,' she said, surprised to hear her thoughts coming out of her mouth. 'There are many remedies but sadly no cure.'

Nola was slow to catch on, regarding Evelyn blankly. There was barely a ripple on the surface of the ocean, a millpond beyond the large picture window. It wouldn't last. It never did.

Earnest Frank led them to a shaded table on the open deck, then went back to fetch three cups of tea. It felt like a good moment to sigh and comment on the gloriousness of the day.

'What a glorious day,' said fizzy Nola, beating Evelyn to it. She took the first bite of her brownie.

'Should we wait for Ernest?'

'Who?'

'Your husband.'

'You mean Frank? No, if I always waited for him, I'd starve.' She laughed. The rest of the brownie disappeared. Through a mouthful of crumbs she said, 'Should we wait for yours?'

'He'll be here soon,' replied Evelyn. She scanned the faces around her but didn't see Henry. She was used to him being held up, in clinic, with paperwork or a particularly tricky patient. How long should she wait? How long before she should worry?

When Earnest Frank returned with the tea, he settled into his chair and sighed. 'Well, isn't this glorious?' he commented.

'Glorious,' they agreed unanimously, for a second time.

The gloriousness of the day made Evelyn feel drowsy. More than once her head nodded and she fought to keep her eyes open. The chatty woman chatted on, oblivious.

'. . . it was such a waste of a complimentary breakfast . . .'

She was in full flow. Something about a ferry. Apparently she hadn't been the same since. Evelyn caught up just as the journey concluded somewhere she didn't quite catch.

'So, Mrs Parker,' said Nola, this time from behind a large buttered teacake, 'you were telling us about the Bay of Biscay.'

Evelyn was reluctant to revisit the misery of that undulating horizon. She felt a stirring of nausea and an undefeatable lethargy that turned her limbs leaden.

~

I'd been feeling perfectly well right up until the captain made his first announcement warning the passengers about the rough seas. From that moment on, however, I developed a heavy-headed feeling and lost my appetite for breakfast. As the day progressed I became increasingly disinclined to move anything other than my swallowing muscles and lay staring at the bulkhead above my bed. Listening to the creaks and moans of the ship as she battled that notorious stretch of water off the west coast of France, it sounded like she was suffering too.

It was my own fault. I'd been forewarned, but the flat waters out of Tilbury had lulled me into a false sense of security. Having tried all combinations of keeping my eyes open, closing them, lying flat on my bed or pacing the cabin, and finding nothing to ease the misery, I decided to venture out onto the deck. If the fresh air didn't work, at least I could throw myself over the side of the ship and end my suffering that way.

By the time I found an empty deckchair in the lee of the funnel, I had all but given up the will to live. All I wanted was for this feeling to pass. My head throbbed and I longed for the relief of a sleep that wouldn't come, tortured by my own body. I sweated and salivated, groaned and yawned. At that moment I couldn't have cared less if I never saw the golden shores of Australia. I prayed for a mercifully swift death and the relief of a watery grave at the bottom of the Atlantic.

I had touched the very edge of sleep when I woke abruptly to the sound of a voice. A man's voice.

'Are you all right, miss?'

It was only polite to open my eyes, but this brought another rush of nausea as they registered a movement that my ears couldn't keep up with. He was standing over me, tall, thin, wearing a dark wool coat and a uniform cap. If he was there to usher me back inside to my cabin, I was in no mood to be polite.

'Perfectly,' I replied, shutting my eyes again.

'May I recommend fixing your gaze on the horizon?'

Saliva flooded my tongue as I opened my eyes again and tried to focus on him. His peak was pulled down low and I could only see the corners of his mouth imitating a smile. Halfway between sympathy and a smirk.

'I would do, if you weren't blocking my view.'

'It is better to keep your eyes open, to occupy them. Your arms and legs too. Occupied, that is. Anyway, may I suggest getting up and walking around?'

Later, I realised that irritability, along with apathy and a sincere wish for death, is a common symptom of seasickness. The daughter of a diplomat, I'd been brought up to be tolerant, and my parents had invested large sums of money to make sure I was always polite to tiresome people. But had I known any swearwords at twenty, I would have used them.

'Thank you for your advice, but I currently have no desire to move.'

I thought he might take the hint, but like a midge on a Scottish picnic he wouldn't leave me alone. He had a small book in his hand, as if to rub in that not only was he unaffected by the motion of the ship but he was also able to read.

'Green apples and crackers then. It's a good idea to have something in your stomach, Miss . . .'

The ship pitched and rolled across a wave, my internal organs sliding to one side to counter the motion.

'Des Roches,' I mumbled, barely moving my lips. *Dear God, please let me die.* When was this going to end?

As if reading my thoughts, he said, 'Only a few more hours, and then if we're lucky it'll be smooth sailing again until we reach the Southern Ocean. It can get quite rough there.'

'Rough? What, worse than this?' I opened my eyes wide at that, and rapidly regretted it as I broke out in a sweat.

He laughed as if I'd made a joke. Admittedly, the sun was shining and there was a group of fellow passengers happily playing quoits a little further down the deck, but surely the sea couldn't get any rougher? Surely?

'Where are my manners,' said the man, removing his hat and extending a slender hand towards me. 'Dr Henry Parker. Ship's Assistant Surgeon.'

I knew this already from his stripes. I'd been studying the booklet given to each passenger by the Orient Line, telling them about life onboard. On the double page, where the staples marked the middle of the book, was a guide to the different badges of rank, from the captain with four stripes, the staff commander with three, the engine department, pursers department, radio officers and catering department. I remembered I'd studied the medical department, whose distinguishing colour between the gold stripes was blood red, described as 'scarlet' in the printed pamphlet.

Accepting his hand, I recoiled at the cool and exceptionally clean-looking skin that was even colder than my own. *Cold hands, warm heart.* I'd always been self-conscious about the temperature of my icy paws as a student nurse, despite the reassurances of well-meaning patients. Did Dr Henry Parker have a warm heart too?

'A touch of autonomic dysfunction, I'm afraid,' he said.

'Excuse me?'

'Overactive sympathetic nervous system.' Seeing my confusion he added, 'Cold hands. It's a curse.'

'I do apologise,' I said, withdrawing my hand.

'No, I'm talking about me. My hands.'

We laughed, both apologising.

'I imagine you're a bit of an expert on seasickness, Dr Parker,' I said, returning to our original conversation in an attempt to relieve the awkwardness.

I noticed his eyes flicker. They were the same stormy grey as the ocean that day, staring unsettlingly into mine. Not so much a leer as a curiosity, as though he was more interested in what was inside my head than beneath my clothes, unlike other men I'd encountered. It was strangely disconcerting.

'Naturally I've developed a certain expertise in treating *mal de mer,* Miss Des Roches.' He sniffed then, a little put out. 'But it is a common misconception that a ship's doctor spends all his time treating the condition.'

'Well do feel free to share some of that expertise, Doctor. So what does an *expert* recommend to end this misery?'

'There have been many remedies trialled over the centuries.'

'Such as?'

'Hot pickles and potatoes, cottonwool in the ear, warm salt water, strychnine, creosote . . .'

'Creosote?'

'It didn't work. Nor did cyanide of potash, chloroform . . .'

'Chloroform. Now that sounds more appealing,' I said. 'I would welcome oblivion of any kind at this moment.'

'In that case, may I recommend an alcoholic beverage? Port and brandy mixed, also known as a "stabiliser".'

'Does it work?' I asked, wondering what time the bar opened. I wasn't a drinker, but I was, as a nurse, an eminently practical girl, even if Florence Nightingale couldn't abide drunk or slatternly nurses on her wards.

'If you mean, will you fall asleep intoxicated and wake up when the sea is flat and calm again? Then yes, very effective indeed, although on waking you might need to repeat the dose. *Poils du chien*.' Seeing my blank expression, he interpreted, 'Hair of the dog, mademoiselle. For the hangover.'

Was I meant to find this amusing? Or was he trying to impress me with his French? If he was, he was wasting his time. As an act of childhood rebellion, I refused to speak anything but English in front of my parents.

Against my better judgement, my mouth cracked into a smile, more at his clumsy and pompous manner than with genuine amusement. I was, however, beginning to feel slightly less wretched, even in the short time we'd been chatting. Distraction was proving to be the most effective remedy after all.

With my twenty-first birthday a week away, I realised there were many things I still hadn't done or been. Neither drunk nor hungover. I'd witnessed death on the wards and laid out many bodies but still knew precious little about life. My parents had sent me to an all-girls school and the only men I'd known, apart from my father and visitors to the embassy, had been the patients on men's surgical or the male doctors who had treated me like a handmaiden. I'd never before met a man like Dr Henry Parker.

'Thank you for your advice, but I prefer not to stoop to such measures.' I jutted my chin then. My mother's mannerism. 'I like to be in control at all times,' I added haughtily.

At that moment the ship dipped and the horizon lurched. I tried to suppress the geyser of bile in my gullet as the ship rose to meet another wave. I swallowed and took long deep breaths that made my head spin before springing up, hand over my mouth, and nearly colliding with Dr Henry Parker in my dash to the ship's railings. There, with the wind whipping my hair into my eyes, my stomach closed and I surrendered my bravery to a final explosion that brought almost instant relief.

To my horror, Dr Henry Parker offered me a white handkerchief embroidered with the letters *HP* to wipe my mouth. I smiled my thanks in his general direction but couldn't meet his eyes. Although I hadn't had the opportunity to study him in any detail, I could tell he wasn't handsome in the conventional sense. His ears were rather prominent, for a start. There was, however, something about him that made my wretchedness feel even more wretched.

'Don't be ashamed, Miss Des Roches. I can assure you that you are in excellent company. Some of the greatest figures in history have shared your affliction.'

It wasn't much of a consolation. I thrust the monogrammed handkerchief into my cardigan pocket. I wished he'd go away, or rather wished he hadn't seen me like this. 'I'm so relieved to hear I'm not alone,' I said sarcastically.

'Homer, Churchill, Christopher Columbus, even Lord Nelson. It is said that Charles Darwin only discovered evolution after he begged to be let ashore from the *Beagle*. Even Lawrence of Arabia suffered motion sickness, riding a camel.'

'A camel?'

'Ship of the desert, Miss Des Roches.'

'Right. Well thank you for the history lesson, Dr Parker, not to mention the physiology and neurology tutorial, but I am feeling much better now.'

'If the symptoms return, you'll find me in the surgery on C deck,' he said, pushing a loose strand of hair behind my ear in an inappropriately intimate gesture. 'Day or night.'

Much as I longed for relief, the thought of exposing my thigh or buttock – indeed, any inch of bare flesh – for a needle left me tingling with unease. He was a doctor, and yet I felt peculiarly shy and self-conscious. Though the nausea had passed, my stomach felt light and fluttery, radiating heat to places that no gastrointestinal complaint could account for.

'That won't be necessary.'

'In that case,' he said, putting his cap back on, 'there is one tincture that is guaranteed to work.'

'Which is . . . ?'

'The tincture of time.'

'How long?'

'A few days in most cases. Although some people suffer *mal de debarquement* when they set foot on dry land again, if they've been at sea long enough. Like motion sickness in reverse.'

'I can assure you that once I reach dry land I do not intend to set foot on a ship ever again.'

'Is that so?' He gave me a knowing look and another half-smirk. He touched his peak and turned to walk away, clutching his rather dog-eared little book. After a couple of steps he turned and added, 'If you change your mind, you know where to find me.'

~

There were two passengers sitting at the table, hanging on her words. The sun had moved round and was shining straight into their faces. Evelyn tried to work out who they were. A rosy-cheeked woman with an empty plate, and a thin, weathered man with an empty scalp.

'And did it work, Mrs P?' said the woman.

'Did what work?'

'Time,' said the man. 'Did you get over your seasickness eventually?' Seeing her confusion, he added obligingly, 'You were telling us about that unfortunate incident in the Bay of Biscay.'

The Bay of Biscay? The calm blue ocean disappearing behind the ship looked more like the Pacific. Evelyn was disorientated.

'I'm sorry,' she said. 'I've digressed.' Digression had become an unfortunate way of life. She wished she could stay on topic, stick to discussing the gloriousness of the day. 'Where was I?'

'You were telling us about the camel, Mrs P.'

'Camel?'

'Yes, as in the ship of the desert. And Lawrence of Arabia,' added the man helpfully.

Evelyn tried to re-join the conversation but her brain was firing blanks.

'We loved the film, didn't we, Frank?'

'Yes, dear. We loved the film.'

'Especially Omar Sharif,' said Nola with a sigh.

Frank blew his nose into his napkin.

'I'm not overly fond of whiskers on a man,' said Evelyn with an involuntary shudder. Aside from the hygiene aspect, given the propensity of facial hair to trap food remnants, there was something about a beard that she found untrustworthy on a man. As if he were trying to hide something. She was grateful that Henry was always clean-shaven. At least he had been the last time she'd set eyes on him. Whenever that was.

8

It's a Long Swim to Manila

BURGUNDY BORDER, GOLD SWIRLS. STARBOARD.

How accommodating of the ship's designers to colour-code the carpets. It was comforting to note that the cruise line catered to all manner of disabilities, including the memory impaired. Fortunately, with all her faculties fully intact, Evelyn always found her own way back to her cabin.

Left at the main elevator, straight on past the mural of Aphrodite.

It was fifty-seven navy-court-shoe-sized steps past Aphrodite to cabin 1006. Evelyn could almost find it with her eyes shut, which was just as well considering how dim the ship's lighting had become in recent years. It was almost like looking through frosted glass, everything appearing cloudy and blurred. Ambience was all very well, but it wouldn't be long before some poor old dear had a fall.

The cabin number was symbolic: 10 June 1954 was the day she and Henry were married. With the entire floor plan of the new ship to choose from, Henry had chosen cabin 1006. A romantic gesture or a pragmatic nod to the less certain years ahead of them? She might never know. It appeared that Henry had not only forgotten where he lived, but also their wedding anniversary.

Fifty-one.

Fifty-two.

She'd arrived, ahead of schedule. It was time to recalibrate the distance to her cabin based on her new walking-faster feet.

Outside the cabin door, Evelyn stalled, trying to work out how to get in. She patted down the pockets of her skirt, searching for a key, all the time wondering where to insert it when she actually found it. There was no keyhole.

Evelyn opened her handbag, looking for some means of gaining entry. She found her mother's tiara, a half-eaten teacake wrapped in a napkin, a packet of mints, a pocket map of the ship and a folded piece of paper. Thinking this might be a clue – instructions of some kind – she opened it to reveal a drawing of a bird flying over the ocean. A parrot? Petrel? No, it began with an A. Abalone? No, that was a kind of snail that lived in the ocean.

'Good morning,' said a voice behind her. Evelyn swivelled, dropping the bird-or-possibly-a-mollusc picture onto the carpet at her feet.

'Darn it,' said Evelyn. She hated bending. It could be so final at her age.

'Here, let me.' It was a young woman with skin the colour of burnt umber and almond-shaped eyes. She wore a burgundy shirt bearing a gold logo that coordinated beautifully with the hideous new carpets but clashed horribly with Evelyn's own tasteful bed furnishing. Next to her was a housekeeping trolley piled high with folded towels and miniature shampoos.

Evelyn noticed how the girl cradled her lower back with her hands, a wince flickering across her face as she straightened up with the flying-snail-or-possibly-a-bird drawing in her hand.

'Are you all right, my dear?' said Evelyn, wondering if the girl had pulled something. At her age she shouldn't be suffering from a bad back. It was heavy work of course, pushing that big cart around, carrying towels, making beds, wielding the vacuum cleaner. Yet the girl looked robust enough.

'It's nothing, ma'am.' The girl fiddled with a folded sheet, her body language suggesting she was busy and would rather be left to get on with it.

Evelyn made a mental note to mention the girl's back to Henry. Musculoskeletal was a particular clinical interest of his and he was never happier as a doctor than when he was piercing some joint cavity with a needle and vial of cortisone. But to be fair to Henry, he had his more holistic moments too and had been known to give detailed – and inadvertently comical – demonstrations of the relevant exercises or stretches.

'Excuse me, young lady,' said Evelyn. 'I seem to have mislaid my key. I don't suppose you have a skeleton somewhere?'

The girl looked confused. Probably a trainee, thought Evelyn. A probationer. She'd go easy on her. Every day is somebody's first day. She wondered how long Florence Nightingale gave her probationers to settle in.

'A skeleton?'

'You know, for breaking into places.'

'May I?' The girl pointed to something hanging around Evelyn's neck on a long ribbony thing.

Lantern-halyard-*lanyard*. A white plastic credit card. It was all coming back to her now.

'How silly of me,' she said, trying to appear light-hearted as she stabbed the white plastic card into the slot in the door handle. 'I don't see so well.'

'After you, Mrs Parker.' The tall girl who clashed with the bedspread pushed the handle and opened the door. To Evelyn's surprise, she followed her into the cabin, holding a pile of folded white bath towels.

Evelyn rested her handbag on the dressing-table-desk and tried to work out what was going on.

'Where's Virgilio?' she said.

The girl called back from the bathroom. 'He went home, ma'am.'

Home? 'But he was only here this morning.' Or was it last night? Evelyn wondered how he'd managed to disembark in the middle of the Pacific Ocean. It was a long swim back to Manila. 'Are you sure?' she said.

'Yes, Mrs Parker. Quite sure. I am your steward now.'

Evelyn squinted at the girl's breast pocket. She even took a step backwards but it was no good.

'I'm terribly sorry, I'm hopeless with names . . .'

'Grace, ma'am.'

Tuesday's child is full of grace. *Grace*. 'And you're my . . .'

'Steward, ma'am.'

Surely Evelyn would remember such a striking young woman. She felt as if she'd skipped a page in the storybook. 'And Virgilio?'

'In the Philippines, ma'am,' said the girl wearily. 'Looking after his mother.'

Virgilio had a mother? Had he mentioned her? *Vera*. Yes, that was her name. The doctors were trying to kill her. No wonder poor Virgilio had had to rush home. To save his mother's life. Immediately he went up in Evelyn's estimation.

She felt a slow, sinking sensation. Virgilio had been such an integral part of their lives that she and Henry had come to think of him almost like family. Naturally, Henry would have seen him off with a handsome tip. He was a generous man. In fact she'd often reminded him not to be too generous. Staying aboard *Golden Sunset* depended on them not spending too much. Or living too long. So far, they'd stayed both solvent and alive thanks to her favourite not-for-worrying people. She had Dobbs to thank for the former, and Dr Johansson for the latter.

The steward-who-wasn't-Virgilio had finished hanging the new towels on the rack. Tuesday's child. *Grace*. Full of.

'This is addressed to you, Mrs Parker,' she said, retrieving an envelope that had been poked under the door.

Grace hovered while Evelyn opened the envelope and pulled out a gilt-edged invitation from the captain. With her very longest arms, Evelyn could just make out the printed words on the invitation. *Requests the pleasure of the company of Mrs Henry Parker to a special farewell drinks party in the Sunset Lounge.*

Farewell drinks? Was the ship being sold off or scrapped already? It was most unexpected. There was no denying *Golden Sunset* was 'a ship of a certain age' but she was hardly geriatric in nautical years. Indeed, she was barely nudging retirement age.

Evelyn was surprised no one had mentioned it. So far this cruise the crew had acted as if it was business as usual, rather than a trip to the breaker's yard. 'Did you know about this being the final cruise?'

Tuesday's child averted her gaze, and nodded silently. 'Yes, ma'am. We're all very sad.' She looked quite choked up, biting her lip. 'But it's for the best.'

How could it be for anybody's best, other than the company shareholders? The full implications of the news settled around Evelyn like a low-pressure weather system. In a matter of days she and Henry would be homeless. She tamed the thought before it got out of control. Now was the time to think clearly and take action.

Evelyn put the invitation into her handbag. There was no time to waste. Rather than waiting for her husband to reappear she would, at her own considerable inconvenience, simply have to go looking for him.

It was time to find Henry.

9

H Is for Hammer Toe

EVELYN PEELED A DRY SULTANA AWAY FROM THE POCKET MAP, leaving a serendipitous stain over the exact location of her cabin. She unscrewed the lid of her fountain pen and set to work finding Henry.

After the cool, conditioned air of her cabin, the humidity outside on the boat deck brought Evelyn out in paradoxical goose pimples. The soupy tropical air felt heavy on her skin.

The ship seemed blissfully unaware of her looming demise, idling towards the next port with barely a wake behind the massive propellers. A post-lunch torpor had settled over most of the passengers. A handful of wound-up children leapt from ornamental dolphins into the main swimming pool while their wound-down parents dozed slack-jawed in the sun. There was so little movement of the ship in the calm seas that the surface of the pool shivered rather than sloshed from side to side as was more usual.

As a regular, Evelyn knew the quietest locations at this time of day, the best places to snooze or read, away from the organised entertainment and the ornamental dolphins. She and Henry had their preferred spots where they could sit side by side and try to amuse one another.

Keeping Henry occupied on long sea days was always going to be a challenge once he'd retired. Living a life of luxury wasn't as easy as it should have been.

'Did you know that retirement has a high mortality rate?' he'd ventured one day when the first wave of anxiety had threatened to spoil their afternoon.

'What are you talking about, Henry?'

'An alarming number of people die when they retire.'

'Every retired person dies. Eventually. It doesn't follow that retirement is a fatal illness.' Evelyn tried to return to her book but Henry was building up towards a full-blown panic.

'My body might have been ready to retire, but my brain isn't. I worry that if I stop using it I'll develop Alzheimer's.'

Sometimes she wished she could take Henry's batteries out. His endless fretting was wearing her down. She closed her book with a sigh.

'Okay then. Let's give that brain of yours something to do other than worry about what it can't control.'

'Like what?'

'A game.'

Henry grinned and rubbed his hands together like an excited schoolboy. 'What sort of game?'

'*I Spy*,' replied Evelyn. His smile fizzled. 'Let's play *I Spy a Diagnosis*.'

Henry's grin returned. 'I like the sound of this. You start.'

Evelyn scouted around for a suitable subject. 'I spy with my little eye, a diagnosis beginning with C.'

'Cardiomyopathy!'

'Where?' Evelyn folded her arms. 'It has to be something you can actually *see*, Henry, otherwise it's just guessing. Strictly speaking, you can't see a cardiomyopathy without an autopsy.'

'Oh,' said Henry, pouting a fraction. 'Like actual *I Spy*, you mean?'

'Of course. Now let's try again. I spy with my little eye, a diagnosis beginning with C.'

Henry bit his lip, scrutinising every passing passenger. When a man limped past dragging one toe on the ground, he shouted, 'Foot drop! Childhood polio!'

The man gave him a strange look and carried on walking.

'That's P, Henry. Polio starts with P.'

'Not childhood polio. What else could it be?'

'Common peroneal nerve palsy,' said Evelyn, already regretting the game. 'Let's try another.'

'My turn! My turn!' Henry was now sitting bolt upright in his deckchair, swivelling his head to take in the passing pathology. 'I spy with my little eye, something beginning with H.'

'Hammer toe?'

'No.'

'Hip dysplasia?'

'No.' Henry's grin widened with each wrong answer. 'Give up?' Without waiting for Evelyn's reply he blurted, 'Hypothyroidism! Dry skin, sparse eyebrows, excessive weight gain.' A flaky-skinned, sparsely eyebrowed lady of ample build pretended not to be offended as she walked past.

What had started as a simple pastime to keep Henry's brain occupied soon became an obsession. The other passengers were variously and mercilessly diagnosed by the retired doctor. The red palms of a heavy drinker. A moon-faced man with Cushing's disease. The osteoporotic old lady with a dowager's hump. H was his favourite letter, and he'd been particularly pleased with himself when he'd diagnosed one poor passenger with not only hyperhidrosis, but hirsutism and halitosis too.

'Darling,' Evelyn said after Henry had pointed out a menopausal woman fanning herself with a menu, 'I think it's wonderful that you're actively engaging your grey matter, and mine, but I think it's gone too far now. Soon there will be no healthy passengers at all on this ship.'

He'd sighed then, a deep Henry sigh, and Evelyn feared he'd be out on the balcony conducting the Philharmonic before dinner.

'I thought it would come naturally to me,' he said with a plaintive look, 'being retired. After all those years of hard work, the long hours, paperwork and stress, I thought I'd welcome being a man of leisure.'

'You're not happy?'

He took her hand then, patting it between his own. 'Oh I am happy, my sweet. It's just that I still want to feel worthwhile. Needed.'

'You mean important, don't you?' This was Henry all over.

'Not so much that. It's more that I want to make a difference. I've always been somebody who made a difference. I want to know that I still am.'

She tried to see it from his perspective. Henry had been somebody all his life.

'I understand. But just because you're no longer a somebody doesn't make you a nobody.'

His bottom lip twitched. 'I couldn't cope with everybody thinking I'm a nobody.'

'No one is saying you're nobody, Henry. But you don't have to prove to everybody that you're somebody. You're somebody to someone.'

'Who?'

'Me, silly.'

They sat in silence for a while. There was plenty Evelyn could have said, about how on the ship, as Henry's wife, there were times when she'd felt like a nobody while her husband enjoyed his privileged position as a professional somebody to everybody.

Henry had kissed her hand then, looking a little more cheerful. 'Everybody is a nobody without somebody special.'

It was as close to a romantic declaration as Henry would ever come. She knew what he was trying to say. Neither of them was anybody without each other. But she still needed to prove that she could also be somebody in her own right.

~

Evelyn reached into her cardigan pocket as she scoured the promenade deck. Her fingers found a collection of objects that she scooped into her palm and inspected as she walked. A red plastic building brick, a tin soldier, a pale blue button and a glass marble. She couldn't think where the items had come from, but she knew that four times round the deck was a mile. Every time she passed Lifeboat 10 she would transfer one object to the other pocket or hand to keep track of the laps. She wondered how many objects it would take to find her husband. The deck felt extra springy today and Evelyn was cautiously optimistic. And when she grew tired she could console herself with the fact that, thanks to her new Finding Henry shoes, her cabin was closer than ever before.

As she walked, Evelyn scanned the sun-lounging passengers, looking for Henry's familiar face or the hard cover of one of his poetry books, behind which she might find him reading. Some passengers wore hats that shielded their faces; others sipped cold drinks or listened to the *tee-tee-tee-tee* of artificial music through giant plastic earmuffs. Many, who were of an age when they no longer fought it, snoozed.

After a building brick, a soldier and a button, Evelyn needed a rest. Spying a rare vacant lounger, she expended her remaining energy in hurrying towards it. Sinking into the chair, she sighed like a deflating inner tube. She could tick off the first area on her pocket map. Henry wasn't on the promenade deck. At last she was getting somewhere, even if it wasn't the same somewhere as her husband.

Evelyn celebrated her small victory by closing her eyes for a few minutes. This wasn't a nap – heaven forbid – simply half-time for her eyelids. She listened to the sounds around her: the distant laughter of children, the wash as the giant hull moved through the water, a singing duo. Her heart was behaving today, keeping time with the beat of the music. There was much to be thankful for. She had the sun on her face, the ocean breeze in her nostrils and her heart in sinus rhythm. Searching for Henry was more tiring that she'd imagined. She needed a few winks to recharge. Not a whole forty, more like twenty.

After only ten or fifteen winks and on the edge of sleep, Evelyn heard the *thump, thump, thump* of running feet. They stopped at the end of her lounger and, opening her eyes, she saw a figure bouncing on the spot, directly in her line of vision. Focusing on the sweaty face made Evelyn feel quite queasy.

The bouncing woman pulled two white strings from her ears, on the end of which dangled a pair of tiny hearing aids. She was clearly out of breath, and yet strangely she continued to jog, spraying beads of sweat like a wet dog shaking.

'Hello, Mrs Parker,' puffed the woman sweatily. She wore a pair of trousers with no legs and a shirt with no arms. It was hard to imagine her wearing much less without it being called swimwear. She must be one of those fitness fanatics who liked to make other people feel guilty.

'Are you having a nice holiday, dear?' Evelyn really wished the woman would go and sweat somewhere else.

To her relief, the woman stopped and leaned forward, hands on her thighs, though still breathing heavily. 'I have to go back to work in a few minutes, I'm afraid,' she said.

Work? Evelyn realised her mistake, eyeing the woman's lithe figure. She must be one of the dancers. Her face was vaguely familiar. Evelyn hadn't actually been to a show for a while. She'd begun to find the throbbing music and bright lights paradoxically soporific, and more than once she'd woken up in a fully lit theatre, with waiters tiptoeing around her, collecting empty glasses.

'I don't know how you do it, my dear.' Evelyn had always admired the coordination of the dancers. Henry had been an enthusiastic audience too, though for different reasons, she suspected. 'Yes, remembering which way the arms and legs go.'

The woman's breathing had slowed, but she was still glistening with sweat. 'I'm pretty sure there's only one way they can go. At least there was when I was at university.'

'University?' They made dancers do a degree these days? Well, well.

'Yes, medical school . . . you know, to become a doctor.'

'You're a doctor and a dancer?' Young women were so much more accomplished these days.

'No, I can't dance to save my life!' The woman wiped her face on the bottom of her top and emerged drier, and smiling.

How strange for a dancer, but then, with the ship coming to the end of her days, the company must be scraping the barrel of entertainment staff. 'Never mind, just copy what the others are doing and no one will notice.'

The woman's eyebrows twitched. 'Mrs Parker, about the little white tablets . . .'

Little . . . white . . . tablets. Now this was ringing bells for some reason. As if to remind her, Evelyn felt her heart pause before firing off a rapid volley of warning beats. How silly of her. This was THE doctor. The one who wasn't Dr Johansson. Now what was her name again?

Red hair. *Viking*. Hiking. *King*.

'Dr King, I appreciate your interest, but I am quite sure there are many passengers on the ship who need your attention more than I do. Besides, I am a nurse and I'm married to a doctor. You might know him, Dr Henry Parker? I really must introduce you. He used to be a ship's doctor too.'

Noticing that several passengers were watching them from neighbouring loungers now, Dr King lowered her voice. 'We open at four. Why don't you pop down? For a cup of tea . . .' This was sounding more promising, thought Evelyn. She was about to enquire about biscuits when Dr King added, '. . . and a chat.'

'Thank you, but I'm not really a chatty sort of person.' Evelyn opened her handbag and pretended to be busy. Her fingers found the packet of mints and she offered them to the doctor. 'Would you like one, dear?'

Dr King shook her head, smiled politely and, poking her mini hearing aids back in, turned to jog off. She hesitated and pulled one ear out. 'I approve of the new shoes, Mrs Parker. Very appropriate.'

Evelyn circled her feet at the end of the lounger, admiring her Finding Henry shoes. She watched the young doctor jog away in a similar pair. It was still a mystery as to who had sent them, but then life was becoming more of a mystery every day, the things that didn't make sense outweighing the things that did. Take Henry, for example. How could a grown man, a doctor, go missing on a ship? A ship's doctor at that.

The whole thing was exhausting. Worrying about Henry. Being old. Trying to remember how a normal person behaved. With all her aches and pains and a bone-curdling weariness, every day she felt like she was coming down with the flu. Evelyn shrank into the lounger and let the reflection from the water dance on her face. Was there something she wasn't remembering properly? If she'd gone ga-ga like one of those forgetful old dears, it would explain things. But she could recite poetry as if she were reading the lines from a book.

I closed my lids, and kept them close,
And the balls like pulses beat;
For the sky and the sea, and the sea and the sky
Lay like a load on my weary eye,
And the dead were at my feet.

See? Word perfect. She uncapped her fountain pen and opened the pocket map. Leaning on the flat side of her handbag, she wrote COLERIDGE. It would remind her to practise her memory exercises every time she looked at the map. Then she drew a tick against the promenade deck. It was where Henry wasn't.

10

Cricketers Make the Worst Sailors

'DRINK, MA'AM?' A WAITER STOOD OVER HER. HE WAS wearing a Hawaiian shirt and holding a tray of sunset-coloured drinks in tall glasses.

It was early in the day to be offering free cocktails, thought Evelyn. It was probably something to do with it being the ship's last cruise. They must be emptying the bars before the ship died.

'I don't drink spirits as a rule,' she said. Evelyn was prepared to make an exception, just this once. In case the company refused to carry her onboard credit over to her next ship. She took two glasses from the waiter's tray. One for her. One for Henry.

A glass in each hand, she sucked on the straw on the left. The flavour exploded on Evelyn's tongue and she reeled at the delicious surprise. She was thirsty after a brick, a soldier and a button round the deck, and the left-sided drink disappeared in a couple of sucks at the straw. Henry had better hurry up, thought Evelyn, eyeing the glass on the right.

Just as she was about to start on the second drink, she noticed a couple standing at the railing. They were partially obscured by a pineapple chunk that straddled the rim of her glass. It was speared with a pink cocktail umbrella that also anchored a glacé cherry, but if Evelyn tilted her head slightly, she could make out two familiar faces. They were peering in her direction.

'Look, Frank,' said the woman, 'it's Mrs P!' She was wearing a busy yellow dress and had a red hibiscus flower poked behind one ear.

Frank, conveniently identified to Evelyn by his wife, appeared self-conscious in a Hawaiian shirt and a pair of shorts that revealed thin white legs. A farmer's tan.

They'd met before, Evelyn was sure of it, but exactly where shimmered like a mirage on the horizon.

'Mind if we join you?' Without waiting for a reply, the woman manoeuvred her yellow behind onto an empty sun lounger adjacent to Evelyn's. 'Frank, you go and find another chair, sweet.'

'Righto,' he said, heading off up the deck.

'I've got him well trained,' said the woman, as if her husband were a performing animal. It had never occurred to Evelyn to train Henry. If she had, maybe he'd be sitting here with her playing *I Spy a Diagnosis* rather than wherever he was.

'B. Give up yet? Baker's cyst,' she imagined him saying from behind his cocktail, pointing to the bulge at the back of a passing passenger's knee.

'Are you sure? What about P for popliteal artery aneurysm?' Of course she only imagined saying this. Henry was the doctor. She was only his wife. A wife who had over the years read and memorised every nursing textbook on her shelf, not to mention *Gray's Anatomy* and most of Henry's medical books, but nevertheless a wife.

'Are you having a nice holiday, dear?' Evelyn struggled to recollect the woman's name.

'So far so good,' replied the woman. 'Sea still looks calm enough, but I've had a big lunch. Important to have something in your stomach, you said. Best piece of medical advice I've heard.' She patted her fleshy yellow stomach and laughed. She was obviously anticipating something the size of a tropical cyclone.

The woman's husband had returned now with another sun lounger, and he set it down on the opposite side to his wife, sandwiching Evelyn.

'Do tell us more,' said the husband. 'We were so enjoying your story about—'

The woman with the yellow stomach took over, not trusting her husband with the second half of the sentence. 'Your voyage on *Orcades*. After you left England to start a new life in Australia. About how you met Henry.'

The outside of the right-hand glass was wet with condensation in Evelyn's hand. She supposed she must have drunk the strange-coloured contents because the straw was soggy and the glass was empty. Her head weighed less than usual too. She closed her eyes and filled her nostrils with a different ocean.

~

We must have passed Gibraltar because I remember sitting out on the promenade deck wearing a poplin blouse and a light wool cardigan. The smart coat that had cost me a month's wages was folded away in my suitcase back in my cabin, and I was still debating whether to give it away, imagining

Australia to be perpetually warm and sunny compared to the grey London chill.

There were tiny waves that barely broke the surface of the ocean, and *Orcades* made light work of them. At last the ship felt stable. The memories of seasickness were growing less vivid, as I imagine a new mother soon forgets the agony of labour once she is holding a newborn in her arms. We'd entered the second phase of the voyage, in which it was boredom that had to be endured. I no longer felt completely wretched but not yet quite normal either.

Making the most of the reprieve in the weather, I'd taken my sketchbook outside, hoping to capture a scene or two as a way to remember the passage. I'd tried to imagine my time on the ship as less of a journey and more of an adventure in itself. To embrace the experience rather than fight it.

Having managed several light meals, I was feeling stronger and more sociable. I had already got to know a handful of my fellow passengers, forming unlikely friendships in the midst of this group of assorted strangers who had little more in common than the same destination. There was something about travelling on a ship that was different to any other mode of transport. Away from civilisation, in close proximity to complete strangers who share that peculiar sense of being in limbo for weeks at a time, a voyage is unlike a journey in a train carriage or aircraft cabin. Time stands still on a ship. Like living for a while in a dream.

With my miniature palette of watercolours I had settled into a quiet spot on a vacant deckchair. There wasn't much in the way of scenery to paint, and I was already bored of the sunsets and watery horizons that took up the first few pages of the sketchpad.

Even the famous Rock of Gibraltar was a disappointment when I painted it, somehow accidental to the scene.

A group of children a little further up the deck drew my attention from the landscape. They were enjoying a sack race, under the supervision of one of the children's hostesses. The outline of a child had begun to appear on my blank sheet of paper when I noticed a man in a white uniform standing to one side. While everyone was watching the children, cheering and clapping them as they stumbled along in their hessian sacks, he was watching me.

Although the officers wore almost identical uniforms apart from their stripes, I recognised him immediately as the assistant surgeon. The Dr Henry Parker who'd watched me vomit and lent me his handkerchief. The supposed expert in seasickness. The same Dr Henry Parker I'd been studiously avoiding since the Bay of Biscay. I caught his eye. Looked away. It was too late; he was already striding towards me.

'May I see?' Without asking, he plucked the sketchbook from my hand and began to flick between the pages. I writhed with as much discomfort as if he'd been appraising my naked body.

'Be my guest,' I said but the sarcasm was lost on the doctor.

'I dare say you will improve with time,' he said. 'Most things improve with practice. These are not bad for a beginner.'

I chewed the inside of my cheek. I hadn't exactly said I was a beginner. As a child I might have stuck my tongue out behind his back, as I used to with pretentious embassy visitors, always in full view of my mother. 'It is merely a hobby, a way to pass the time.'

'I take it you're feeling better, Miss Des Roches?'

'Yes, thank you.'

'I am so relieved to hear you've gained your sea legs at last.' I noticed him glance at my unstockinged legs below my skirt hem. I crossed them demurely at the ankles and pulled my skirt down a fraction.

'Do you paint, Doctor?'

'No. I am merely an admirer.' He held my eyes for a moment longer than was comfortable. 'I consider myself more of a poet.'

I noticed his front teeth were chaotic, his lips and tongue catching on them as he spoke. So much of his immediate appearance suggested an Englishman that when he spoke I was taken aback as much by his unexpected Antipodean accent as his demands to examine my sketchbook. I hadn't noticed it the last time we'd met, when I'd parted with my stomach contents.

'Banjo Paterson?' I knew only one Australian poet. One poem, in fact. *The Man from Snowy River.* Slipping the clutches of a boozy-breathed Santa Claus at one embassy Christmas party, I'd played with the daughter of the Australian ambassador, who, as the visitor, had chosen the game, an elaborate re-enactment of the bush poet's famous work, adapted for two eight-year-old girls.

'Samuel Taylor Coleridge, actually,' he replied, drawing himself up to his full height.

'*The Tale of the Ancient Mariner*?'

'Rime, Miss Des Roches. *The* Rime *of the Ancient Mariner.* One hundred and forty-three verses of it.'

He handed back my sketchbook. I snapped it shut and clutched it against my chest. 'Well I'm sure you're very busy, Dr Parker. I wouldn't want to keep you from your patients.' Piqued, I stiffened and readjusted my spine. *How dare he.*

Dr Henry Parker didn't take the hint. He seemed rooted to the spot at the end of my deckchair. 'I'm in no hurry.'

I was trapped. At sea in the middle of an endless four-week voyage, I could hardly tell him I had somewhere else I had to be. We'd exchanged barely more than a few sentences and yet this pompous young man was already maddeningly under my skin. The more I tried to scratch, the more he itched. Human eczema.

There was an awkward silence, which Dr Parker was in no hurry to fill.

'I will return the handkerchief,' I said. 'Once I've had it laundered.'

'There's no need. I have several.'

More silence.

'Do you make a habit of saving young women who are travelling alone?'

'Not as a rule.'

'Are you married, Dr Parker?' I don't know why I said it. Under normal circumstances it would have been a perfectly acceptable small-talk opener, but I regretted the words as soon as they left my lips.

'No. Not married. I am next in line for a promotion, to surgeon. I'll have my very own ship soon.'

'And are the two mutually exclusive?'

'Not necessarily, but the wives of ships' doctors are a unique breed. It's not for everyone.'

'I see. And yet I'm sure there are many women who would jump at the chance to live such a glamorous life.' I gambled with sarcasm and lost.

He looked at me, scrutinising me closely. 'Yes?'

I was suddenly aware of my hair, and set to tidying the loose strands around my forehead. I tried dismissive this time, a safer bet. 'I imagine there are women like that.'

'Prepared to make that sacrifice?'

'No doubt. Those without careers, naturally.'

It was still a time when women gave up nursing after they married, and of my cohort at St Thomas' the previous year, several had already left the profession to walk down the aisle. What a waste, I'd thought as I'd wished them well.

'What about you, Miss Des Roches? Do you have a career?'

'I am a nurse,' I said. I stood up at that point, delighted to find that I was virtually the same height as Dr Parker. 'Apparently Australia is crying out for nurses.'

'Nursing is an admirable pursuit for a young woman,' he said, as if I'd told him I was taking up embroidery or stamp collecting.

'And not one that should be taken lightly,' I snapped. 'I presume you have heard of Florence Nightingale?' He nodded. *'It seems a commonly received idea among men and even women themselves that it requires nothing but a disappointment in love, the want of an object, a general disgust, or incapacity for other things, to turn a woman into a good nurse.'*

I watched him push his hands into his pockets and sway backwards and forwards on his hips as though enjoying some joke at my expense. 'Well said, Miss Des Roches.'

His deliberately enunciated consonants were beginning to irritate me; his attempt at cultivating a BBC accent, I imagined. At that moment there was nothing I wanted more than to throw him over the railings into the water and never see that haughty expression ever again.

'And you, Dr Parker, you've never considered a career as a *proper* doctor?'

To be fair, he didn't flinch as he pulled another mono-grammed handkerchief from his pocket and, removing his uniform cap, began to mop his brow. His hair, short around the sides as was the fashion, with a flattened quiff of sandy hair on the top, hadn't fared well beneath his hat in the heat.

'On the contrary, I was offered a surgical rotation at Oxford after finishing my degree there. I turned it down,' he said. So, he had fancy letters after his name, letters that spelled out what a twit he was.

'And you gave up all that to run away to sea?'

His expression changed and he stared into the distance with a wistful look. 'My father's ancestors arrived with the First Fleet in 1788. My mother is descended from survivors of the Spanish Armada. The sea is in my blood.' Apparently the fact that his heritage included eighteenth-century criminals and unfortunate Spanish sailors was sufficient justification for him to turn down a prestigious surgical training at Oxford. He took a step back and put his cap on again.

'I take it you'll be heading to London after we dock in Sydney then?' I pushed away a whiff of disappointment.

'Along with the Australian cricket team and half of the Empire for the coronation,' he said, smiling again. I sensed we were back in safe territory once more. 'Too valuable a cargo to leave to the amateurs, and I hear those cricket fellows make the worst sailors.' With that he tapped the side of his nose as if sharing a piece of gossip.

We were standing very close, both now holding the varnished handrail and looking out at the endless curve of the earth. I could feel my heart beating differently, lively and mischievous. Hot blood sluiced through my atria and ventricles with every contraction. I felt the sharp snap of the aortic and mitral valves. I could conjure instantly the diagram from the textbook and feel the urgent pumping of blood to every corner of my body.

The awkward silence returned.

'Well, I mustn't hold you up, Dr Parker.'

'I will leave you to your sketching.' He took a small book from his shirt pocket and gestured towards me with it. 'And I will go and bother Samuel Taylor Coleridge instead.'

11

A Very Irate Passenger

EVELYN COULDN'T UNDERSTAND WHY SHE WAS LATE. LIKE sand plummeting through an hourglass, the day had run away from her. Furthermore, having gone to the trouble of writing herself a note on the back of one of the envelopes, she was even more frustrated to arrive amongst the stragglers.

DINNER 8 pm DO NOT BE LATE.

The envelope was there in her handbag, alongside the pocket map, the mints, the bad-luck seagull, a teacake and her mother's tiara. She'd left another, lying on the dressing-table-desk.

HENRY – I AM LOOKING FOR YOU. STAY IN THE CABIN UNTIL I RETURN. SOMETHING IMPORTANT TO DISCUSS. E.

It was a long shot, a remote chance that she and Henry could simply be missing each other. Like passing ships on an actual ship. It was best to cover all the possibilities.

Dinner was well under way, every table filled with diners already tucking into their delicious meals. There was a low-pitched bass of conversation, accompanied by the percussion of cutlery and crockery in motion. Warm air escaped from the bodies and hot plates, the overcompensation of the air conditioning making the foyer feel chilly.

The indecipherable telling-the-time thing hung from Evelyn's wrist and offered no clue as to why they'd moved second-sitting dinner forward. Beyond holding her handkerchief under the wristband, the thing was as good as useless.

Was it possible that she'd missed clocks? Usually when the ship crossed a time zone, the daily newsletter would fore-warn the passengers and the clock change (known as 'clocks' among the ship's company) spoken of in the dining room that evening. It was hard to miss, but not impossible. She'd even done it once, early in her career as a wife, winding her clock forward an hour instead of back and turning up to breakfast before the sun was up. That was in the days when she was young enough for people to laugh it off.

The worst thing about being late was that punctuality had always been her strong suit. Matron had often praised her for her prompt arrivals. It came of self-discipline, something she'd adhered to, determined to live her life on board as more than one long holiday. Evelyn had always forged her own schedule – office hours of sorts – by breaking down the day into hour-long segments. An hour for breakfast. An hour to walk a mile around the deck. An hour for this lecture or that craft class. A weekly visit to the hairdresser lasted an hour. In the afternoons, for reading and penning letters to her mother in the D deck writing room, she allowed two hours. On sea days she allocated an hour on the bed after lunch, in the early days of their marriage making love when Henry slipped back to the cabin, then in later years preferring a good book instead.

Outside the restaurant, Evelyn was greeted by a young waiter wearing a tricolour waistcoat and holding a plastic dispenser.

'Good evening, Mrs Parker,' he said, squirting clear jelly into her palms.

It was cold and for a moment Evelyn couldn't think what to do with it. The waiter helpfully demonstrated that she should spread it across her hands.

'Is this absolutely necessary?' Evelyn felt instantly light-headed with the fumes from her now wet and chilly hands.

'New hygiene regulations, ma'am.'

'Good heavens.' Evelyn had not reached her dotage by being riddled with germs. Good old-fashioned soap and water had kept her clean enough to survive every virus since 1932. She noticed a grubby-looking young man sneak past the waiter, however, and rapidly changed her mind.

Every nurse ought to be careful to wash her hands very frequently during the day. If her face too, so much the better.

Things spread quickly on a ship: bugs, rumours, panic. It was best to take precautions. Remembering Florence Nightingale on the subject, Evelyn rubbed the gel vigorously between her palms, and finished with a pat of her cheeks, as she'd seen Henry do with his aftershave. It stung, but she felt very clean, and exceptionally ready for dinner.

She paused to examine a new thought. Henry's aftershave. Sadly, Evelyn could more easily call to mind Henry's scent than she could the exact arrangement of features on his face. She wondered if a sniffer dog might be more use than a pocket map if she was going to find her husband.

'I'll see myself to my usual table,' said a clinically sterile Evelyn, sidestepping a second waiter who offered to escort her.

This was one time she didn't want to make a grand entrance, happy to skulk to the table and either find her husband there waiting for her or else tick it off as another place that Henry wasn't. Admittedly there were other restaurants on the ship where passengers could eat casually without fixed seating. But this kind of dining wasn't for Henry. He'd tried pizza once and hadn't got on very well with it. She made a mental note to cross off the pizzeria on her pocket map. And the self-service ice-cream-cone station for the same reason.

'Madam, please wait,' called the waiter after her.

Evelyn lifted the skirt of her dress and accelerated, her Finding Henry shoes offering pleasing traction against the dining-room carpet.

Left at the first table, follow the row to the windows.

Evelyn had barely made the first left when she felt a hand on her arm.

He holds him with his skinny hand ... Hold off! unhand me, grey-beard loon! Evelyn swung her handbag, hitting the waiter on the shoulder. He let go and began to massage the site of the impact. Obviously she hadn't meant to cause an injury but the bag was heavier than usual and had developed surprising momentum.

'Please, Mrs Parker. I have a table for you over here.'

'*Our* table is over there. We always sit at the same table. Twenty years we've been sitting at the second table past the pillar.'

'But, madam, your usual table has been taken.'

'Taken? Where has it gone?'

'Occupied, madam. By a VIP.'

Evelyn could feel her heart beating erratically. It was all over the place, as was her evening. 'But my husband and I are Very Important Passengers too.' Soon to be Very Irate Passengers.

Surely if a former ship's doctor and his wife didn't command VIP status aboard the ship – the ship on which they had lived since it was launched – she didn't know who did. To Evelyn's dismay, reinforcements arrived and a second round of placation began.

'I am terribly sorry, Mrs Parker,' said a man. Reassuringly for Evelyn, he was wearing a shiny tie instead of a tricolour waistcoat. At last she might get somewhere. 'Please let me explain.'

He went to lead her by the arm, but Evelyn brandished her handbag and was pleased to see him flinch and clasp his hands in submission. She wasn't one to resort to violence as a rule, but the stress of losing Henry had brought out an emboldened and unusually forthright side to her. For a split second she recognised the feisty young nurse who'd booked herself a passage to Australia. Her heroine Florence Nightingale had had a reputation as something of a contrarian, a woman not to be trifled with. Evelyn considered it a worthy aspiration. She imagined herself in a long dark dress, wearing a white lace cap and apron.

'This is outrageous!' The new emboldened Evelyn was determined to stand her ground, regardless of the looks she was attracting from the other diners. 'I have been evicted from my table!' She raised her handbag a fraction. 'A defenceless old lady!'

The man in the shiny tie shied at her raised voice. His name badge said Bruno and displayed an Italian flag.

Beyond the pillar, her steadfast landmark, Evelyn could see the table for two in its usual position, bathed in the peachy caress of the setting sun. The sunset that was rightfully hers and Henry's. A portly man in a suit had his back to her. He was sitting in Henry's usual seat. Opposite, where Evelyn always sat, was a woman who looked half his age. They were tucking into their entrees, oblivious to the unfolding commotion.

Following her gaze, the Italian tried to explain. 'That's the managing director of the company. He's on board for the cruise.'

'I don't care if he's King Neptune, tell him and his daughter they're sitting at *my* table,' said Evelyn, indignant.

A hush fell over the dining room, leaving the Italian holding his breath, unsure of what to do next. The managing director looked around briefly, patted his mouth with his napkin then returned to his dinner.

'Between you and me, Mrs P,' said a woman appearing from nowhere, 'I don't think that's his daughter.' She had big giggly teeth and a kind face. The background noise of eating and drinking resumed. 'Now why don't you come and join Frank and me over here?'

Frank and the giggly, bubbly, fizzy woman. Evelyn knew she knew them from somewhere. Fizzy cola. *Nola. And Frank.*

'I wouldn't want to intrude,' said Evelyn.

'Don't you worry. We've nearly finished but I'm sure we could squeeze in another course to keep you company.'

'I wouldn't want you to overeat on my account.'

'Nonsense. We'd be more than happy to. We only requested first sitting dinner so we can get to the show and be in plenty of time for the midnight buffet.'

'*First* sitting? You mean you've been eating since six-thirty?' Evelyn imagined if Nola talked less, she wouldn't need two sittings to finish her dinner.

'This *is* first sitting, Mrs P,' said Nola gently. 'It's only seven o'clock. I think you're a tad early.'

Early? A whole hour early. Evelyn was relieved she wasn't late after all. This was proof that she wasn't going dotty. She still had time to be on time for Henry. Better than that, to be early. She was pleased she hadn't made a scene.

An extra place was made at Frank and Nola's table, and a nervous-looking waiter handed Evelyn a French-themed menu. She placed her handbag under her chair, comforted to know that all her important things were within easy reach.

The ship's printing press must be faulty again because the menu was blurred. Luckily she already knew that French night meant a choice of beef consommé or twice-baked goat's cheese soufflé, followed by *boeuf bourguignon* or *carré d'agneau rôti* with *Napoléon de légumes*.

Her dining companions were already on their desserts. In the old days passengers would only be served the same course the captain was currently eating, rather like the Queen at a banquet. Things were more relaxed nowadays, and the waiter offered to fetch her whatever she fancied. Nola was tucking into chocolate mousse and Frank, *tarte tatin*. Evelyn didn't want to hold them up and, ironically, wasn't a big fan of French cuisine. She ordered vanilla ice cream.

'Vera used to get terrible heartburn if I fed her too late,' Nola was saying as the waiter returned with the ice cream.

Vera? Evelyn was none the wiser. She felt as if she'd joined the conversation after a pit stop and was trying to warm up her new tyres. Henry had always felt more comfortable with wheels than balls, and as a big motor-racing fan he enjoyed nothing more than a fifty-lap snooze in front of the grand prix on the ship's sport channel.

'Nola is a wonderful cook, Mrs Parker,' said Frank through a mouthful of shortcrust pastry. 'The doctors were sure all that home-cooked food was the reason Vera lived so long.'

'If I'd known that, we might have been on this holiday years ago,' muttered Nola.

'My mother was a big cheese eater, Mrs Parker,' said Frank proudly.

Evelyn spooned ice cream into her mouth but her thoughts had drifted back to Florence Nightingale.

'*Cheese is not usually digestible by the sick,*' she said thoughtfully. '*But it is pure nourishment for repairing waste; and I have seen sick, and not a few either, whose craving for cheese shewed how much it was needed by them.*'

'We're big cheese eaters too,' said Nola. 'Aren't we, Frank?'

'We certainly are,' he replied, patting the back of her hand. 'Big cheese eaters.'

They sat in companionable silence, bonded by their mutual appreciation for cheese. Evelyn liked these people. They were her new friends. She'd lost Henry but discovered Frank and Nola instead. And Vera. And cheese.

All too soon, Evelyn's dessert was gone, her spoon left resting in a creamy puddle at the bottom of the dish. At neighbouring tables diners were leaving, their meals finished, ready to join the scrum for the best seats in the show lounge.

'Once upon a time,' said Evelyn, thinking out loud, 'dinner was the highlight of the day. The main event if you like.'

'Is that so?' Nola ran her finger across her dessert plate and licked off the remnant chocolate. 'I bet you've had dinner with some interesting people in your time, Mrs P.'

~

On my twenty-first birthday I arrived in the restaurant to find Dr Henry Parker sitting at the head of my table. The captain was entertaining a table of well-to-dos on the other side of the restaurant and several other of the senior ship's officers were similarly holding court at their own tables. I was embarrassed to find this particular member of the ship's company dining with me, remembering the awkwardness of our previous meetings. I still had his monogrammed handkerchief. My fellow dining companions, on the other hand, were already making quite a fuss of him.

'Miss Des Roches, this is Dr Parker, the assistant surgeon. He's joining us for dinner.' The self-appointed spokesperson for our table was a wealthy widow from Tunbridge Wells whose daughter and son-in-law had emigrated to Melbourne a couple of years before. Despite being twice his age, the widow flirted with our guest in a most unedifying way. 'We're very honoured to sit at your table, Doctor.'

'May I suggest that it is the other way round, that the doctor is sitting at our table?' I acknowledged Dr Parker by way of a brief nod and turned my attention to the menu.

Dr Parker loosened his collar with a finger. 'You are quite right, Miss Des Roches,' he said. 'Please forgive my intrusion.'

I could feel his eyes on me. I studiously avoided meeting them, determined not to interact with him. He'd already watched me throw up, criticised my sketches and patronised me. He was rude, condescending and aloof. Exactly the kind of man I would never marry. Not even if he asked me.

Table twenty-seven was in the very centre of the restaurant, a rectangular table for six, although there had only ever been five of us seated around it. My fellow diners, apart from the merry widow, were a couple from Surrey and their fifteen-year-old son, Edward. Having spent the previous ten evenings eating dinner with them, I had started to relax and enjoy their company.

The conversation was usually light, the widow proving somewhat of a mimic, and highly entertaining company. The teenage boy, a mathematical genius by all accounts, for the most part stayed silent and tongue-tied, with a habit of staring at me. If I ever caught his gaze and smiled, he would turn beetroot red and look hastily at his plate. His father kept him on a tight rein, prodding him to sit up straight several times during each course.

The young lad seemed quite relieved to have a new diner at the table, as Dr Henry Parker soon became the focus of the evening, even drawing attention away from Edward's perpetual slouching. It was as though he came to life in Henry's presence, and the two fell almost immediately into a kind of mental jousting. An intellectual arm-wrestle. It soon became clear that I was the one they were trying to impress.

The merry widow proposed a toast to coincide with the arrival of the main course.

'Here's to Dr Henry Parker, our distinguished guest.'

'The pleasure is all mine,' said the young doctor. He looked at me as he said it. 'Mr P. G. Wodehouse maintained that in an emergency the ship's doctor could always be located playing deck quoits with the prettiest girl on board.'

If it had been his intention to embarrass me, then he would have been disappointed because if my nursing training had taught me one thing, it was how to suppress a blush.

He continued, 'This is not entirely true, because invariably the prettiest girl becomes the domain of the chief officer, and the doctor is obliged to act as wingman and entertain her friend. Or seek more intellectually robust company.'

They all laughed at this. All except me. Was I the robust company? I was relieved that Dr Parker obviously relished my intellect, but his honesty, on the night of my coming of age, cut my young ego to the quick.

While I seethed and broiled, the other adults continued to interrogate Dr Henry Parker, shooting a barrage of the obvious questions at him like a firing squad. What did he do all day? What did he recommend for seasickness? Was there a morgue on the ship? I only prayed that no one was planning to take advantage of our captive medic and offer up ailments for free advice.

I sat back and took it in. Took him in. He looked even younger than he'd first appeared when we met on the deck. In his mess kit of short white jacket fastened with gold buttons, I thought he looked like a waiter. His spectacles, as thick as milk bottles, were smudged with fingerprints, and I wondered how he could possibly see through them. His voice was more tenor than baritone, his build more that of a cricketer than a rugby player, though I doubt he played either. When he laughed, a fop of reddish hair fell across one eye and he had the habit, I noted, of smoothing it into place with the back of his thumb.

The widow was positively cooing over him, this failed Oxford surgeon whose ancestors had been convicts and shipwrecked sailors. If I hadn't been so hungry, I would have left the table. But we still had corned ox tongue served with steamed potatoes and green beans followed by melrose pudding to come. And yet another philosophical debate between young Edward Partridge and Dr Parker, this time over the nature of human consciousness.

To young Edward's intense embarrassment, his mother was regaling Dr Parker with the story of how she'd gone into labour in the first-class carriage between London and Edinburgh and had given birth just as the train passed York. I had no idea how the conversation had arrived here, having spent the last few minutes daydreaming into my consommé.

'Have you ever had to deliver a baby on the ship, Dr Parker?'

I expected him to laugh and dismiss my question as ridiculous.

'If it can happen in a railway carriage then I suppose it could certainly happen on a ship. Everything that happens ashore can potentially happen at sea.'

I lost my opportunity to outshine Dr Parker when a birthday cake arrived at the table complete with twenty-one candles and a chorus of waiters. Following a rousing rendition of 'Happy Birthday' in which the merry widow sang an ear-piercing descant, I blew out the candles.

Dr Parker insisted on ordering a bottle of champagne to be shared at the table. I noticed he covered his own glass, urging the waiter to refill mine instead. Naturally I thanked him and the other diners for their best wishes. I chatted and laughed with wellwisher after wellwisher, suddenly finding myself the reluctant centre of attention. All the while I felt Dr Parker's eyes on me, his piercing gaze setting my whole body on fire. When the champagne bubbles tickled my nose and made me sneeze, twice, he smiled at me as if it was the most endearing thing he'd ever witnessed. I smiled back in spite of myself. It was as if we were the only ones in the dining room. Alone, surrounded by seven hundred strangers.

12

Man Overboard

'I'D LIKE TO REPORT A MISSING PERSON.' EVELYN RESTED HER handbag on the reception desk.

The junior assistant purser who was manning the front desk, a handsome young man with a thick accent, smiled tolerantly. 'Good morning, Mrs Parker, how are you today?'

'I am very well thank you, but that is beside the point. The point being that I can't find my husband.'

'Very good, very good,' said the receptionist.

'I can assure you, young man, that it is far from *very good*. In fact, it is the exact opposite of *very good*. It is *very bad* indeed.' It was important to speak slowly and clearly when addressing someone with an accent.

The young man maintained his smile while his eyes turned towards the computer screen. 'Try not to worry, Mrs Parker. I'm sure he will turn up.'

Another passenger had appeared behind Evelyn and was ushered forward to the desk by another receptionist, with a 'Thank you for waiting, how may I help?'

So far, Evelyn noted, she hadn't been offered any help whatsoever in her own predicament. She wasn't usually one to express her frustrations in the customer feedback forms, but she had a fountain pen full of blue-black Quink ink in her handbag and she wasn't afraid to use it.

'It's all very well to tell me not to worry, but my husband has disappeared into thin air. Dr Henry Parker. Perhaps you've heard of him? He was a ship's doctor, you know.'

'I know who your husband is, Mrs Parker.' The reception man smiled. More accurately, his mouth was smiling. His eyes were not.

'Then why aren't you looking for him? How does one organise a search party? Or a sniffer dog?' Evelyn was sure there must be a policy for such a circumstance. After the *Titanic* sank in 1912, they invented a procedure for just about everything aboard a ship. 'Can't we simply pretend that Henry is an iceberg?'

The young man looked up from his computer screen and swallowed. 'I'm not sure I follow.'

'There must be a standing order when it comes to missing ships' doctors. It is an emergency.'

'It's not strictly speaking an emergency. Not like a man overboard, for instance.'

Evelyn was growing tired of this. No one seemed to be taking Henry's disappearance seriously. Unlike the plumbing emergency the couple at the desk had just reported, which the other receptionist had promised to act on immediately.

'Henry is more important than a blocked toilet, you know.' She saw the young man smirk. 'What if he *has* fallen overboard?' She opened her handbag and took out her mints, unwrapped one and put it in her mouth.

'Then we'd initiate the man-overboard procedure.'

'And how exactly is that done?' Evelyn suddenly wished she'd paid more attention to the last emergency muster drill. There was no time to return to her cabin and consult the safety notice on the back of her cabin door.

The receptionist took a deep breath. 'If you actually *witness* somebody fall overboard, you must shout "MAN OVERBOARD", alert a crew member, throw anything that will float into the water and keep the person in your sight at all times.'

'I see,' said Evelyn, chomping the mint between her back molars. 'A bit like this, you mean . . . "MAN OVERBOARD!"'

The mint shot out of her mouth with the last syllable. It skidded across the desk, narrowly missing the reception man. He sprang back from the sticky missile, his eyes wide. Several passengers who'd been milling around the atrium turned to stare. Evelyn's new approach seemed to be working. There were already more people taking notice than there had been before she started shouting.

'Mrs Parker, please . . .'

She offered the packet. 'Would you like one?'

'No, thank you.'

'Look . . .' she squinted at his name badge and guessed, '. . . Julius, I wonder if I might be entitled to a second opinion on the situation with my husband?' This was getting very tedious, and more serious by the minute. 'Would you be so kind as to fetch me someone with more stripes?'

Evelyn's new, more direct approach had the desired effect, and a youngish woman with a reassuring number of stripes appeared from the back office.

'Is there a problem?'

'As a matter of fact there is. Dr Henry Parker has disappeared into thin air and nobody is taking it seriously.'

'Are you sure? I thought I saw him a little while ago. He was heading for the boutique . . .'

The young man with the accent jumped in, '. . . the buffet, wasn't it?'

'Yes, the buffet. You see, Mrs Parker, there's no need to worry. Henry is safe and well. Now is there anything else we can help you with today?'

Evelyn narrowed her eyes. Henry had a tailor in the city and never ate in the ship's buffet on account of his ineptitude with serving implements. He could sew up a child's eyelid with a suture as thin as a human hair, but faced with a tower of profiteroles and a set of buffet tongs, he would go to pieces.

'No. That'll be all . . .' Evelyn closed her handbag and hooked it over one elbow, growing an inch with indignation. 'For now.'

Short of throwing a couple of sun loungers over the side of the ship as the young man had so helpfully suggested, she couldn't think how else to get anyone to take her seriously. With all resources mobilised in response to the bathroom crisis on deck nine, and yet no one apparently in the least concerned about a missing passenger, Evelyn wasn't surprised that the *Golden Sunset* was heading for the scrapheap.

She was, however, left juggling two scenarios, each equally troubling. Either the purser's staff were completely incompetent, or they were deliberately fobbing her off. It occurred to her for the first time that their bungling might simply be a ruse. A cover-up. Did the crew know something she didn't?

13

Water, Water Everywhere

PAGE 86, NOTES ON NURSING: *LIES, INTENTIONAL AND UNINTEN-tional, are seldomer told in answer to precise than to leading questions.*

Evelyn debated going straight back down to reception and demanding to know what they were hiding from her. She tried to imagine what Florence Nightingale would do, an intelligent woman, ahead of her time in so many ways. Not one to leave an important matter in the hands of others. There was nothing for it but to carry on searching for Henry herself.

Fifty-two Finding Henry paces past Aphrodite, Evelyn found her cabin door wide open. She checked the number twice to be sure. There were feet poking out from behind the bathroom door, just visible from the alleyway. Ankles the colour of burnt umber, ending in white shoes. Confused, Evelyn stepped over them and, peering round the bathroom door, saw a woman on her hands and knees surrounded by wet towels.

'What is going on?' Evelyn said.

The young woman attached to the feet turned and smiled.

'I'm sorry, Mrs Parker. There has been a small flood in your bathroom. I am just cleaning it up. I won't be long.'

A flood? How very unusual. Evelyn's chest tightened, her heart thumping behind her ribs.

'Where is Virgilio?'

The woman sat back on her haunches and sighed. 'Manila, ma'am.'

It was news to Evelyn.

'Who are you?'

'I am Grace, your cabin steward,' said the girl with the feet, the one who used to be Virgilio.

Grace. *Tuesday's child.* A tiny memory sparked but soon fizzled like a broken match.

'That's a lot of water.' Evelyn looked on as the girl wrung out another bath towel's worth of water from the floor into the shower tray.

Evelyn had lived through many disasters on board ships: floods, fires, engine trouble. Flooding was a common problem, or at least it used to be. Modern ships were more reliable. Not like the good old days when emergency stations were called almost every cruise for some mechanical drama or another. Cruising was much more fun back then.

Tuesday's child stood now, pulling herself up in the cramped bathroom space by grasping the sink. She didn't look quite as agile as she should for her age, and Evelyn noticed how her burgundy shirt was rather snug on her otherwise slim body. Too much stodge in the crew canteen. She'd mention it at the front desk, or on second thoughts, after this morning's fiasco, she would go straight to the captain instead.

With the mopping and wringing operation taking up valuable space in the cabin, Evelyn stepped out into the alleyway. There was nothing out of the ordinary, no clue as to the cause of this ship-borne catastrophe, the doors to the neighbouring cabins quietly closed.

'Why is my cabin flooded and none of the others?' she called to the girl.

The girl emerged, her arms heavy with saturated towels. She looked up from under her thick lashes and bit her lip. Such a lovely young face, but the girl looked tired with crescent shadows under her beautiful dark eyes.

'When I came in, the shower was running. The washcloth had blocked the plughole.'

This was troubling news to Evelyn. Who would do such a careless thing?

Henry. *Silly old fool.*

'Have you seen my husband?' He'd been behaving very strangely recently. Wandering, getting lost. Now he'd left the shower running. If he could flood the bathroom, what else was he capable of? She had to find him before something terrible happened.

The bathroom was steamy but otherwise pristine. The raised threshold at the entrance had contained the deluge and, what's more, the hideous carpet that didn't match her bedspread looked disappointingly dry.

Water, water every where
And all the boards did shrink

'I'll bring you fresh towels, ma'am,' said the girl.

All that exertion in mopping up the flooded bathroom had left her glowing. Evelyn liked her new steward, Tuesday's child.

She had a gentle but efficient way about her. Would make a good nurse in whatever country she was from.

'You should be doing more than mopping floors and putting chocolates on pillows.'

'I'm sorry, ma'am. I'm a little behind with the beds. On account of the flood.'

'Have you thought about nursing, my dear?' said Evelyn, following the young steward who wasn't Virgilio out to her cart to fetch dry towels and then following her back again. 'Strong girl like you, willing, practical . . . never mind. What did you say your name was again?'

'Grace, ma'am.'

'Are you married?' Evelyn followed the girl to the bed and helped her straighten out the sheets.

'No, ma'am.'

'Tighter,' said Evelyn, tutting at the girl's first attempt to fold the corner at the foot of the bed. 'That's better. Very good. Do you have a boyfriend?'

They plumped a pillow each, straightened the bedspread.

'I do have a fiancé. We'll be getting married soon, once we've saved up enough money to build a house. He's training to be a teacher because there's a shortage of qualified teachers on my island. I have to keep working until he finishes his course.'

'A teacher. Saving up. How lovely.' Evelyn wasn't normally one for small talk, but she'd become much more chatty since Henry disappeared. 'How old are you?'

'I am twenty-one, ma'am.'

'Now there's a coincidence. I was twenty-one once.' Evelyn slumped into her armchair, feeling a hundred and twenty-one after all the pillows and corners.

'Can I do anything else for you before I leave?' Tuesday's child moved sideways towards the door, reminding Evelyn of a crab.

'Pass me my handbag, would you, dear?'

She placed the beige leather handbag on Evelyn's lap as requested. The clasp fell open as the contents resettled into the cramped space inside.

Evelyn rifled through, finding the packet of mints near the bottom.

'Would you like a mint?' she said to buy herself thinking time. There was something on her mind but she couldn't think what it was.

'No thank you, ma'am.'

Fountain pen. Envelope. Pocket map. Lantern-halyard-*lanyard*. A teacake. Her mother's tiara. Folded piece of A4 paper. *The bad-luck seagull.*

'I need your help with something very important,' said Evelyn, unfolding the paper triumphantly to reveal a partially coloured-in drawing. She couldn't settle until she'd found the answer to her puzzle. She handed Grace the drawing. It was important, though she couldn't think why. 'Do you know the name of this bird?'

~

'Did you know there are thirteen species of albatross, Miss Des Roches? They say that some can follow ships for days on end. The scientists have marked birds and found them up to six thousand miles away from their breeding grounds. The wandering albatross has a wingspan of ten to twelve feet. In other words, perfectly adapted for life at sea. Cormorants are a different bird altogether. Some say they represent the souls of dead sailors.'

I had noticed Dr Henry Parker out of the corner of my eye. I pretended to startle at his voice, gouging a semi-convincing pencil line across the bird's hooked beak. When my hands started to shake, I quickly closed the sketchbook, trapping the pencil between the pages.

It had become our own private deck game. While the other passengers whiled away the remaining hours and days of the journey with giant chess pieces, tug-of-war or quoits, the assistant surgeon and I had fallen into a routine of sorts. I would take my sketchbook to the aft end of the deck to a sheltered deckchair away from the cool Antarctic wind. The same spot every day, the place where magically, at the conclusion of his morning clinic, the assistant surgeon would happen to appear and pass comment on the weather or admire my drawings.

In the distance, the horizon looked smudged, as if I'd started to rub it out with my eraser. A storm approaching. I judged we had less than five minutes before it hit.

'So Dr Parker, not only are you a poet and an expert on seasickness, you are also an ornithologist. There is no end to your talents.'

'I merely pay attention to the things that fascinate me.'

'Seasickness fascinates you?'

'Only the patients.'

'Well I am happy to report that I am no longer suffering the *mal de mer*. As you so rightly predicted, I have acclimatised.'

'Like the albatross, perfectly adapted to life at sea.'

I frowned. 'You're comparing me to an albatross? That's not very flattering. I thought they were meant to be bad luck for sailors.'

'On the contrary, sailors consider the albatross to be good luck, a symbol of God's creation, of nature and innocence. It is only bad luck if you capture and kill one.'

'But is innocence always preferable to worldliness, Doctor? Isn't it better to have the benefit of experience? Especially on a ship.'

'Once innocence is lost, it cannot be restored. The Ancient Mariner had to endure the consequences of his decision to shoot the albatross. The wind dropped, his men died, his ship sank.'

'But he learned his lesson and made it home safely, didn't he?'

He was standing right in front of me now, cloud-grey eyes with a flare of sun. 'He did. A wiser man.' He produced a wrapped package from behind his back. 'Happy birthday, Miss Des Roches. I'm sorry it's a little late.'

I took the gift and untied the long white bow I recognised as wound-packing gauze. The crinkled brown paper fell open. Inside was a book with a brown cloth cover, bevelled edges and gold lettering. The spine was all but worn away, the corners soft and rounded by handling.

The Rime of the Ancient Mariner, by Samuel Taylor Coleridge, illustrated by Gustave Doré.

Inside, on the first blank page, he'd written, *To Evelyn, On the occasion of your twenty-first birthday. From Dr Henry Parker. Orcades, 1953.*

'I couldn't possibly accept this,' I said, seeing that it was a first edition, printed in 1876. 'It's . . .'

What? Too valuable? Too personal? Too . . .

'I hope you don't mind me inscribing it,' he said.

By writing inside the book, he knew I couldn't decline his gift. I still hadn't told him my Christian name. He hadn't asked.

The formality of our interactions had been part of the game. Part of the thrill. But of course my full name was printed on the official passenger list. If he'd cared to look me up.

The book was old and tatty, but it was priceless. It was one of Dr Parker's personal possessions, a cherished and well-loved thing, and in giving it to me he had shared an intimacy that left me moved and a little confused. My mother, on the other hand, had given me a pair of kid gloves. Hers was the only present I opened on the morning of my twenty-first birthday, alone in my cabin. I wondered if I'd ever wear them in the Australian climate, except to handle my infrequent dealings with her.

'Thank you. I don't know what to say.'

Dr Parker was oblivious to the approaching weather front. His features had softened and he was smiling. He looked rather pleased with himself, as though once again he had the upper hand. 'Just tell me what you think,' he said. 'When you've had a chance to read it. I thought you might like the illustrations too. Inspiration, perhaps?'

I promised that I would. I tried to ignore the approaching squall, the first fat drops of water on the tip of my nose and Henry's glasses.

'Brace yourself,' I said. 'I think we're about to be caught.'

'It's too late. I already am,' he replied as weather engulfed us.

14

Wagging Tongues

WITH A GLORIOUS AFTERNOON STRETCHING OUT IN FRONT of her, Evelyn had no intention of going ashore. Wherever the ship happened to be docked, she'd been there already. Been, seen, done. Leave the exploring to the young folk, who still had room, the capacity to gather new memories. She barely had storage space for the ones she'd already made.

She must have nodded off because she'd dreamed of Henry. They were dancing. Henry treading on her toes as they twirled around the crowded dance floor. In the dream, she didn't feel the pain of his size tens trampling hers. She was trying to ask him why she had no sensation in her feet, but even shouting she couldn't make herself heard above the band.

Evelyn wasn't normally one to drop off, but sleep was becoming an increasingly inviting place. In her dreams she always found Henry. The waking world made less and less sense as the shapeless days passed. It was as though she was gradually falling into a long, deep sleep, slipping further and further from reality, one head nod at a time.

When she'd closed her eyes the ship had been in port and the sun directly overhead. The ship was moving now and it was dark outside, the sun replaced by stars. She was wide awake and needed something to do. Evelyn wandered around the cabin, looking for ways to while away the inconvenient night.

She would have to start packing soon, with the ship about to be decommissioned like an old nag heading for the knacker's yard. It was such a shame. *Golden Sunset* was still a real lady, holding herself together with class and dignity compared to the brash floating hotels that people flocked to these days.

Her eye skipped from object to object in the cramped cabin, taking in all her things. Hers and Henry's. The placement of objects was like the arrangement of features on a familiar face. But something was wrong. There was something missing from the bookshelf, an eyebrow, or a nose. *Cassell's Modern Dictionary of Nursing and Medical Terms* was still there, as were W. T. Gordon and Alice M. Pugh. Florence Nightingale was leaning at an angle, as if she'd had one too many on duty. Evelyn pulled the dusty tome from the shelf, blew away a cobweb and opened a page at random.

> *To a nurse I would add, take care that you always put the same things in the same places; you don't know how suddenly you may be called on some day to find something, and may not be able to remember in your haste where you yourself had put it, if your memory is not in the habit of seeing the thing there always.*

Evelyn was about to return Florence to her place when she noticed a hardback bound in brown cloth, pushed up against the bulkhead, partially obscured by A. Millicent Ashdown SRN's *Complete System of Nursing*. She shoved Millicent and her three hundred and seventy-four photographs, diagrams, charts and illustrations aside and rescued the forgotten book.

Bringing the book to her nostrils, she breathed in the damp, woody, tobacco smell of old paper. There, on the first blank page, Henry's first tentative inscription of her name. Hoping it might act as a lucky charm, a talisman, Evelyn tucked *The Ancient Mariner* into her cramped handbag. Eating the last of the stale teacake freed up some extra space, Samuel Taylor Coleridge appearing quite content, nestled between the tiara and the remaining mints.

What would happen to all her things? Evelyn pictured the ship driven aground, winched up the beach in Pakistan or Bangladesh or wherever, the torches hungry for her steel, sparks spraying like a farewell fireworks display. Where would she go? Tears shivered in the corners of Evelyn's eyes but she wouldn't shed them however lonely and frightened she felt.

Evelyn had always been comfortable in her own company. Even as a child she'd been happy to fill her loneliness with imagination, her rich inner life of stories and invisible friends a welcome escape from the real world and parents who were consumed by making each other unhappy. She'd had few friends except for the convenient children of other dignitaries. At her exclusive school, she'd been seen as aloof and left out of other children's games and conversations. Evelyn was swaddled by all the trappings of wealth, yet impoverished in every human connection. Even privilege couldn't buy her friendship.

As the wife of the ship's doctor, she'd thrown herself into the role, leaving little time for loneliness. With so many other people on board, she was rarely alone. There were always plenty of other women who, like her, were married to their husbands' jobs. The wives of the captain, chief engineer, or the staff captain provided brief friendships. Shipboard friendships, like romances at sea, were intense and all-consuming. The relaxed atmosphere of a ship allowed strangers to share secrets and forge deep, if short-lived, connections. It reminded Evelyn of the war, when lives were lived in the moment, and the next and the next. After her friendless childhood she let down her guard and threw herself into the intimacy of these new relationships. Other women, who ashore would be little more than casual acquaintances, became best friends. One after another after another.

Eventually the cycle of greeting and farewelling took its toll, and Evelyn conceded to a life of polite yet superficial engagement and civility. Out of self-preservation, she had sought solace in her own inner world and her husband.

Without friends to mirror her passing years, however, it was easy to forget she was ageing. She simply forgot that she was old, the hostile mirror her only reminder.

Evelyn scoured the cabin for photos of Henry, hoping to conjure up a likeness of her most up-to-date husband. His hair would be grey by now, white even, like her own, and she supposed he still wore his glasses. In her most vivid memories of him, Henry was twenty-seven, eyes clear behind his perpetually smudged lenses, his pale skin soft and unblemished by the sun. He'd always favoured the shade, so that in spite of a life of travel around the tropics, she imagined he would have been spared the worst of the warts and wrinkles that appeared with age.

She scanned the photo frames, from the earliest shot of Henry in his uniform, a stripe and a half on each shoulder, through to later photos as a couple, Evelyn in a series of gowns, a museum-worthy progression of fifties and sixties and seventies fashion, and Henry with two then three stripes. Black and white photographs in their younger days; their latter in full Technicolor. A small boy featured in several of the photos, growing into a larger boy who reminded her of Dobbs.

The final photograph was taken in front of the grand staircase in the atrium, a favourite location for the ship's photographers to capture formal portraits. Age became Henry. He'd grown into his ears, and his white hair gave him a distinguished air. Having finally ditched his milk-bottle glasses for a pair of modern spectacles, Henry was handsome. He'd been quite a catch, once upon a time. Probably still was. But who was that old woman standing next to him, thinning hair lacquered into scaffolded fullness and large diamond earrings hanging from her drooping earlobes?

Misery settled on Evelyn like the thick skin of a pudding as she realised the woman in the picture was her. It all made perfect sense now. Why hadn't she seen it before?

Henry was having an affair.

She slumped into the chair, winded. All those years, gone. Wasted. Her heart throbbed like a new bruise.

The humiliation of it was too much to bear. She'd seen it played out all too often. The months away from home, out of sight, out of mind. The endless temptations, the oblivious spouse. The wagging tongues, the whispered whispers.

Had she been naïve in assuming that since she sailed with him all year round temptation wouldn't find him, and heartbreak, her?

Evelyn's broken heart splintered, tiny shards travelling through her arteries until every body part ached with sadness. She remembered this feeling. Jealousy. Rage. Despair.

Whom could she trust when she had nobody?

Evelyn hauled her balcony doors wide open and filled her lungs with ozone.

Her one faithful friend, lifelong companion and confidante.

The one who understood, who always listened but never passed judgement.

The sea.

~

The second half of my voyage to Australia is less clear in my mind. It is as though I skimmed through the last few chapters, eager to see what happened without paying full attention. In my memory there are pages still stuck together, things I simply can't recall. I remember the emotions and feelings rather than the events themselves. My heart softened towards Dr Henry Parker as the ship approached Fremantle. By Melbourne I felt something that I imagined was love.

I'd boarded *Orcades* to escape post-war London and a stifling childhood. By the time I disembarked four weeks later, I was engaged to an Australian doctor and heading for a life I had never envisaged. Looking back, it's much harder to explain why such a determined and independent woman changed course so suddenly. At the time I'd reasoned that I could always have a second chance at a career, but with the ship about to carry Henry away to the other side of the world, I had to decide, before it was too late, whether to follow my head or my heart.

We had a quiet wedding in a registry office. Henry's parents were already dead and my mother was too frail to travel. We accosted a pair of sightseers to be our witnesses and to take our photo afterwards. Me shivering in a thin tea dress as a cool southerly blustered in, and Henry, stiff and formal in his uniform.

There was no honeymoon – Henry was called back early from leave when another doctor left. A promotion to his very own ship at last. It didn't bother me. I assumed that as newlyweds our lives would be one long honeymoon, travelling the world in luxury.

The first few months after the wedding were idyllic and I never once regretted giving up my nursing career. Each morning, waking up in some glamorous new destination, I'd thank my lucky stars that I'd been saved from the drudgery of bedpans and night shifts under the auspices of some battleaxe matron. Being Mrs Henry Parker carried status and an undeniable cachet, albeit frequently a companionless one. I, like the other post-war brides of my generation, had been led to believe that my role in life was simply to make my husband happy.

It was during a cruise from Sydney to Canada and America that I began to feel the first pang of boredom and insecurity. Henry was especially busy in the hospital and I tried to keep myself occupied with my routine of walks and shipboard activities. I had written endless letters to my mother, filled several sketchbooks and read just about every book on the shelves of the library. Anything to engage my brain, to distract it from the unhelpful thoughts it kept returning to. I began to ruminate over Henry's frequent absences. Insecurity soon turned to suspicion.

Madeline Ashton was a very glamorous and worldly American pianist who was travelling alone on the ship. It was in the days before cruise ships carried proper entertainment staff and she soon became the darling of not only the other passengers but most of the male officers too. She was beautiful and talented and before long had a loyal following.

I'd learned to play the piano as a child, at my mother's insistence. My recitals were part of the show she liked to put on for visiting dignitaries. But nothing kills off a child's musical enjoyment faster than a parent's aspirations. It wasn't long before I was bored with being wheeled out like a circus act and began to deliberately miss notes. The more wrong notes, the more attention I received. Mother was furious. It was a great game, but one that didn't last. When my parents divorced, the piano was sold.

Late one evening, all dressed up, I got sick of waiting for Henry to finish work and decided to head out on deck alone. The piano bar was a popular spot for passengers after dark. When I arrived, Madeline Ashton was well into her set. Her voice was smooth and silky. She oozed sensuality and sex. I'd tried to emulate her sultry pout in the mirror but I'd looked as if I was suffering an allergic reaction instead.

After spectating from the back of the room through several numbers, I made the decision to approach her at the end of the show and ask if she would tutor me. I'd already cooked up a plan to surprise Henry with a recital in his honour, for our anniversary.

On this night, instead of mingling, she slipped away. I watched her leave through a side entrance and saw my chance. She was remarkably quick given the precarious red heels that were her trademark. I followed her down the main staircase and tried calling out, but she didn't look back.

To my surprise, she stopped at E deck and headed midships. Towards the hospital. It was closed at this hour, although it was possible that Henry or one of the nursing sisters was still inside tending to a patient, writing up notes or restocking the pharmacy shelves.

The door opened as soon as Madeline Ashton arrived. Someone was waiting for her. Expecting her. I hid behind a laundry cart parked outside the passenger ironing room and watched my husband let in this glamorous single woman without a word.

My heart tore in two. A beautiful woman in the peak of health meeting the ship's surgeon late at night? My body turned to water. My legs and arms tingled and I couldn't breathe. I've heard it said that a woman always knows when her husband is having an affair, but up until that moment I'd been blissfully unaware. I longed to go back to that time before I knew, to a time when I still trusted Henry. I remember that feeling of utter desolation, of being detached from my own body as I tried desperately to disbelieve what I had witnessed with my own eyes.

Frozen by indecision, I slumped to the ground behind the cart. I needed proof, knowing that I couldn't move from that crouched spot until I'd watched her come out again. I tried to imagine every possible innocent explanation, but when she emerged some time later, smoothing down her dress, I crumpled. Knowing at that moment that my life would never be the same again, I watched Henry follow her. They stood in the alleyway, facing each other, neither saying a word. He took her hands in his, and they stood looking at each other for several seconds before she leaned over and kissed him on the cheek.

Terrified they would hear my heart clattering against my ribs, I crouched in a ball like a small child playing hide and seek. I remember Madeline Ashton's red heels as she walked by, piercing the deck with each stride, like icepicks through my heart.

~

Evelyn grasped the polished mahogany railing on the edge of her balcony. Her tongue was salty but she wasn't sure if she was tasting spindrift or her own tears. No, never tears. The star-smudged Milky Way stretched towards the morning, still far away.

> *Alone, alone, all, all alone,*
> *Alone on a wide wide sea!*
> *And never a saint took pity on*
> *My soul in agony.*

'Oh, Henry,' said Evelyn. 'Where are you?'

Had he really left her for another woman? She was quietly impressed he still had the energy for an affair at his age. But could her Henry really be that cruel? When they were so close to the end of their lives, would he let her live out the rest of hers in such torment?

How easy it would be to slip over the edge of the ship. Like falling weary into bed. To surrender to the cool clutches of the waves and an eternal sleep in the arms of the ocean.

Inside, Evelyn saw the life they'd made together. All the miles they'd travelled, the countries they'd visited, all the wonderful things they'd done were there in that cabin. And at a time when many of their age were checking into nursing homes, separated, their houses and possessions sold from under them, she and Henry still travelled in style. They had a steward who mopped up their flooded bathrooms, and more food than they could possibly ever eat. They even had special people to worry on their behalf. There was live entertainment every night and a different port of call almost every day. This was the life they'd chosen. The sea was their life. This was how they'd planned to end their days too. Aboard a ship. Together.

Evelyn ran a brush through her hair, her resolve strengthening immeasurably with a squirt of expensive eau de parfum. She hadn't sacrificed her best years so Henry could simply upgrade her for a newer model when her upholstery started to sag. He was making a fool out of himself, and her. Evelyn hadn't come this far to only come this far.

The dress she chose was risky. Shimmering silver, low cut and fitted over the hips. It had always turned heads in the past. With a side fastening, the dress was at least easy to get into. A little too easy, because even when the zip was done all the way up, there was a worrying redundancy in the fabric that billowed where her bust and hips should have been. The satin hem gathered on the floor. Evelyn was sinking inside her own body, her bones settling like an ancient building. Thankfully her foundations were solid and reliable even if she couldn't feel them.

She eyed her Finding Henry shoes neatly paired by the cabin door. She loved the way the soft canvas hugged her feet, the way the rubber soles cushioned her joints from each jarring step. But when she found Henry canoodling with his mistress in the piano bar, she wanted to make an impression. She wanted to turn his head, show him what he was missing. She wouldn't win back his heart in sensible shoes.

Forcing her cottonwool feet into a pair of heels she found gathering dust at the back of the wardrobe, Evelyn at last felt a sense of purpose. The height threw her weight forward onto her knees, but at least the hem of her evening dress was no longer dragging on the ground. With an extra two inches, Evelyn felt invincible, if a little unsteady. She was off to the piano bar, to find Henry. The only concession she was prepared to make, in the circumstances, was to take the elevator rather than the stairs.

15

A Nurse Who Rustles

To LOCATE A GRAND PIANO ABOARD A SHIP SHOULDN'T BE too hard, thought Evelyn. She slipped her lantern-halyard-*lanyard* over her head and nestled the handle of her handbag into the crook of her starboard arm. Containing so many important things, it was bulky and heavy, forcing her to lean to port to counteract the extra weight.

The pocket map was comprehensively marked in blue-black with a number of potential 'places of interest' to be investigated. Her money was on the piano bar. She still hadn't worked out what she was going to say to Henry when she found him, whether or not she found him in the arms of another woman. Her heart was skittish with excitement, and dread.

A giggling young couple greeted Evelyn in the alleyway before disappearing into the cabin next door. Judging by their eagerness to get inside, they must be newlyweds, their individual foibles still charming to one another. But love was like that. It was short-sighted and sometimes made people do things that seemed foolish in hindsight.

There was no sign of the girl who wasn't Virgilio, either in the alleyway or the pantry. She liked this girl. The girl who wasn't yet married to the man who wasn't yet a teacher. There was something about her, apart from her prowess at mopping floors. When every passing moment felt like another page torn from the photo album, for some reason Evelyn had held on to everything she knew about this girl. Everything except her name. She had, if not a sixth sense about her, then at least a fourth or fifth.

The ship was moving a little tonight, no more than she was comfortable with in normal attire, but the shoes had shifted Evelyn's centre of gravity, each roll of a wave a mini battle to stay upright. What's more, the taffeta of her long skirt was shrink-wrapped around her ankles. She could almost hear Florence Nightingale complaining.

A nurse who rustles (I am speaking of nurses professional and unprofessional) is the horror of a patient, though perhaps he does not know why. The fidget of silk and of crinoline . . .

The dramatic entrance Evelyn had planned was looking less dramatic. Having walked the length of two decks, which felt more like four in her Winning Back Henry shoes, Evelyn was growing impatient with the lack of piano. It was only when she'd passed the photographic shop for the second or third time that she realised she was lost. Not lost exactly, since it was virtually impossible to get lost at home. More astray. Off course. Adrift.

Back where she'd started in the atrium, Evelyn decided not to throw good steps after bad and headed to reception.

'Where is the piano?' she asked the receptionist, a helpful-looking young man.

'Good evening, Mrs Parker,' he replied in an accent.

'I'm looking for a piano.'

'A piano?'

'Yes, a piano.' Evelyn fought the urge to break into song, finding old musical lyrics suddenly easier to recall than why she was looking for one.

'It's in the piano bar.' The receptionist corrected his smirk and cleared his throat. 'Deck ten, forward.'

Evelyn's arm ached and she let the handbag dangle by her side. She managed to bang into one or two passengers who were taking up too much space and found her way to the front of the elevator queue. When the doors opened, however, it was full of soft-bodied passengers pressed together like marshmallows in a jar. She tutted her judgement. She blamed elasticated clothing for the overcrowding in modern-day elevators.

When the next elevator arrived she stepped into an unexpected greeting from a smiling couple.

'Hello stranger,' said the woman. She wore a green sequinned dress that reminded Evelyn of a mermaid's tail. Her husband, a warty-headed man, was grinning straight at her.

Evelyn tried to darn the hole in her threadbare memory. They'd met before, she was sure of it. But what did she know about this couple, of the two thousand passengers aboard?

It came to her. 'How is Vera?'

'She's dead, Mrs P,' said the woman.

Evelyn was shocked. Vera dead? 'Oh I'm so terribly sorry, my dear.' What a terrible thing to happen. Especially on holiday. They'd be taking the champagne out of the ship's mortuary at that very moment. 'You'll be heading home from the next port, I presume?'

'Home? Not on your life,' laughed the woman. 'We're having the time of our lives! Aren't we, Frank?'

'Yes, dear. The time of our lives.'

Evelyn shouldn't have been shocked. Grief had been different in her day, but with times changing so fast it was hard to keep up with modern attitudes.

'Have you found Henry yet?' said Nola.

'I'm off to meet him now,' said Evelyn. 'I'm going to surprise him in the piano bar.'

'Do you mind if we join you?' said Nola. 'We love the piano, don't we, Frank?'

'Yes, Nola, we love the piano.'

Frank and Nola. Frank. And. Nola.

Like chewing a tasty morsel she couldn't bear to swallow, Evelyn repeated the names of her two friends as they made unsteady progress towards the piano bar. The heels had been a mistake, and she longed for her Finding Henry shoes. Walking was more difficult than she ever remembered. She pictured a toddler, wobbling and lurching towards her outstretched arms. Flanked by Frank and Nola, however, she felt secure enough. Walking sticks and wheeled walkers were for old people. She had Frank and Nola.

They arrived to the tinkle of piano keys and a lush female voice. The bar was crowded with expensive-smelling passengers, some sitting at small tables, others scattered around the plush velvet banquettes that lined the walls. In her memories a fug of cigarette smoke hung from the ceiling like a London fog. She pictured a dewy-eyed Madeline Ashton in a sequinned gown, crooning behind the raised lid of a baby grand, a coupe of Dom Pérignon within her reach. Henry, she suspected, would be hiding on the periphery, perched discreetly on a bar stool watching her with the chief officer. Evelyn was torn. To find

Henry in the thrall of another woman or hold on to the ideal of a faithful husband, albeit one who was still lost?

'Why don't you ladies find a seat and I'll fetch us some drinks?' said Frank.

'There's a table over here with a good view.' Nola gently guided Evelyn towards a polished table with three vacant chairs. Evelyn noticed she didn't paw her arm as other people tried to do, but offered her own as a support.

As Evelyn settled into the chair and jettisoned her not-for-walking shoes under the table, she felt uneasy. Nothing was how she'd imagined. There was no smoke. The handful of passengers who still liked to puff on a cigarette were now confined to a shameful corner of the promenade deck where they were subjected to the scrutiny and undisguised judgement of passing health fanatics. Behind her, Evelyn heard cackling women at the bar, noisily toasting the absence of their husbands. She scanned the other tables, the rim of passengers around the bar and the shady corners. There was no sign of Henry. Evelyn wasn't sure whether to be disappointed or relieved.

'And for you, Mrs Parker, what would you like to drink?'

She couldn't remember the last time she had drunk alcohol. It was ironic given that most of the time she felt drunk anyway – light-headed and wobbly with no recollection of what she'd done the night before.

'Let's splice the mainbrace,' she replied. She ordered champagne. For no reason other than when Henry walked in she wanted him to see her drinking champagne with strangers. It would make her look sophisticated and alluring.

'Coke for me, luv,' said Nola. *Fizzy cola, Nola.*

To Evelyn's dismay, when the waiter arrived with the drinks on a silver tray, he brought the champagne in a tall flute.

There was no way, with her father's nose, she could emulate the cool sophistication of Madeline Ashton as she sipped from her coupe. But beggars couldn't be choosers when it came to champagne. She tipped her head back more than was ladylike and after a couple of practice slurps managed to get some of the champagne into her mouth. The rest went up her nose, making her sneeze. Once. Twice. Always twice. Like a double-barrelled shotgun, Henry used to tease.

The ever-ebullient Nola somehow managed to talk over the sound of the piano, alternately sipping her drink and nibbling handfuls of coloured rice-flavoured snacks between paragraphs. Evelyn couldn't really hear what she was saying. Adjusting her hearing aids unhelpfully amplified the crunching and slurping noises from Nola's mouth rather than the all-important words.

From where she was sitting, Evelyn had a good view of the singer. She wasn't Madeline Ashton but a woman of lower middle age wearing a black dress and large sparkly earrings that hung like chandeliers. Her voice was so syrupy that it set Evelyn's teeth on edge but she didn't recognise any of the tunes.

'Have you seen him yet?' said Nola. 'Henry. Is he here? We're so looking forward to meeting him. After all the stories you've told us. We're beginning to wonder if you've made him up.'

'Yes, what does he look like?' Frank glanced around as if he might recognise the man he'd never met before in the crowd.

Evelyn tried to think. Which Henry was she looking for? The young man with one and a half stripes and a copy of Coleridge in his pocket; middle-aged and world weary with three stripes; or the old man he must be now? The Henry who had betrayed her with Madeline Ashton? Or the one who had deserted her and vanished into thin air?

'Difficult to describe,' she said sadly, a new worry snagging the moment like a broken nail down a silk dress. If she couldn't remember what her husband looked like, how would she know when she'd found him?

There was only one thing that Evelyn knew for sure. In her handbag she found her fountain pen and the pocket map and, leaning on the polished table, she was able to strike through her first question mark. Henry wasn't in the piano bar.

The woman who wasn't Madeline Ashton finished singing, thanked the audience and disappeared. Evelyn watched Fizzy Nola drain the dregs from her glass, crunching the ice cubes between her teeth.

'Time for bed, Fred,' said Nola.

Evelyn was embarrassed. She'd been calling the husband Frank all night when he was actually Fred.

'Yes, we've got to be up early for a tour in the morning,' said Fred who wasn't Frank after all.

'A tour?'

'They're taking us to visit a copra plantation, followed by a basket-weaving demonstration.' The woman who was hopefully still Nola sucked the juice from her lemon slice and dropped it into her empty glass. 'After a traditional lunch in the village we're stopping to look at some waterfalls on the way home.'

Evelyn was none the wiser. Basket-weaving, lunch, waterfalls. It could be anywhere.

Once upon a time she used to read up about the places they were visiting, loved listening to the port lecturers as they shared insights into the ancient cities or fascinating cultures at the various ports of call. Always on the front row with her notebook, Evelyn would prepare to extract the most out of each port of call, however brief.

Over her years and miles of travel, she'd gained an in-depth knowledge of the major European destinations: Venice, Rome, Barcelona. She'd climbed Vesuvius and scaled the Duomo, strolled the seafront in Cannes and watched the ballet in St Petersburg. She was as at home shopping in New York as in the glass factories of southern Ireland. But the way things were going recently, she'd soon need a guided tour to find her way to bed.

'Shall we see you back to your cabin, Mrs P?' said Nola as if reading her thoughts.

The truth was that Evelyn was too tired, too bone weary to refuse. All this thinking had worn her out. Thinking about Henry and where he might be. Worrying about what she was meant to be doing. Even normal conversation had turned into a crossword puzzle in which everything she wanted to say required her to solve a clue.

She consoled her worries with a passage from Florence Nightingale, who as ever had hit the nail on the head. *Apprehension, uncertainty, waiting, expectation, fear of surprise do a patient more harm than exertion.*

Evelyn discreetly tried to squash her feet back into her shoes under the table. Apparently someone had stolen them and left an identical pair in their place, only a size smaller. Unable to feel anything but a burning numbness in her feet, Evelyn forced them into the cramped shoes. It had a name, this condition of her extremities. She scanned the filing cabinet of her memory for the pages of *Cassell's*. She tried a few out loud. Pernicious nephropathy? Pemphigoid encephalopathy? Ephemeral osteopathy? It was no good. None of the words sounded right together. The more she reached for the answer, the further away it moved. It would come to her eventually.

The champagne had gone to her head, the sensation in her feet now spreading to the rest of her body. Rising from the chair, Evelyn felt as though she was trying to balance on ice skates.

Then like a pawing horse let go,
She made a sudden bound:

Nola grasped her shoulder. 'Whoah there, Mrs P, are you all right?'

'Steady on, old girl,' said Frank, or possibly Fred.

It flung the blood into my head,
And I fell down in a swound . . .

Evelyn swayed. Righted herself. Overcompensated.

Past the point of no return, more horizontal than vertical, she noted the pattern on the carpet – burgundy border, gold swirls, *starboard* – before crashing into it.

16

Bound by the Hippocratic Oath

She could hear voices, faraway voices, as if she was eavesdropping through a closed door. Someone was standing over her, forming a silhouette against the light. Then an even brighter light shone straight into her eyes. Like looking straight into the sun. She winced and tried to turn her head away.

'Pupils equal and reactive to light,' said a voice.

Dark again, the sun burning a bright negative into her eyelids.

Evelyn moved her arm. It hurt. She tried the other arm, which didn't hurt quite so much, then tried to lift her head. Pain again. Bruised. Like an apple. Apples in the orchard. Apple pie. Crumble.

'Apple crumble,' said Evelyn.

'Don't try to move, Mrs Parker.' The voice again.

'You've had a fall.' Another voice.

Opening her eyes, Evelyn could still see the sun branded in her vision. She looked for familiar landmarks: the framed photographs, the faded paperback books on the shelf, the Russian dolls Henry had bought her in St Petersburg, the blue bedspread, the hideous carpet that didn't match.

'Do you know where we are? What is the name of this place?'

Evelyn couldn't help. She was as lost as they obviously were. The cold white clinical walls reminded her of somewhere. It smelled like a hospital. St Thomas' perhaps. Yesterday. No, before that.

'Can I have a clue?' said Evelyn. Twenty questions. Charades. Cluedo.

'You're in the ship's hospital, Mrs Parker.'

'Where is Henry?' Evelyn tried to sit up again, but the sheets were tightly tucked in around her like string around a parcel.

'Please lie still.'

'What's happening?'

'You've had a fall.'

Evelyn turned her head to follow the voice. The sun had faded and she could see a woman. A white uniform. Red between the stripes of her epaulettes. Red for blood.

'Would you like me to draw up more morphine, Hannah?' There was another woman standing on the other side of the bed with not quite as many stripes. She looked at Evelyn, this lesser-striped woman, and said, 'How's your pain, sweetheart?'

Sweetheart? 'My name is Mrs Henry Parker . . .' The rest of her scalding rebuke was lost in a jumbled skein of sounds that wouldn't form words. She was floating on her back in a warm bath. It was quite a pleasant sensation, as long as she didn't try to move.

What was that? At the foot of the bath, dark and shiny. It was slithering towards her. Eyes like a snake, mouth like a fish, tail curling from side to side as it wriggled and writhed around her feet. She tried to kick it away. Crawling up over her ankles, then shins, towards her knees now.

By the light of the Moon he beholdeth God's creatures of the great calm.

A strangled sound escaped from Evelyn's throat. '*Water snakes!*'

'Now, now, Mrs Parker, there are no snakes here.'

'You're quite safe. Relax.'

'Oh, but I can see them clearly.'

O happy living things! No tongue
Their beauty might declare

Evelyn wasn't frightened, far from it. She plucked at the blanket, trying to reach the shiny head of the first snake.

There was a sting, a pressure in her forearm. A cold trail along the vein. Then someone turned on the hot tap and the bath began to fill with warm water.

~

When she opened her eyes, the water snakes had vanished. The room was empty.

'Henry?' she called. 'Are you there?'

He'd been and gone. She'd missed him again.

With no portholes or windows in the room, it was impossible to tell whether it was day or night. A crack of light framed the door, enough to see her evening dress draped over a plastic chair in the corner. On the smooth polished floor, her no-good-for-winning-back-Henry shoes stood to attention.

Evelyn's tongue found her dry, cracked lips. She was so thirsty. And tired. Terribly, terribly tired. She was lying in bed, her entire skin encased in white cotton. The starched fabric crinkled as it moved over plastic. She lay very still and listened.

Outside, she heard voices. A Morse code of short, high-pitched sounds interspersed with long, low replies. They grew louder and before Evelyn could work out what they were saying, two people entered the room. She recognised their faces from somewhere but couldn't think who they were.

'How are you feeling, Mrs P?' said the woman. She had round cheeks and kind eyes. 'We've been so worried, haven't we, dear?'

A man stood just behind her, awkward in a dinner suit. He had thinner cheeks but his eyes were kind too. 'So worried,' he repeated.

The white uniform lady with not so many stripes appeared and began rearranging the bed covers where the water snakes had been.

'Your friends have been here all night,' she said, re-parcelling Evelyn's legs.

The couple nodded solemnly.

'You went down so suddenly,' said the woman. She flailed her arms like a windmill by way of demonstration, making Evelyn flinch as she slapped her palms together to reproduce the moment of impact.

Evelyn still couldn't think who these people were. One generous, verging on wasteful with words, the other so frugal. Whoever they were they belonged together, she decided, their talking budget well balanced. One fizzy, one earnest.

Frank and Nola. Her Frank and Nola. Evelyn sighed with relief. They were her people and they had come to take her home.

'You must be exhausted, Mrs P,' said Nola, yawning. She took Evelyn's hand and gave it a gentle squeeze. 'Close your eyes and have a little rest. Everything is going to be okay. There's nothing for you to worry about.'

Evelyn found the words soothing. She liked having her hand held more than she would have imagined. These were more of her not-for-worrying people. She felt safe and reassured. Was this what it felt like to be cared for, looked after? To be nursed?

'Henry . . .' Evelyn began.

'Shh,' shushed Nola. 'Rest now.'

'About my husband,' mumbled Evelyn. 'I need to tell you what happened next.'

~

The weather took a turn for the worse on the night I watched another woman kiss my husband. The rest of the cruise was miserable, the ship battling against tides and headwinds as she made her way up the west coast of America. The sinking barometer reflected the state of my marriage. For days Henry and I barely exchanged words.

The hospital was busier than ever, and Henry spent long hours patching up the various casualties from the storm and relieving passengers of their seasickness. He would slip into bed long after I had fallen asleep and be gone again before breakfast. I had tried to quell my misgivings, my suspicions, but it was too late. What was seen could not be unseen.

'I could help out,' I said to him on the one morning I'd woken to find him shaving before work. 'Surely there is something I could do to make myself useful?'

He poked his head around the bathroom door, his face half covered in shaving cream, razor poised like a scalpel in his hand.

'The company wouldn't allow it, Evelyn.'

'But I'm a fully trained and registered nurse.'

I longed to get stuck in, to draw up the drugs, slip needles into skin. I wanted to unroll a crisp new bandage around an ankle, making sure to keep the pressure firm and the overlap even. I swung my legs out of bed and tidied my hair as if preparing for a shift.

'But you're not registered *here*. There are all sorts of processes involved if you wanted to work on board a ship.'

'Well, why not request the paperwork and I'll get started.'

Henry disappeared back into the bathroom and emerged a few minutes later, fresh-faced and smelling of citrus, spice and leather.

'I thought we had an agreement,' he said. 'I'm not even sure the company employs married women as nursing sisters. And even if it did, Evelyn, your posting could be anywhere in the fleet. We'd be apart, on different ships, on opposite sides of the world. Is that what you want? To not see each other for months on end?'

'No,' I said, weaving the sheet between my fingers. 'Of course not.'

'Well then,' he said, his final words on the matter left hanging. He pecked me on the forehead as he departed, as if placating a truculent child.

I was missing my daily walks and fresh air. The deadlights had been closed for days and, with no natural light through the portholes, I was coming down with cabin fever. There was only so much reading and letter writing I could do. Even Florence Nightingale was under the weather, lying facedown on the cabin floor next to the bed. I had turned to *Notes on Nursing* for words of comfort and found the Lady with the Lamp as frustrated with the state of Scutari Barrack Hospital in the height of the Crimean War – the rats, unemptied chamber-pots, and inedible food – as I was with the self-indulgent misery that comes with neglect.

I would earnestly ask my sisters to keep clear of both jargons now current everywhere (for they are equally jargons); of the jargon, namely, about the 'right' of women, which urges women to do all that men do, including the medical and other professions, merely because men do it, and without regard to whether this is the best that women can do.

I slammed the book shut and threw it across the cabin. I had fallen out with Florence, tired of her preaching. This was the 1950s yet it might as well have been the 1850s for all the progress that women had made in the workplace. Would there ever be a time when a married woman could have a career *and* a husband? A time when she didn't need to choose, and then stand by that decision for the rest of her life? It wasn't fair, but just because I had made my bed, it didn't mean I had to lie in it. Neatly folded hospital corners or not, I was fed up with being taken for granted, making do with scraps of attention from my husband. I'd sacrificed everything, only to have him flaunt his infidelity as he paraded his mistress so brazenly, right under my nose.

If he thought I would ever be content to stay quietly in my cabin, looking pretty with a ribbon in my hair and turning a blind eye to his bad behaviour, then he had clearly under-estimated Mrs Henry Parker. Enough was enough.

By the time I made it down to the hospital, the waiting area was already full of passengers retching into bowls, holding icepacks against sprained limbs or clutching blood-soaked towels against their heads. Admittedly, it wasn't an ideal time to confront my husband but I couldn't hold back any longer.

This too was a matter of life and death. The life or death of our marriage.

I mingled with the waiting passengers until the nursing sister's back was turned, then snuck past. I rarely visited Henry at work, preferring to give him his space, but the smell of disinfectant and clinical white walls made me tingle. Far from feeling intimidated, I felt emboldened and sure of myself. I was ready to stand my ground.

Bending down, I put my ear to Henry's consulting room door and listened. If he was consulting, my rage and indignation would simply have to wait until he was finished.

I heard voices, Henry's and a woman's. I couldn't make out what they were saying, but as I listened, the pitch of the woman's voice suddenly changed and I could tell she was crying. More Henry. More crying. Silence.

Then without warning the door opened, my ear still pressed against it. Straightening up I came face to face with my husband and, standing next to him, a puffy-eyed Madeline Ashton.

Henry didn't say anything. He escorted Miss Ashton out and spoke to the nurse briefly, before marching back towards me. His expression was implacable, but knowing him as I did, I could detect the gathering storm behind his glasses.

He closed the door and gestured for me to sit. The chair was still warm from my husband's lover.

'What is going on?' he said quite calmly.

I tried to keep my response measured. 'I could ask you the same thing.'

Henry removed his glasses and pinched his brows between his fingers as he did when he had a migraine coming on.

'I know I've been neglecting you this cruise,' he said, 'but I am the ship's surgeon. You can see how busy I've been.'

I folded my arms, unappeased. 'Some of your patients look perfectly healthy to me.' I jutted my chin.

'What is this about, Evelyn?'

'You tell me.'

'I don't have time for riddles. Tell me why you're angry.'

This was my moment, the moment when things would change forever. Accuse my husband of betraying me, and the vows we'd exchanged? Or stay silent and tolerate his dalliances, as I'd seen so many other wives do?

'*Miss* Ashton.'

'What about her?'

'I saw you, Henry. I saw her leave the hospital the other night. What was I supposed to think? She *kissed* you!'

He regarded me for a moment, then to my surprise he fell to his knees and took my hands in his. The skin around his knuckles was raw from washing his hands between patients. There were hollows beneath his eyes as he stared into mine. Without his customary spectacles, I was looking into the eyes I saw each morning, the same eyes I made love to. These were the eyes I'd fallen in love with.

'There are things I can't tell you,' he said. 'You know as a doctor I am bound by the Hippocratic Oath. I cannot discuss my patients.'

She must be no gossip, no vain talker; she should never answer questions about her sick except to those who have a right to ask them.

'I know you can't break confidentiality. It's just that I . . . I don't want to lose you, Henry.'

He smiled then. 'Don't you worry, my dear. I'm not going anywhere without you.' Henry bent to kiss my hands and I was left with the top of his head. I hadn't noticed it before, but his hair was already thinning around the crown, his pink scalp clearly visible like a sandy bottom through shallow water. 'One day, when we have family there will be months when we're apart, when you'll have to cope on your own. And I know you're more than capable of doing that and hopefully of trusting me too.'

When he looked up, there were tears in his eyes. If it hadn't been for the sound of someone heaving into a bowl outside the door, it would have been the perfect moment.

Henry, bound by professional oath, never told me himself why Miss Ashton had become a regular patient that cruise. Ships being hotbeds of gossip, however, it wasn't long before I learned the truth.

On the final day of the cruise I overheard two stewards talking whilst sneaking a cigarette on the promenade deck. By deliberately slowing down as I walked past, I garnered the gist of the details over two successive laps.

Miss Ashton had left the ship at the end of the cruise after discovering she was in the family way. The two stewards had been less euphemistic. She'd tried to take some pills but quick action by Henry had saved not only her life but the baby's too. She had family in California, and Henry had wired ahead and arranged for her to stay with a discreet and sympathetic aunt. Rumours abounded as to who the father might be. I had my suspicions. Had the chief officer once again claimed the prettiest girl on the ship? I'd never know for sure.

When Henry climbed into our one-and-a-half berth bed late that night, he lay staring at me in the dark, the contours of his face thrown into relief by the moon reflecting through the porthole. The storm had blown itself out and the seas were calm once more.

He smoothed my sleep-tangled hair away from my face and brought his lips to mine. And as exhausted as he must have been, Henry made love to me with such unhurried tenderness that all my doubts simply melted in the warmth of his body.

17

Cold Hands, Warm Heart

A CHOCK OF SUNLIGHT SHONE THROUGH THE GAP IN THE curtains and into Evelyn's face. She lay quite still, fully awake, trying to get her bearings.

It had been the most awful dream, nightmarish visions of snakes and icepicks. She'd found Henry. Then lost him again.

Evelyn tried to sit up but her body felt bruised and her limbs boneless, as if she was recovering from some delirious childhood fever. Turning her head, she noticed a tray next to the bed. Her bed. In her cabin. A teapot, milk and a plate full of crumbs. Henry must have drunk the tea, eaten the toast and left again, not wanting to wake her.

Henry. Something was very wrong. Something to do with her husband. She was falling, hurtling down, backwards towards an uncomfortable truth. Henry was missing.

She tried to remember the sequence of movements required to get out of bed. She managed to push the covers away but a pain in her left shoulder made her pause, semi-upright. How odd, she thought. Perhaps it was a touch of rheumatism. Common at her age.

When the pain subsided, she continued to work her way free of the bedclothes, like a caterpillar emerging from a chrysalis, and shuffled to the bathroom. For a moment she couldn't think how to flush the toilet. There was no handle. No instructions. This was ridiculous. She could hardly complain at reception after twenty years in the same bathroom. Luckily there was a circular button on the bulkhead above the seat. She would simply have to call the steward, the one who wasn't Virgilio. She was good with floods, and hopefully toilets too.

Instead of summoning her cabin steward, the button caused a loud sucking noise that Evelyn recognised with relief. As she washed her hands in the sink, she noticed the reflection in the bathroom mirror.

She grasped the basin for support, stealing herself for another look. An old woman stared back in horror. One brow was grazed and swollen. Her tissue-paper eyelid, so thin that she could almost see with her eyes closed, was ballooned with blood and fluid. Raising one bony fingertip to her face, Evelyn watched her mouth open in disbelief as she prodded the tender purple flesh. What on earth had happened? She reached for mental pictures but drew only blanks. Stones tumbled in her stomach. Panic squeezed her chest.

Evelyn turned to find a young woman peering in through the bathroom door. 'Sorry, ma'am, shall I come back later?'

'Where's . . . ?'

'Manila, ma'am. Did you finish your breakfast?'

Breakfast. Virgilio. Manila. Henry. Evelyn's thoughts galloped away like a riderless horse. What was wrong with her face? Why was she in so much pain? Where was Henry?

'Dr King called in to check on you earlier this morning, but you were sleeping. She was worried after you discharged yourself against medical advice. She wanted to keep you in the hospital for observation.'

In hospital? Discharged herself? None of it made sense, thoughts refusing to line up into a coherent explanation.

'I don't know a Dr King,' she said. 'Dr Johansson is my doctor, and there's Henry, my husband. Did you know that he's a ship's doctor?'

Evelyn recognised that look of exasperation. It was the current norm with the younger generation. Along with their ill-mannered familiarity.

'I'm not really supposed to do this, but would you like me to help you get showered and dressed?' The girl's name badge said she was Grace. *Tuesday's child.*

No wedding ring, Evelyn noted. Fingers were swollen and the veins bulged in her otherwise slim legs. Too much salt. Too much standing.

'No thank you,' said Evelyn. 'I might give it a miss today.'

Her head throbbed. She longed to lie down and simply watch the clouds through the window, letting her thoughts play on an endless loop like the ship's television.

'I don't mind. Really. I used to look after my grandmother. Back in my village.'

'Grandmother?' Evelyn pictured a burnt umber version of herself surrounded by bright-eyed babies. A matriarch. A fount of knowledge and wisdom which she would pass on to her descendants in return for a loving final home in the bosom of her family.

'Yes, she is ninety-one and still very strong. You remind me of her, Mrs Parker. She is very kind. And very clever.'

Kind and clever. Evelyn would have loved to have been a grandmother. What a better place the world might be with kind and clever women of her age – grandmothers – in charge.

'How long have you been on board this ship, dear?' Evelyn noticed the girl pulling down the front of her shirt. She'd grown out of it.

'Seven months, ma'am.' She looked exhausted. Evelyn wondered if the poor girl would even last until the end of the cruise, what with pushing that housekeeping cart around and folding towels into monkeys.

'Not long to go, then you can have a nice holiday,' said Evelyn. If looking after her 91-year-old grandmother could be classed as a holiday.

'I am getting married during my next leave. Just a few more weeks to go and we will have saved enough.'

'I love weddings,' said Evelyn. She'd only been to one, her own, but she liked the idea of them.

The girl backed away. 'Sorry, ma'am, I have to finish the other cabins. Shall I help you back to the bed?'

Evelyn shook her head. Her swollen, bruised and grazed head. She dismissed the girl politely, telling her that she could manage perfectly well on her own. *Tuesday's child. Full of grace.* About to be married, a whole new adventure waiting. She tried to remember that feeling, when the world was still waxing and not waning.

How had Henry proposed? Romantically, down on one knee with a diamond ring concealed in his pocket, a bottle of champagne at the ready? She searched for a moving speech, a declaration of eternal love and devotion, but couldn't find a memory that matched. With her brain increasingly like a lint trap for the trivial and unimportant, why couldn't she remember such an important milestone in her life?

The cabin door closed softly behind the girl. Alone again, and with her head slowly clearing, Evelyn scanned the cabin. She needed to find something. A particular thing. Except she couldn't think what it was.

Everything was in its usual place: the books, the Russian dolls, photographs. Someone had tidied the desk, making two piles of paper. On one side was a stack of the ship's daily newsletters. The top one was the most recent and, if it was to be believed, they were at sea today, expecting a maximum temperature of twenty-seven degrees Celsius and light winds, increasing later from the south. The other pile consisted of unopened envelopes from that dreaded nursing home. The threat of ending up somewhere similar hung around her neck like the Mariner's bad-luck seagull. She shuddered. Those places were for people named Doris and Wilfred or Edna and George. People who liked reminiscing and singalongs. Old people who sucked custard through their teeth.

On the bed, someone had left a triangular bandage, folded and knotted into what looked like a sling. Evelyn tried it for size, and as she slipped her sore left arm into the folds of white woven fabric, she felt the muscles in her shoulder relax and the mysterious pain dissolve.

Something else caught her eye. Not out of place, but a new thing, in a new place. A white card with writing on it. An invitation of some sort. *Farewell drinks.* That's right. She remembered now. The ship was terminal. The company was throwing a party to celebrate. She checked the date against the top of the pile of daily newsletters. Assuming her deliveries were up to date, the party was tonight.

In the meantime, there was so much worrying to do. It was time to knuckle down. Evelyn went to replace the invitation where she'd found it, on top of her television set, leaning against a lump of wood. Was this the thing she'd been looking for? It was a carving of two turtles, a mother and her baby, an object that obviously held some sort of sentimental attachment, space being at such a premium in their cabin. But it was a long time since she'd seen it. Sitting on the edge of the bed she stared at the turtles. Where had they come from? And what did they signify?

Evelyn turned the carving over and over in her hand like a bar of soap, feeling for its meaning. She brought it to her nose and inhaled. Her sense of smell wasn't what it used to be but she could still detect something. Wood. Smoke. A hint of coconut.

'I remember you,' she told the turtles, smiling. *I remember you.*

~

After Miss Ashton disembarked, Henry became the model husband. The Henry Parker version of a model husband at least. Fair weather helped, and for the next several voyages it was smooth sailing for the ship and for our marriage. I'd forgiven Florence Nightingale and placed her back on the shelf next to Samuel Coleridge, with W. T. Gordon and Alice M. Pugh for company. I knew she'd keep them in order.

I was back into my daily routine of walks and reading, attending lectures and accompanying Henry to dinner in the evenings. My brain needed something to do, like a small child who was inclined to mischief when bored. As I walked my laps I worked on memorising more Coleridge, more Florence.

One port day, Henry rushed back to our cabin after his morning clinic and announced we were going ashore together. He'd been supervising a new assistant surgeon and, having satisfied himself that the young chap was suitably competent to cover for a few hours, had decided to take a day off. It was long overdue. I'd become accustomed to exploring on my own, seeing the sights and shopping in the local markets, so to have Henry's company was special.

'Do hurry, Evelyn,' he said, packing his swimming shorts and towel into a knapsack. He tossed my broad-brimmed straw hat across the cabin with a grin. Then he produced two black oval masks complete with snorkels. Goodness knows where he'd managed to find them. He put one on and began mimicking a swimming motion with his hands. 'Have you guessed yet?' he said, sounding like he was already underwater. I laughed, more at his boyish excitement than his miming skills.

I could barely keep up with Henry as he sprinted down the gangway as if he'd been released from a long internment. The humidity had already brought him out in a sweat by the time we'd negotiated our own private taxi for the day.

'Where are you taking me, Henry Parker?'

'Wait and see,' he replied from the front seat of the taxi. He'd had a quiet word with the driver as we got in, and I trusted that at least one of them knew where we were heading and, more importantly, how to get back before the ship sailed at four o'clock. 'I thought we'd get off the beaten track and do a bit of exploring,' he said.

Bouncing along the unsealed island roads, I'd never felt further from the streets of London, and never happier. For a moment I felt guilty, thinking of my mother wasting away in her Paris apartment. I thought of my father and wondered whether he'd have approved of the choices I'd made. This wasn't what I'd envisaged when I'd kissed him goodbye outside Selfridges on the day of the smog, but I was living the kind of life that most married women back home, chained to their Hygena kitchens, would envy. I knew I should be grateful and most of the time I was. I'd like to think that my father would have been proud of me.

'Can't wait to see where you're taking me. I didn't know there were any ancient ruins, galleries or museums on the island.' I'd always thought of Henry as more of the beaten track sort.

'There's something I want you to see. It'll be worth it, my dear, I promise.' He swivelled round to smile at me from the passenger seat. A little boy with a big surprise.

Just then the taxi hit a pothole. The rebound catapulted Henry out of his seat and he hit his head on the ceiling of the taxi. We laughed. I remember laughing a lot that day.

Finally, after what seemed like hours, the towering sawgrass and creeper-lined road opened out at the whitest beach I'd ever seen. The water was so blue that I wanted to cry at the sheer untouched beauty of it. The picture-postcard beach was deserted. We had it all to ourselves.

The driver parked the taxi under a broad-leafed tree and promptly fell asleep on a patch of adjacent grass.

'Come on,' shouted Henry after neatly arranging his socks and lace-up shoes beside the taxi's wheel. 'Last one in's a rotten egg!'

I watched him reach the sand in a couple of strides, then spring gazelle fashion from one soft white scalded foot to the other until he reached the cool wet sand near the water. Then Henry being Henry, in the middle of a deserted beach he wrapped his towel around his waist and, shuffling discreetly out of his shorts, donned his swimming costume.

More English than the English. I thought of my father, and how much he would have liked Henry. How much Henry reminded me of my father.

By the time I'd changed into my own black and white checked bathing suit, Henry was already wading knee deep in the water, staring wondrously at the shoals of tiny fish circling his thin, pale legs. He turned and smiled at me, a big, crooked, happy grin.

In that moment there was no rumination over what had been or fretting about what lay ahead. There was no past and no future. Only Henry and me, on this perfect beach.

'Hold on,' I shouted, grabbing the Coppertone from the knapsack. 'You'll be needing some of this, otherwise you'll be burned to a crisp.'

The surgical nurse must be ever on the watch, ever on her guard.

Henry waded back and stood dutifully with his back to me, his skin as white and flawless as milk. I warmed the lotion between my palms and began to spread it across his hairless back.

As I massaged his left shoulder I noticed him wince and tense his muscles.

'Sore?'

'Cold hands,' replied Henry through clenched teeth.

A touch of autonomic dysfunction. And a warm heart, I wanted to remind him.

I rubbed harder, feeling the tensing of the muscles beneath my fingers then the release.

'Better?'

'Much,' he said. 'You've got healing hands, Sister Parker.'

'Why don't you let me release some of these knots when we get back to the ship?'

He tested the shoulder, tracing a large circle with his elbow. 'There's no need. It's just a sprain. It'll pass.'

'More likely a sub-acromial bursitis, don't you think? Your rotator cuff is quite wasted on that side. I'd say it's been bothering you for a while.'

His smile fell away and a shadow passed across his face. 'I don't think so, Evelyn.'

I could feel Florence Nightingale peering over my shoulder, shaking her head.

It is constantly objected, – 'but how can I obtain this medical knowledge? I am not a doctor. I must leave this to the doctors.'

I'd received top marks for anatomy. The other girls had begged me to help them pass their examinations, teach them mnemonics to learn the bones of the wrist or the twelve cranial nerves. I just remember things, I told them. It's a gift.

'You should see a doctor,' I joked, trying to lighten the mood once more.

To my relief, Henry's straight face cracked. 'What, that pimply-faced rookie who joined us last cruise? I'll take my chances.'

'It's not so long ago that you were the pimply-faced rookie.'

It was true. He'd risen through the ranks quickly, and I could tell he was thrilled to have been promoted to ship's surgeon already. I was proud of him, naturally, but as time went on it was becoming more difficult to broach the subject of what would happen once we started a family. But this wasn't the time or place to begin that conversation.

'Turn around,' said Henry. I did as I was told. He took the Coppertone and smeared my shoulders. As usual his hands were cool in spite of the midday heat, but I surrendered to my husband's firm circles. He lifted each strap in turn, working the lotion methodically down my arms. Then, without a word, his hands circled my waist and came to rest, cradling my lower abdomen. There was nothing to feel, it was too early for movements, but we both knew. We were about to cross the threshold into a new phase of our lives.

Henry kissed the back of my neck, took me by the hand and led me into the shallows.

'Come on,' he said. 'Let's look for turtles.'

~

It was past three when we emerged, crisp and tight across our backs from that underwater paradise. It was as though time had stood still as we watched the multicoloured fish dart in and out of the coral. I remember Henry's face through his fogged-up mask as he pointed to the dark shape swimming past. A turtle and, close by, its baby.

The taxi driver did his best to navigate the potholes and puddles, the road an unlikely combination of both dust and mud. I felt Henry silently urging the taxi forward, every so often glancing at his watch. I saw his jaw tighten as we slowed to pass a crowd of people walking at the side of the road, women in bright dresses carrying baskets and bundles of washing on their heads, and barefoot children dragging sticks in the dirt. Some smiled and waved, others looked on with faint bewilderment as we weaved between them and the stray dogs that were everywhere on the island.

When we arrived back at the dockside, the ship's black-domed funnel was already billowing thick smoke, heralding an imminent departure. Henry paid the taxi driver and we ran towards the gangway. With burning lungs, I sprinted those last hundred yards, urged on by good-natured shouts and jeers from the bridge. At the bottom of the gangway I paused to catch my breath, but when I looked back, Henry wasn't with me.

I began to panic. Had he been kidnapped by dock workers and held for ransom? Or fallen off the dockside and drowned, weighed down by his army surplus knapsack? Had he had second thoughts and, like the *Bounty*'s mutineers, decided to stay in paradise?

I heard the chief officer, a friend of Henry's, shouting from the bridge wing. 'Dr Parker, I must insist you hurry, sir!'

The insults and wolf-whistles rose to a crescendo as a figure appeared in the distance, running. There was something in his hand. At the foot of the gangway, against a backdrop of cheers and applause from the waiting passengers already aboard, he handed me the wooden carving he'd delayed the entire ship to buy.

'For you,' he said. 'And our baby.'

18

You Can't Put a Ship on a Boat

THE TOOTHPASTE HAD AN UNUSUAL FLAVOUR AND FORMED
a soapy lather in Evelyn's mouth. She spat into the basin and
screwed the cap back onto the tiny white bottle. She was excited
about the farewell drinks party. And now she had exceptionally
clean teeth.

She and Henry had been there at the very beginning, when the
champagne bottle smashed against the white hull. It was fitting
therefore that they should be sailing on its final voyage too.

Catching a glimpse of her reflection in the mirror on the
back of the bathroom door, Evelyn saw she had a black eye.
How long had that been there? Had she bumped into the door?
Fallen out of bed? Surely no one would think Henry capable
of such a monstrous thing? She would have to come up with
something convincing or hope it had gone by this evening. In
the meantime, there was plenty left to do. Not only did she
need to locate her husband who'd presumably been sent his
own invitation but there were two other people she needed to

track down before the party. The invitation had been addressed to *Mrs Parker plus guest*. In blue-black Quink ink, Evelyn had amended the wording, adding a shaky S. *Mrs Parker plus guestS*. Plural.

The front desk was the obvious place to start. It felt like midmorning and there was already a long queue of other passengers waiting to ask ridiculous questions. Sometimes Evelyn wondered how the junior assistant pursers managed to keep a straight face. The idiocy of some passengers had become the urban legends of cruise ships.

'Do the crew go home at night?' or 'What time is the midnight buffet?'

Her particular favourite was hearing passengers referring to the vessel as a 'boat' rather than a 'ship'. Although the young staff let it go, the captain was usually more of a stickler for terminology.

'Who's driving this boat?' Evelyn had overheard an inebriated man ask, seeing the captain in the bar one night.

'Sir, she is a ship, not a boat,' the captain had replied, as if the man had just asked to sleep with his wife.

'Ship, boat, what's the difference?'

'You can put a boat on a ship, but you can't put a ship on a boat.' The belligerent passenger had been left red-faced, and Evelyn had considered it as good a put-down as she'd ever heard.

But no one was asking about boats or ships ahead of her in the queue. There were requests to change money, the inevitable complaints about the ship's plumbing, and two harassed-looking parents reporting a lost child.

'He'll turn up,' Evelyn wanted to say to the parents. They always did, usually full of ice cream. It happened all the time. Kids liked to explore. Hide from their parents.

The receptionist reassured the panic-stricken parents that there had been no reports of anyone seeing a child climbing or falling overboard. He then tried to placate them by offering to put out an announcement over the tannoy.

'What if somebody has taken him?' wailed the child's mother. 'What if he's been kidnapped?'

Evelyn rolled her eyes behind the woman's back. Kidnapped? Honestly, some people had such vivid imaginations. This was a ship. There were two thousand people on board and none, to her recollection, looked like pirates. And if there were pirates on board, disguised as crew members or ample-waisted retirees, what would they do with a hostage? Where, on a ship, would they hide a small child? Or a grown man, like Henry?

The arrival of a slightly dishevelled little boy holding the hand of a young mending-the-engines officer interrupted Evelyn's train of thought, but not before a new idea had taken root. As predicted, the missing child was full of ice cream. In this case strawberry flavoured, the boy having been found shivering in a cold room just off the M1, the main corridor that ran the length of the ship in the crew-only area. Relief soon turned to chastisement as the parents embraced the ice-cream smeared face of their young explorer. Evelyn gave them a wry smile.

The receptionist called Evelyn forward to the desk where she stood, mute. What on earth was she doing here?

'Can I help you, Mrs Parker?'

Evelyn opened her handbag, hoping to find a clue. The clasp sprang open, revealing all manner of objects. The tiara. An unopened letter. A fountain pen and a spare bottle of blue-black Quink. Mints. Coleridge. A wooden carving of a turtle and its baby.

She spread the items across the desk, searching for inspiration.

The receptionist scratched his head. Evelyn did the same. No, none of these things were the thing.

'Was there anything in particular I can help you with?' The young man picked up the turtle carving and examined it from several angles before returning it to the counter top.

She hated to be rushed. 'It'll come to me,' said Evelyn. Her thoughts scattered like a shoal of fish from a shark.

The young man drummed his fingers on the counter. Evelyn felt her heart accelerate to the same beat. She trawled the depths of her handbag and came out with a piece of white cardboard. Aha!

'I've come about this,' she said, placing the card triumphantly on the desk in front of the young man. She saw him inhale in an exaggerated fashion and exchange glances with the woman standing next to him behind the counter.

'It's an invitation,' he said.

Of course it was an invitation. She could read. Evelyn was irritated but then she knew not everyone was as sharp as her.

'That's right,' she said slowly. 'An invitation.'

'It's for tonight.'

'Yes, dear.'

'Would you like directions to the Sunset Lounge?'

No, she had her map for finding places. That's not why she'd come. She looked at the invitation again, searching for clues. *Mrs Parker plus guestS.*

'I need to find someone,' said Evelyn.

The receptionist relayed her request to a person in the back office. 'Mrs Parker is here,' he shouted, 'and she's trying to find someone.'

Evelyn thought she heard somebody snigger, but the young man's face was quite serious. Almost too serious. She would mention his impertinence to the captain. It wasn't what she'd come to expect after so many years as a passenger, or 'guest' as they were now referred to. *Guest.* Now that rang a bell for some reason.

Fizzy cola . . . 'Nola,' said Evelyn. *Earnest and* . . . 'Frank.'

The receptionist looked a little surprised but, to his credit, turned straight to his computer to look them up. 'Cabin number?'

'If I knew that, I wouldn't be here, would I?'

'Do you have a last name for Nola and Frank?'

'I don't know, that's why I'm here.'

Reinforcements with more stripes arrived to help the young man. The line was building behind Evelyn as she tried to be as helpful as she could. 'I think they're retired,' she said. 'Nola's short and smiley and likes colouring-in. Frank's head is covered in those weather spots. They're here because Vera is dead.'

To her own amazement, Evelyn had quite a clear picture of not only her friends' appearances, but other important and no doubt helpful details. 'She has a yellow dress with flowers on,' she added as it came flooding back to her. Or was it green?

Before long, to Evelyn's relief, the front desk had a whole team of staff trying to track down the elusive Nola and Frank.

After several minutes, the young receptionist said, 'Leave it with us, Mrs Parker, this might take a while. Is there a message you'd like me to pass on when we find them?'

Evelyn pushed the invitation back across the desk. 'Could you make sure they get this as soon as possible?'

19

The Lightest Spot in the Room

'WOULD YOU LIKE ME TO HELP YOU PICK A DRESS FOR tonight, Mrs Parker?'

'Tonight?'

'For the farewell drinks party.'

Evelyn watched the girl – Tuesday's child, full of Grace – as she tidied the cabin with practised efficiency.

'What farewell drinks party?'

Grace handed Evelyn an envelope, one of the many unopened Dreadnought Home for Retired Seafarers mailings. On the back in blue-black Quink, someone had written in scratchy letters: *6 pm, SUNSET LOUNGE, FAREWELL DRINKS.*

Tuesday's child was looking particularly weary, as if she'd barely make it to Wednesday, let alone the end of her contract. Evelyn knew how much her family would rely on the money she sent home, and there was the wedding too.

Evelyn was becoming quite fond of the girl, even though she wasn't Virgilio. But she was worried about her too: with those swollen fingers and puffy eyelids, Evelyn could tell there was something wrong with the girl. She was hiding something. Low protein? Kidney problems? Or something more sinister? This was a tricky spot diagnosis, one she would have to work a little harder on. Especially if she was going to get there before Henry.

Henry.

'Have you seen my husband?'

Grace sighed. 'How about we concentrate on you?'

Evelyn imagined that being a personal stylist was a welcome change from picking up towels after lazy passengers. She was pleased she could add variety to the girl's day. It was yet another unsung role of the ship's doctor's wife.

The first item hanging on the rail was a piece of white woven fabric, tied in a knot to form a loop. Evelyn didn't recognise it. A scarf or wrap? She removed it from the hanger and put it over her head. It was the right shape and size for a sling and, come to think of it, her left shoulder was quite sore. She would ask Henry when she saw him. There was no need to bother Dr Johansson with it. He'd been very busy this cruise. She couldn't remember the last time she'd seen him.

'Is it painful, your shoulder, ma'am?' Tuesday's child, full of Grace was beside her now, brows pinched. 'Only, Dr King advised you to rest that arm.'

'Dr King? But Dr Johansson is . . .' The sentence dwindled before she could complete it. The conversation sounded stale already. Evelyn had a party to go to and there was no time to waste going over old ground.

'How about this?' Grace pulled out a hanger bearing a dark blue calf-length dress with sleeves. When Evelyn nodded her approval, the girl slipped it off the hanger and undid the zipper for her to step into.

'I'd forgotten I had this dress. I can't think why I don't wear it more often,' said Evelyn, putting one foot at a time into the dress, holding on to the girl to keep her balance. She appraised the overall look in the long mirror. 'Not sure this goes with it.' Evelyn removed the sling-wrap-scarf and tried to ignore the mysterious black eye. 'Better.'

'You look very smart, ma'am. It's perfect for the farewell party.'

Farewells were always bittersweet, thought Evelyn, the loose thread of a memory dangling in front of her. 'It's important to have the right dress, when you say goodbye.'

~

I barely recognised my mother, lying pale and drawn against the satin sheets in her apartment. When I'd last seen her, she'd been wrapped in her new life back in her native Paris. Now, barely three years later, she was a frail shell of a woman.

I put the wrapped flowers I'd brought on the table next to the bed. 'How is the pain, Mother?'

'Unbearable, *chérie*. I'm in a living hell.'

Her chic apartment, although stuffy and dark behind the drawn curtains, didn't exactly look like a living hell. But then we all have our own private purgatory. And my mother's came with a live-in staff of three.

'It's a slipped disc, Maman. It's hardly terminal. Perhaps if you got out of bed and moved a little . . .'

'What would you know?'

'I am a registered nurse, in case you'd forgotten.'

My mother sniffed then, building up to one of her withering put-downs.

'*Was* a nurse, Evelyn. Was.'

'Once a nurse, always a nurse.'

'You could have been a doctor if your father hadn't filled your head with all that Florence Nightingale nonsense.'

I'd inherited my mother's brain, I knew that much, but thankfully not its capacity for bitterness. She'd studied litérature at the Sorbonne and had seen herself as an intellectual until my father had 'locked her away in a gilded cage' as she put it. She'd never seen her role as an ambassador's wife as a career, more an imposition.

My father couldn't have functioned without her. A large part of his diplomatic role fell on her shoulders. Her skill in entertaining and forging connections with the other embassy wives was something he had taken for granted, his career coming to an end when their marriage did. They were truly a partnership. Vicar and vicar's wife. Rabbi and rebbetzen. Two sides of the same coin.

'You're entitled to your opinions.' I unfastened my coat and draped it over a chair. It was time to go into battle. 'But I will not have you bad-mouth Florence. Not only was she the mother of modern nursing who probably saved the lives of thousands of soldiers in the Crimean War and afterwards, but she was also a gifted mathematician, statistician and social reformer. And let me remind you that, despite what she might have cautioned about "women's rights", she was a feminist.'

My mother receded at that, turning her head towards her pillow. '*La féminisme?*' She sniffed. 'Perhaps you should have paid more attention to her.'

'Oh but Mother, I did pay attention,' I said, moving determinedly towards the long windows that overlooked the Marais. '*There are five essential points in securing the health of houses: One. Pure air. Two. Pure water. Three. Efficient drainage. Four. Cleanliness. Five. Light.'* With that, I threw open the thick velvet curtains, blinding her with the morning sun. Lifting the catch, I pushed open the windows that had been sealed like a sarcophagus for months. Looking back at my frail mother cowering beneath the bedclothes, I was worried that the fresh air might blow her away. *'Noxious air,* foul odours and *effluvia* will do you no good at all, Mother.'

She shielded her eyes and said, 'If you're so clever, why did you marry the first man who asked you? Were you worried you'd never get another offer? So much for *la féminisme.'*

I strode to the bedside and gently lifted her fragile frame forward to plump the pillows, afraid that even the lightest touch might bruise her skin as it would a flower petal.

'A patient's bed should always be in the lightest spot in the room; and he – or she *– should be able to see out of the window,'* I said.

'No one likes to be left alone in their old age. Abandoned by their own flesh and blood.' Mother sniffed.

'One likes to suffer out all his suffering alone, to be as little looked after as possible. Another likes to be perpetually made much of and pitied,' I muttered beneath my breath.

'I was hoping you'd come to say sorry, Evelyn.'

Sorry for what? For being happy?

'I came to say goodbye. Henry and I are buying an apartment in Sydney. I won't see you for a while.'

Her response stung. 'Have you gained weight?'

Tears quivered, threatening to spill onto my hot cheek, but I held them back. Instead, I took a deep breath and smoothed my hands down over the front of my dress. It was a little less fitted than my usual style, but with none of my other dresses reaching around my middle now, I'd had to buy something presentable to visit my mother.

'Yes, you're right, Mother. I have gained weight, and I'm about to gain a lot more. I'm pregnant, Maman. Henry and I are expecting a baby.'

I hadn't planned to tell her so abruptly, hoping that there might be at least time for a cup of tea and a few strained pleasantries before I broke the happy news. I saw tears in her eyes. If only they'd been tears of joy.

She sniffed again but turned her head away this time. 'Have Dr Billiet call, would you? And tell him I need something stronger for the misery.'

It is a much more difficult thing to speak the truth than people commonly imagine. Dear Florence was right.

I fetched a vase, filled it with water and arranged the flowers.

'Take them away. You should know that I'm allergic to roses.'

Later, Henry arrived to rescue me, greeting his mother-in-law with a kiss on her stretched forehead. He held my hand as if I might break as we descended the broad staircase from her apartment at the conclusion to our visit.

'Honestly,' he said, shaking his head. 'Who is allergic to roses?' He added, 'I like your dress, by the way. The colour suits you.'

'My mother says it washes me out,' I said with a rueful smile. 'And apparently I look fat.'

'Both excellent signs under the circumstances,' my husband said and squeezed my hand.

I was relieved when we left, later picking up the ship in Le Havre before it headed for Sydney via Trinidad and Panama. It was my last major voyage. Soon, I would be too far along to travel aboard. The plan was for me to disembark in Sydney and wait in our rented place on the North Shore for Henry to finish his contract. If we timed it right, he would be home for the birth. We were due to depart on 22 August. A Friday, considered by superstitious seafarers the unluckiest day of the week to set sail. But I had no reason to be superstitious. My life was as close to perfect as it had ever been. I had a wonderful husband, a life that most women could only dream about and, now, a baby on the way.

My mother died a few months later of a massive pulmonary embolism, caused by immobilisation and self-pity. It would never have happened on Florence Nightingale's watch. *He ought never to be in his bedroom except during the hours when there is no sun.*

I never told Henry my mother's parting words, after he'd nipped out into the boulevard to hail a taxi. I'll never forget what she told me, how it hurt me more than the back of her hand had ever done when I was a child.

'Keep an eye on that husband of yours.'

20

Fly Me to the Moon (and Back)

THE SUNSET LOUNGE WASN'T WHERE IT SHOULD HAVE BEEN. How odd of them to change the entire ship's layout, thought Evelyn, just as it was about to be decommissioned. After several fruitless circuits of deck eleven, she was back at the main staircase. Luckily, she was wearing her Finding Henry shoes, otherwise she would have been heading for a serious sit-down.

The invitation had gone missing and Evelyn was relying on the handwritten note on the back of an envelope to tell her where she was meant to be going. It was one of the ones from the Dreadnought Home for Retired Seafarers. They really were most persistent.

Cross-referencing the envelope and her pocket map, she deduced she was actually in the right place. But on the wrong deck.

A small group had already assembled by the time she exited at deck twelve. The Sunset Lounge was used for special functions like birthday parties or the occasional wedding conducted by the captain. But looking at the twenty or so people milling around, it seemed a rather modest gathering for a farewell party for what was once the flagship of the fleet.

'Here she is,' someone shouted.

To Evelyn's surprise, as she entered the lounge everyone turned and began to clap. She looked behind her but there was no one following.

A woman stepped forward and guided Evelyn towards the small raised stage at the front. 'We were getting worried,' whispered the woman. *Fizzy cola, Nola.* 'We knocked on your cabin door earlier, but there was no answer.'

'I was in Paris, saying goodbye to my mother,' replied Evelyn. She noticed Nola gesture to a bumpy-scalped man, who positioned himself on Evelyn's right.

'Thank you for inviting us,' said the man. 'We are very honoured indeed.' *Earnest Frank.*

On the stage, assorted officer stripes waited in line like a piano keyboard. Evelyn recognised the captain immediately. He had the same world-weary look she'd seen in so many other captains over the years. All that handshaking, the 'grip and grin' stance as the photographers snapped away. It must take its toll eventually. Repeating the same jokes at every welcome night. All that baked Alaska.

She and Henry had sailed with dozens of different captains over the years, watched many of them grow up, from skinny deck cadets straight out of college, to third, then second officers, first officers, chief officers and finally, with expanding waistlines and receding hairlines, self-assured men in command of their own ships. Women too. Sailing under the first female captain of *Golden Sunset*, Henry had declared, 'It's simply marvellous that the ladies are having a crack at it too, these days.'

There were several other breeds of stripes present, in addition to the driving-the-ship variety: eating-drinking-and-sleeping stripes, mending-the-engine stripes, and radioing-for-help stripes. Evelyn looked for Henry in the line-up, but where he should have been there was a young woman wearing three blood stripes on each shoulder. She seemed familiar, and smiled when she caught Evelyn's eye.

Frank and Nola ushered Evelyn to a chair on the raised stage area. She recognised it as a dining-room chair sprayed gold. It reminded her of King Neptune's throne at one of the many Crossing the Line ceremonies she'd attended. She wondered how many more times she'd witness the ritual dunkings and drenchings, fancy dress and general silliness that were part of the traditional initiation ceremony whenever a ship crossed the equator.

When the captain gestured for her to sit on the gold chair, Evelyn said, 'We must be further north than I thought.'

A ripple of nervous laughter skirted the crowd. Sensing an audience, she added, 'It's many years since I've been a slimy pollywog, you know. I'm a shellback now. KISS THE FISH! KISS THE FISH!'

Everyone laughed again, more than was necessary. Evelyn scanned the rest of the faces. To her surprise, she knew them all. The Italian who wasn't Olivier. The security officer who was good at counting, with tears in his eyes. The obstreperous receptionist and the other one with more stripes. Her people.

Uneasy, Evelyn took her seat, balancing her handbag on her lap. It was much heavier than she remembered and the stitching holding the handles in places had started to unravel. Everybody was looking directly at her, as though they were waiting for something. It was most disconcerting. She smiled back generically.

'Now that we're all here, I'd like to say a few words on behalf of the Sunset Cruises board of directors.' A man wearing a dark suit and a tie in company colours (that clashed horribly with her blue dress) was speaking into a microphone. Standing beside him was his daughter, which Evelyn thought unusual for a business trip.

The man went on to say the words. Then a few more. And several more after that. Considering he only had a few words to say, he took a very long time to say them, as was the norm when a man in a suit was in charge of a microphone.

Evelyn yawned. She wasn't really paying attention. She was more worried about the glass of champagne that had found its way into her hand or, more specifically, what she was going to do with her nose.

The words droned on. Luckily a waiter appeared with a plate of savoury snacks and Evelyn was able to get most of one into her mouth. The sound of the snacks thankfully drowned out the man's tedious words. *Cheese flavoured.* She was so pleased she'd come. Evelyn signalled to the waiter and helped herself to more of the snacks. Hoping no one was looking, she popped one into her mouth and emptied the rest of the plate into her handbag, wrapped in a *Golden Sunset* napkin.

'We have calculated that she has sailed all the way to the moon and back again!'

Gracious me, thought Evelyn. The moon and back was a long way. No wonder the ship was looking tired.

'Fly me to the moon,' Evelyn sang.

She and Henry used to like dancing to that one. She looked around for the waiter with the plate of nibbles. They really were delicious. It crossed her mind to throw a party, to celebrate when she finally found Henry. There would be large-nosed champagne glasses and plenty of cheesy snacks. Retrieving the envelope from her bag, Evelyn unscrewed the lid of her fountain pen and wrote herself a note. *PARTY FOR HENRY*. As an afterthought she added, *CHEESE*.

The suit-and-tie was still prattling on. Evelyn yawned again and wondered out loud how long it was until dinner. Hungry, she allowed herself one more of the cheesy snacks from her handbag. The rest were strictly for later.

'She has become somewhat of a fixture, one might say. Well known and well loved.'

People were clapping again. Evelyn joined in, though it was tricky with her handbag and all the things on her lap. The security guard was mopping his eyes with a handkerchief now. *Poor love.* Evelyn delved her hand into her bag and came out with the rather diminished packet of mints.

'There, there,' she whispered, offering the packet in his direction. 'Have a mint, dear. You'll soon feel better.'

Even with her not-for-seeing eyes, she noticed the fluff and other assorted matter stuck to the top mint. She was sure he wouldn't mind. Luckily, foreigners were generally less fussy about that sort of thing.

'Thank you, ma'am,' he said, extricating the fluffy mint.

'Pass them round, dear. It looks like everyone could do with a little suck.'

The suit coughed into the microphone. 'Er, where was I?'

'Have a mint, young man,' said Evelyn, gesturing for the packet to be passed in his direction. 'It'll grease your throat.'

'Anyway,' he continued, now with a mouth full of mint, 'as I was saying, details of a major refit and rebranding of the *Golden Sunset* will shortly be announced but, in the meantime, I'd like to propose a toast to . . .'

Evelyn was relieved to hear that the man was finally getting to the point. She stretched and checked the watch she couldn't read.

'Mrs Parker.'

'Mrs Parker!'

Suddenly Evelyn was in an echo chamber, her name coming at her from all directions, people holding up their glasses in salute.

'We're very sorry to see you go and wish you all the very best in your new home. *Ashore.*'

The captain stepped forward with a bouquet and a peck on the cheek. Evelyn recoiled from both. She held the flowers at arm's length, examining them as if they were radioactive. The captain, of all people, should know that flowers were bad luck on a ship.

'Flowers, umbrellas, priests and dead bodies!' she shouted, instead of 'Thank you.'

All were unwelcome on a ship. She seemed to know more about ships and their traditions than the crew did. Indeed, she hadn't made it to however old she was by disrespecting tradition.

'We'll be sending someone to help you pack,' said the eating-drinking-and-sleeping stripes. He shook Evelyn's hand and summoned one of the ship's photographers to capture the moment.

Evelyn crunched her mint and swallowed the rubble. 'I don't understand . . .' she said. Had someone said *ashore*?

What she didn't understand was drowned out by a rousing three cheers and a rendition of 'For She's a Jolly Good Fellow'.

Evelyn grappled for meaning, but it was as though her thoughts had curdled into amorphous blobs of incoherence. Her world was a shattered mirror, the pieces too sharp and dangerous to reassemble, her reflection now too distorted to make sense of.

'Are you all right, Mrs P?'

Evelyn felt a reassuring hand on her shoulder, and with it a welcome moment of clarity.

Sweetly, sweetly blew the breeze –
On me alone it blew.

It wasn't the ship that was being scrapped after all. It was her, Mrs Henry Parker, who was heading for the beach in Bangladesh.

21

Trouble on Men's Surgical

THE TASTEFUL ARRANGEMENT OF LILIES, GINGERS, HELICONIAS and birds of paradise filled the cabin with suffocating pollen. It was an omen. No wonder flowers were shunned at sea, thought Evelyn, sneezing twice. She pictured them floating like a funeral wreath, marking the spot where she and Henry might have jumped hand in hand into the watery afterlife. It was an unspoken pact between them: to end their days together, at sea. Had Henry gone ahead, crossed to the other side, without her?

It was dark outside but she couldn't sleep. A ship could travel vast distances and its passengers never experience jetlag, and yet Evelyn's entire body clock was topsy-turvy, trying to adjust to two time zones – the past and the present – simultaneously. During the day she fought to stay awake, riding great waves of fatigue. At night she paced, restless and sleepless. She'd come to dread the hours when others slept.

The craving for 'return of day', which the sick so constantly evince, is generally nothing but the desire for light, the remembrance of the relief which a variety of objects before the eye affords to the harassed sick mind.

Like a general inspecting troops, Evelyn ran her finger along the shelf where her books stood to attention. There was nothing amiss, nor in the gallery of framed photographs that chronicled two lifetimes at sea. Dr and Mrs Henry Parker. Some way behind the others was a stiff portrait of her parents, their expressions suggesting they'd both rather be elsewhere.

Evelyn perused the wardrobe. Some of the things in there hadn't been moved for years. What was going to happen to them? What was going to happen to her? She couldn't remember if she'd eaten dinner or not, or even what day it was, but the suit-and-company-tie-wearing man's words had embedded in her consciousness like shrapnel, as if they'd been fired from a rifle. At the end of this cruise, she was leaving. Being evicted, thrown out, tossed overboard. Shipwrecked.

All she knew was that time was running out. She needed to find Henry before turnaround day. And if her pile of daily newsletters was to be trusted, she only had a few days left.

Evelyn reached for the furthest hanger on the rack, the one inside Henry's mess jacket. She slipped the jacket from the hanger and buried her nose in the yellowed fabric. Was it her imagination that still conjured his scent? Could she trust her own brain to tell the truth? And if she couldn't trust herself, whom could she trust?

She laced her feet into her Finding Henry shoes, tied the belt of her Sunset Cruises dressing-gown into a double knot and unfastened the gold buttons on the front of the mess jacket. Her left shoulder was sore and she lowered that arm gingerly into the first sleeve. Always the bad arm in first when dressing, she recalled from her training. The reverse on undressing. Henry was never broad-shouldered, even as a young man, and the mess jacket fitted perfectly. Evelyn admired her reflection in the long mirror. She felt buoyed. Henry's jacket was just the lucky talisman she needed. With her Finding Henry shoes and now her Finding Henry jacket, she was cautiously optimistic.

Evelyn emerged unseen from her cabin. It was late and the other passengers would all be tucked up in their berths, digesting their four-course dinners. The conditions were perfect. This time she was determined to find her husband and wouldn't return to the cabin until she had. Armed with her pocket map and handbag full of cheesy snacks and other essentials, Evelyn had never felt more prepared.

The pantry door was locked. There was no sign of Tuesday's child, or the one who'd already gone back to Manila to save his mother. For once, Evelyn was relieved. She had a mission and, now, a deadline. Under the cover of darkness she could systematically search the ship, using her pocket map, and tick off the remaining areas.

Finding the reception desk unmanned, she marked a Quink ink tick against it and moved on without stopping. Evelyn was convinced that the money-changing-direction-giving-plumbing-reporting stripes were somehow in on the whole thing. It was the way they all knew her name, and the looks they exchanged in her presence that made Evelyn suspicious.

It made perfect sense now. *They* were all in on it, the entire crew, but she felt sure that the man in the suit-and-company-tie was the real instigator, the ringleader. He was the criminal mastermind behind this plot to get rid of her. All so *they* could rebrand the ship for younger people. *They* didn't want old-timers like her and Henry cramping their style and ruining their corporate colour scheme. *They* had already taken Henry. Now *they* were after her.

Fired up, Evelyn made excellent progress on her mission. She arrived at the main elevators without seeing another soul. The ship had a different personality at night, content to transport without having to entertain its sleeping passengers. When Evelyn pressed the button, the doors opened immediately and she had the elevator all to herself.

Once inside, she froze, unsure of what to do next. The elevator seemed equally unsure, waiting passively for further instructions. The pocket map offered several suggestions. Evelyn studied it carefully.

How would Florence Nightingale go about such a task? Evelyn pictured a dour-faced woman in a long dark dress and white apron with her hair parted and scraped back into a lace cap. 'Come on,' she imagined her saying. 'What are you waiting for? There are rounds to do. To the wards!'

'Yes, Matron!' Evelyn squared her shoulders and selected a deck.

She double-checked the pocket map, and when the doors opened she turned left and headed aft, towards men's surgical. There would be drain sites to check and dressings to change. A catheter bag to empty. But to her surprise, instead of rows of metal-framed beds and pyjama-wearing patients, Evelyn found row upon row of brightly coloured, jingling machines. She headed towards them, a moth to a flame.

No one looked up as she walked between the rows of dinging and flashing boxes. There were only a couple of patients out of bed, sitting in tall chairs, their eyes fixed on the spinning symbols. Queens, jacks, cherries, strawberries. They reminded Evelyn of the snakes she'd watched rise from the baskets in Cairo hypnotised by the sound of the charmer's pipe, and the crowd mesmerised as the pickpockets mingled amongst them.

Evelyn approached the nearest patient and tapped him on the shoulder. 'You really should get back into bed before you burst your stitches. If Matron catches you . . .'

The man looked strangely at her then returned his attention to the flashing lights. On his own head be it. Personally, she wouldn't want to get on the wrong side of Florence Nightingale, but the patient seemed unperturbed.

To her right, the big green operating table was covered in numbers. The surgeons must be lazy in this theatre, thought Evelyn, seeing a row of chairs on each side. There was even a large roulette wheel at one end. She remembered Henry telling her about how the ship's mortuary used to double as a champagne fridge. Could this be another dual-purpose room? Gambling and operating. A place to lose one's appendix and one's money.

'Can I help you, ma'am?'

Evelyn turned to the voice. It was a young Filipino man, in a uniform she hadn't seen before. He didn't look like a surgeon. More of an orderly.

'Look sharp, Matron's on her way.'

He seemed worried, his eyes wide and ready to dart in another direction at any moment. 'Ma'am?'

'There'll be hell to pay if she finds the post-ops out of bed.'

The man – Evelyn could just make out his badge, which said *Cashier* – looked her up and down, apparently unsure of what to do next. 'Are you lost?'

'Of course I'm not lost. I might be a bit rusty but I still know a Sengstaken tube from a Spigelian hernia.'

'Yes, ma'am. Would you like me to escort you back to your cabin?'

'Cabin? Good heavens, no. I've only just got started.'

'Would you like to play while you're here?'

Evelyn thought about this for a moment. There was a first time for everything. Even a busy nursing sister could have a few minutes off duty while Matron's back was turned.

'Why not,' she said, smiling at the cashier. 'But I'll warn you, I've never done this before. I'm a complete novice at deliberately losing money.'

'I'll need your cruise card,' he said, pointing to Evelyn's chest.

There to her surprise, hanging around her neck, was her key card thingy, attached to a blue lantern-halyard-*lanyard*.

'Fancy,' she said.

The young man led her to a vacant machine where he invited her to sit on a raised seat and, inserting her cruise card into a little green slot, pressed some buttons. 'How much would you like to bet, ma'am?'

Evelyn scanned the possibilities. They ranged from $10 up to $300 and 'other'.

'Ten dollars, please.' Henry would disapprove however much she spent. She knew that they had to be careful when it came to money, try not to outlive their financial longevity. But it was a tricky equation to balance, not knowing with any certainty either how much money or how many years she and Henry had left between them.

'Okay, it's all set up. You just need to press the button.' The cashier backed away, leaving Evelyn's finger hovering over the button.

'Righto,' said Evelyn, rubbing her hands together.

'Shall I stay in case you need a hand?'

'Don't let me hold you up,' said Evelyn. It's what people said when they wanted to get rid of someone. 'Those bedpans won't empty themselves.'

Sensing him behind her, Evelyn was about to give the young orderly his marching orders, but when she turned he was behind a glass screen in a booth talking into a telephone. It was most disconcerting, this funny feeling that she was being followed. Perhaps it was just her guilty conscience. After all, if Matron found her playing on the money-depositing machines, she'd be out on her ear. Best make it quick.

'Forgive me, Henry,' she said under her breath then pressed the button as the orderly had shown her.

The lights flashed and the dings dinged as the rows of delicious fruit spun in front of her eyes. The symbols lined up, some matching, some not. She pressed the button again and again until she had three cherries, a Q and a $. Numbers flashed. Evelyn pressed the button again. Four strawberries and a dragon this time. Watching the spinning pictures was fun for a while, but she soon grew bored, the spinning fruit eventually making her nauseated. There didn't seem to be any point to it, and with Matron hot on her heels she must press on.

She slid down from the chair and, seeing the cashier's back turned, pressed the button one final time, for the fun of it.

Evelyn had only taken a couple of steps when she heard the machine spring to life. *Ding, ding, ding, ding.* She started to hurry, lights flashing, and the bells of the malfunctioning machine ringing behind her. Evelyn broke into a half-jog. What if she'd wrecked the money-depositing machine? Would they expect her to pay for it? Best evacuate swiftly, thought Evelyn, scurrying towards the exit before anyone noticed.

Sticking to the less brightly lit public areas as a precaution, Evelyn relaxed her pace when she reached a vaguely familiar place. The area was filled with empty chairs and tables, and there was a piano in one corner. A shiver went through Evelyn. It was many years since she'd been here. Inside the nurses' home at St Thomas' Hospital. It had changed considerably since 1952.

Resting her handbag beside her on the red velvet upholstered stool, she lifted the shiny mahogany cover and admired the perfect row of ebony and ivory. The grand piano was certainly an improvement on the old upright she remembered playing each Christmas. Instinctively, Evelyn's fingers found the right keys. Muscle memory, she told herself. It wasn't as though she could remember any of the notes. Then out of the darkness, sound. A note. Pure and clear. Then another, and another. She paused, looked around. The other girls were in bed, asleep. Evelyn didn't want to wake any of them. They all had a busy day ahead, starting with a physiology lecture, then a cookery demonstration, and finally splint padding and bandaging. Perhaps if she played very quietly . . .

With Christmas around the corner, she'd best practise some carols. Before she knew it, Evelyn's fingers were dancing and skipping across the keyboard, the music coming from a place she had thought long lost. Beyond memory.

After several hearty renditions, Evelyn's hands were growing tired. She stretched her knotty finger joints and returned them to the keys. This time the notes brought tears to her eyes, the sound so ethereal that it seemed to be coming not from her but through her.

Clair de lune. It was her father's favourite.

A chill came from nowhere and Evelyn's fingers stilled, resting softly on top of the keys. Her chest ached, as if her heart would no longer fit inside. Beyond the windows, the moon kissed the tops of the waves. She wasn't in the nurses' home. This was a ship. And somewhere in this floating maze, Henry was waiting.

22

All at Sea

THE HANDBAG WAS SLOWING HER DOWN. EVELYN TOOK A breather in somewhere called the Jazz Club and set about rearranging the contents. Transferring her mother's tiara from the handbag to her head freed up valuable space, as did eating three cheese-flavoured snacks she found wrapped in a napkin. She also found her fountain pen and, relieved to be back on track with her mission to find Henry, she turned her attention to her pocket map and crossed off more potential hiding places. Progress was slower than she'd have liked, but Evelyn knew that a nurse must be systematic and methodical. There were no short cuts.

Conciseness and decision in your movements, as well as your words, are necessary in the sick room, as necessary as absence of hurry and bustle. To possess yourself entirely will ensure you from either failing – either loitering or hurrying.

Evelyn traced her finger along the deck, past two wobbly ticks and a question mark. Uncapping her pen, she updated the map, turning the query into certainty with a single stroke of Quink ink. It was time to extend the search to deck twelve. Evelyn's finger paused next to the obvious starting point. The club.

Why hadn't she thought of it before? Her father had been a member of an exclusive club in London. It was a place where men went to escape from women. She'd never set foot inside one, for that very reason, and yet Evelyn had a mental picture of oak-panelled rooms filled with cigar smoke, where pocket-watch-wearing gentlemen sipped single malt whisky in tall-backed leather chairs free from the scrutiny of their wives.

'I'll be at my club,' her father used to say in his new English accent. All along, had Henry simply been 'at his club'?

Evelyn calculated she needed to head forward, half the length of the ship, and up the forward elevator. It meant crossing several public areas, risking discovery. She didn't want to raise any suspicion. Not with the authorities out to get her. The only option was to stick to the darkness of the outside decks.

The heavy wooden door that led to the promenade deck closed behind Evelyn. It had been a struggle to open on account of her left shoulder. She couldn't think why it was suddenly so painful. A sling would help, but she didn't want to bother the medical staff at this hour. Given the probable state of her finances, she could only afford to be in pain during regular office hours.

Untying the white waffle belt from her dressing-gown, Evelyn fashioned it into a lopsided figure of eight and draped it around her neck. The arm went nicely into the smaller loop and felt instantly better.

Outside, the air was blowing in the wrong direction. Evelyn could taste the salt as the wind tried to force the breath back down into her lungs. She shivered inside Henry's mess jacket. Her nose dripped and her dress flapped around her ankles like signal flags against a mast. The sky was now dark and solid where the moon had been. It took a minute for Evelyn's eyes to adjust to the dim light shining through the ship's windows.

Which way now? Buffeted by the salty spray of the black ocean, Evelyn struggled to get her bearings. Eventually, she worked out the direction of the waves and headed as if to the front carriage of a moving train. One Finding Henry foot in front of the other, she leaned into the stiff breeze and moved forward.

Evelyn hadn't noticed the movement before but now she had to grip the handrail to steady herself as the ship rode the bucks and kicks of the waves. She'd seen enough weather to know when it was about to turn and this really wasn't a night to be outside. Which was why, when she saw the dark outline of a man in the distance, she decided it was her duty to warn him.

One hand on the rail, she made her way towards the man. As she approached, she saw he was leaning over the railing, forehead resting on his hands, and shoulders shaking. She recognised that posture, knew all too well the misery.

'Unless you've experienced it,' said Evelyn, 'you'll never know how awful it is.'

The man started and, with a loud sniff, turned his head to look at her. The wind muffled his reply, his mouth exuding moist sucking sounds instead of actual words.

The wind blew the smell of stale liquor right into her nostrils.

'If the brandy didn't work, there's no hope I'm afraid.'

He looked at her without really seeing. 'The signs were all there, but I was in denial. I just buried my head in the sand.'

'You'd be better looking at the horizon, in my experience,' said Evelyn.

The man gazed out to sea, his eyes damp and distant. 'I thought it would get easier with time.' Pulling a handkerchief from his pocket, he dabbed his eyes then blew his nose.

'How long have you been suffering?'

'A year to the day.'

'That is a long time,' she said. She put a hand on his back in sympathy. 'You might want to try drugs next. A lot of people don't like the idea, but they can really help. As long as you're not squeamish about needles.'

'Drugs?'

'Yes, the ship's doctor sees this all the time. A quick shot in the backside and it's all over. I'm a firm believer in it. My husband is a ship's doctor.' The man's eyes widened. Evelyn could just make out his face in the dim light. He was in his sixties, she imagined, his hair thinning and body thickening with age. 'Why suffer?'

'I was wondering if I should give it a bit longer. People tell me that time heals.'

'Not with this, I'm afraid.' Evelyn rubbed the man's back. He didn't object. 'If you were going to feel better, it would have happened by now.'

The man hiccupped. 'I just don't think I can go on like this.'

Evelyn had an idea. 'Look,' she said, 'I know it feels like the last thing you want to do, but you'd feel so much better with a full stomach. In fact, I'm sure the midnight buffet will be open. How about a ham sandwich and a nice slice of sponge cake?'

'I've no appetite. I've hardly eaten a thing in weeks.'

'*A spoonful of beef tea, of arrowroot and wine, of egg flip, every hour, will give them the requisite nourishment, and prevent them from being too exhausted to take at a later hour the solid food, which is necessary for their recovery.*'

'I'm afraid eggs don't really agree with me.'

Evelyn was losing her patience. Some people just didn't want to help themselves. Without hiding the irritation in her voice she said, 'In that case, the only way you're going to feel better is to get off this ship once and for all.'

The man sighed deeply, staring into the chunky waves below. 'That was my plan, until you came along.'

'Have you packed?'

'Packed? No, I hadn't really thought about packing.'

'Guest services can give you a hand if you need,' said Evelyn. 'Only they like to service the cabin as quickly as possible, ready for the next passenger.'

'Oh.'

Evelyn added, 'I expect your wife will have it well in hand.'

The man's lower lip began to quiver. 'If I had a wife . . .'

Evelyn could have kicked herself, noticing now that the man wasn't wearing a wedding ring. The look of defeat. The pathetic helplessness. He wasn't seasick – he was divorced.

'Never mind,' said Evelyn. 'Plenty more fish in the sea. A good-looking man like you should have no trouble finding someone else.'

Men really were no good on their own, thought Evelyn. She'd read somewhere that divorced women lived longer than married ones, whereas the opposite was true for men.

'I'm sure you'll cope,' said Evelyn. 'Learn one or two simple recipes, nothing fancy, and you're away. Just think, you get the whole bed to yourself and no more fights over who writes the Christmas cards. It could be the beginning of a wonderful new chapter in your life.'

'My wife,' he sobbed. 'I lost her.'

'Lost her?'

'A year ago.'

At last, it made sense. 'I see,' she said. They had something in common. Here was a kindred spirit and the opportunity to offer some words of comfort. 'I've lost my husband too.'

'Really?' He was wiping away more tears now. Looking at her hopefully with his bloodshot eyes. 'It's so good to find someone who really understands what I'm going through. Talking helps.'

Together, they stared out into the salty darkness.

'I'm sorry, where are my manners? I'm Gordon Bulstrode.' The man extended his hand. Gordon. *As-in-Henry's-favourite-gin.*

Evelyn shook it. 'Mrs Henry Parker.'

'If you don't mind me asking, how long has it been since you lost your husband, Mrs Parker?'

'Difficult to say exactly.'

Was it hours, days or, as she was beginning to suspect, much longer? If she could only remember the day he disappeared, she might be able to find him. But like a fish, she was rotting from the head down. There was terrifying wilderness where all her most important thoughts should have been.

Sensing Evelyn's discomfort, he said, 'I'm sorry, Mrs Parker. I didn't mean to pry.'

'You're not prying. It's nothing like that. It's just that I get a bit muddled about specifics.'

'I like to think my wife is swimming with the dolphins.' The man gestured towards the waves that rose and broke at the side of the ship's hull.

'Oh? Did she go on an organised tour?' Evelyn wondered if travel insurance would cover something like that.

'I brought her ashes with me. I scattered them this morning. She loved the sea, so it seemed like the right thing to do. It was all completely above board. There was a lovely officer present and the company issued me with a certificate, giving the coordinates of where we dropped her. As a memento.'

Ashes. Evelyn caught up, just in time. 'I'm sorry for your loss.' She held back from saying that swimming with the dolphins didn't seem a bad place to end up.

The man took Evelyn's hand, the one that wasn't in her dressing-gown-belt-sling, and squeezed it gently. 'And I'm sorry for your loss too.'

Her eyes widened as she considered a new thought. Was Henry even alive? Whether he'd slipped quietly over the side unnoticed to his watery grave, or whether her memory had simply erased the painful truth, it really made no difference. Was that why the crew had been treating her differently, if not exactly with pity then certainly forbearance? Because something terrible had happened that had rendered her stupefied with the shock? Somewhere in the shadows, Evelyn sensed grief lurking, waiting for her.

The pang, the curse, with which they died,
Had never passed away:
I could not draw my eyes from theirs,
Nor turn them up to pray.

'Do you know Samuel Taylor Coleridge?' said Evelyn.

'I'm not sure. Which cabin is he in?'

'He's in here.' Evelyn patted her handbag. 'He's always with me.' A little piece of Henry.

They stood side by side, braced against the ship's railings, each lost in their own thoughts. She had to keep searching. The only way to prove that Henry was still alive was to find him.

'There's a storm coming,' said Evelyn eventually, sensing a shift in the direction of the wind. 'You mark my words.'

'In that case, we'd best get back inside. Are you coming?'

'No, not yet. I'm on my way somewhere.'

Gordon-as-in-the-gin turned to Evelyn and offered his hand once more. 'It's been lovely to meet you, Mrs Parker. And thank you. I feel so much better after talking.'

People rarely had time to listen these days. The less time Evelyn had left, the more valuable it was when it was lent to others.

Always sit down when a sick person is talking business to you, show no signs of hurry, give complete attention and full consideration if your advice is wanted, and go away the moment the subject is ended.

'Well, I mustn't hold you up,' she said, releasing her hand from the gin-man's.

23

Swimming the One-Armed Breaststroke

THE CLUB WASN'T QUITE WHAT EVELYN WAS EXPECTING. FAR from the genteel oak-panelled space she had envisaged, it looked more like an alien spacecraft, all noise and pulsating lights. Perched at the very forward end of the ship, the glass-domed structure throbbed like a pimple on the ship's forehead. It wasn't the sort of place she expected to find Henry but, then again, that was the very reason she needed to tick it off her list.

Mesmerised, Evelyn moved towards the kaleidoscope of ever-changing colours. She and Henry had watched Nature's most impressive light shows at sea. They'd seen the Northern Lights at Tromsø, and the green flash of the sun setting on an unobstructed horizon. They'd seen shooting stars and Halley's comet, and once, just once, they'd witnessed St Elmo's fire as a storm spawned flames from the mast of a passing ship. But this was something else entirely. This was spectacular.

Following the wraparound deck, Evelyn skirted the club like a cat eyeing up a goldfish bowl. She placed both hands on the giant glass windows, feeling the beat of the muffled music. The dull bass note travelled up through the deck, bypassing her no-feeling feet and entering her body at mid-shin. The urge to move to the beat was irresistible, primordial even. Inside, illuminated by bursts of colour, were dozens of people who were doing just that. It was raw and tribal, a war dance or ancient ritual preceding a sacrifice or battle. The sheer energy recharged Evelyn's age-weary body. She felt invincible.

After a full circuit around the goldfish bowl, she found the entrance. Hot sticky noise sluiced through the glass door as Evelyn pulled it towards her with her good arm. She stood unnoticed at the periphery, trying to take it all in, the throng of sweaty bodies pressed together on what looked to be the dance floor. There seemed to be more limbs than people, arms above heads as if climbing invisible ropes, and feet marching on neon squares.

The strobing searchlights reminded Evelyn of London in the Blitz. Wide-eyed, she watched the passengers of all ages writhing in time to what she supposed passed for music.

Oblivious to their new audience, the dancers danced, laughed, sang along and spilled drinks over each other. And every one, dressed in white. Like some modern-day pagan ritual.

Evelyn had seen enough. Unless Henry was trapped within the crush of bodies, he wasn't here. Nor was it a likely place for him to hide, a sedate shuffle to a four-piece his preferred evening entertainment. But the glimpse of a male officer in the middle of the dance floor stopped Evelyn in her Finding Henry tracks. His build and profile were familiar; however, before she could get a good look at him or count his stripes, he'd gone again, consumed by the many-armed and -legged beast.

Edging closer, she caught sight of the officer again. Yes, she knew it! Three stripes. The lights were changing so quickly it was difficult to discern the colour between the stripes. Was he a mending-the-engines officer, a steering-the-ship officer or a plug-and-socket officer? Or was it Henry, having a last knees-up in his uniform?

She craned her neck for another look but nearly collided with an elderly couple attempting to jive to the throbbing music. The three-striper disappeared once more, like a drowning man swallowed by the waves. A rapid sidestep saved Evelyn from the path of a sweaty man as his overenthusiastic moves ejected him from the clutches of his partner.

Before she knew what was happening, a group of heavily made-up young women wearing what looked more like underwear than overwear had scooped her up and transported her to the middle of the dance floor. They wailed like banshees, dancing around Evelyn as if she were a totem. It was utterly terrifying, but at the same time terribly exhilarating. Unfortunately, surrounded by mostly undressed women, she lost sight of Henry, his stripes vanishing in the crowd.

With no means of escape, Evelyn had no choice but to join in. Taking her cue from a woman wearing red lipstick and what looked like a crepe bandage, Evelyn waved her good arm above her head as if she was hailing a taxi.

She soon found that this style of so-called dancing was more difficult than it looked. No sooner had she picked up the required sequence than the self-appointed lead dancer would change the moves. One minute she was jumping up and down on the spot, the next covering her face with her arms as if fending off an attack. At one stage Evelyn wasn't sure if she should copy or go to her rescue.

Not having set steps, the dance was confusing, but at the same time quite liberating. Evelyn soon noticed that the more mistakes she made, the more the young women woo-hooed and encouraged her. To her delight, they even started to follow her moves. Dusting cobwebs. Shaking out a winter coat. Swimming a one-armed breaststroke in an imaginary pool. Soon they were all brushing a pony's forelock and wiping their feet on a doormat.

Every now and again Evelyn caught sight of the officer who looked like Henry performing similarly in an adjacent circle. If only she could get a better look at his face.

The music changed and Evelyn thought she'd found her moment, but as the new beat took over, the squeals and cobweb dusting exploded. Everyone seemed to recognise the song, the premise of which appeared to be to act out the letters Y, M, C and A with jerky movements of the arms, some frenzied bouncing on the spot and a lot of shouting. By the third chorus, Evelyn had caught on, though her arm was getting tired and her spelling had started to slip. She was grateful when one of the young women caught her eye and mouthed, 'Are you all right?'

Evelyn cupped her ear. Her hearing aid merely amplified the strangled trumpet in the background and she hadn't a clue what the girl was trying to say. Even with lip-reading, however, Evelyn could tell she was slurring her words.

'I said, are you all right?' The woman screamed into Evelyn's cupped ear.

'There's no need to shout, dear,' shouted Evelyn, seizing the interval between an A and the return of the next Y.

'Wanna sit down?'

Evelyn nodded and followed the woman as she parted the crowd and led the way to a quieter area of tables and chairs. Young folk today had no stamina. But someone had to keep the poor girl company while she caught her breath. Perhaps it was the shoes she was wearing, a pair of high heels that made Madeline Ashton's icepicks look positively orthopaedic. Yet again, Evelyn was relieved to be wearing her Finding Henry shoes. Wherever they'd come from, they were proving the perfect footwear for just about any occasion on the ship. Including the jumping-and-spelling dance.

The waiter had just finished clearing away the empty glasses from a small round table with two vacant chairs. The girl slumped into one and kicked off her not-for-dancing shoes. Back on the dance floor, her friends were urging her to return with energetic arm gestures and catcalls that would have made a football final sound subdued.

Evelyn was bewildered by these young ladies, and at the same time fascinated. It was as though she was studying a new, highly evolved subspecies of female, one that appeared perfectly adapted to the environment, if a little louder than its predecessors. If she'd had a daughter, was this how she'd look? Heaven forbid. It crossed her mind that if she'd behaved like this, Henry might have disappeared years ago. But then, these young females were attracting plenty of male attention, and enjoying every moment of it. Florence Nightingale might have hauled them over the coals for their slatternly behaviour, but it wasn't Evelyn's place to do so.

She lowered herself into the other chair, grateful to take the weight off her Finding Henry feet. Evelyn weighed less than she ever had as an adult, yet her body felt heavy, weighted down by the accumulated years.

'It's a bit loud, isn't it?' shouted the woman.

'I'm sorry I can't hear you,' said Evelyn. 'It's a bit loud.'

The woman threw back her head and laughed. Her bosom jiggled and threatened to pop over the neckline of the white garment that was too long for a top and too short for a dress.

'It's my birthday today,' she said.

'Many happy returns, my dear. How old are you, dear?'

'I'm twenty-one. Key to the door and all that,' slurred the young woman, circling her unusually orange-skinned legs. 'I feel like I'm already over the hill.' The young lady looked like she'd rather be lying down.

'What a coincidence,' shouted Evelyn above the racket. 'I was twenty-one once too.'

She meant that she too had celebrated her own coming of age on a ship. There'd been no cobweb dusting and she'd worn an actual dress, but she remembered that feeling of being between two worlds, leaving one life behind and heading for another. But she'd never reached her destination. It was as though her entire life had been spent in transit, always with Henry as her travelling companion. Without him, she was alone, trying to read a map that no longer made sense.

'Still no idea where I'm heading,' shouted the birthday girl.

Evelyn found this strange considering the ship's itinerary was clearly indicated in the daily newsletter.

'What do you do, dear?' Evelyn noticed it was the first thing modern-day people asked one another when they met, men and women. She congratulated herself on her newly discovered conversational skills.

'Apart from keeping that lot under control, you mean?' She nodded towards the other inadequately clad young ladies who were now gyrating suggestively under the watchful gaze of several young men. 'I started doing law at uni, but I don't think it's for me. I'm keeping my options open.'

To have options, in the singular or plural, wasn't a luxury Evelyn's generation ever enjoyed. The only choice they'd had as women was to work or marry. She envied her new young friend her life, full of possibilities and opportunities. It was too late now to have regrets, to think how things might have been different if she'd been born fifty years later.

'Are you married?' she asked.

'Me, married? No way. That's one of the options I'm keeping open, if you know what I mean.'

Evelyn didn't. Though her mother had accused her of throwing herself at the first man who'd proposed, Evelyn knew there was more to it than that. There must have been, even if the details had faded beyond comprehension. She wasn't one to fall for flattery, not now, not then.

'It's different nowadays, I imagine.'

'Yeah, got a fair few frogs to kiss before I find my prince.'

Evelyn realised she had only ever kissed the one frog. She pictured Henry's underbite tessellating perfectly with her overbite, their tongues meeting and the graze of his evening stubble against her cheek.

'There's no hurry,' said Evelyn. 'Plenty of time to settle down.'

'You remind me of my nan. She's very wise. Like you.'

'I don't know about that, dear.' Evelyn felt anything but wise. A wise woman would know where her husband was, or else have lost him on purpose.

'You here on holiday?' The options-open young lady seemed genuinely interested.

'Not exactly. My husband and I live on board.'

'Cool! You live on the ship! Is that even a thing?'

'I can assure you that it is indeed a thing. We've been very happy.'

'*Been* happy?'

'Sadly all good things must come to an end. It's our last cruise.'

'So you're finally going home?'

Home. Evelyn considered the word. What did home mean? The place where one lived? Not bricks and mortar, certainly, for theirs had been made of steel and glass. If home meant family, then this ship and all its crew and passengers were the only home she could remember. But if home was the place where she and Henry were together, side by side as man and wife, then she was already homeless.

'Eventually,' she said. As long as she could find Henry.

A slow song had started and miraculously the young lady's friends had each paired off with a young gentleman. One lad was cupping his dance partner's buttocks, another looked as if he was giving mouth-to-mouth resuscitation to his. They all looked very happy.

'To be honest, they're a bit much for me.' The woman was watching her friends on the dance floor. 'They're just out for a fun time. Sometimes I wish I could curl up with a good book and have an early night instead. But that's not why you come on a cruise, is it?'

'Some do,' said Evelyn. 'The best thing about ships is that you can do whatever you want to. There's something for everyone.' She patted the young woman's knee. 'Lots of quiet nooks and crannies to hide in. The secret is knowing where to find them.'

Out of the corner of her eye, Evelyn spied the officer-who-might-be-Henry slip away through a side door. She couldn't let him escape without seeing his face. She stood, grasping the table until the blood reached her head once more.

'Perhaps I'll leave you youngsters to it,' she said.

The young woman smiled a wry smile that was somehow beyond her years. 'And I'd better make sure this lot get back to their cabins in one piece, hold their hair while they throw up, hand out the painkillers in the morning. Always there to put the pieces back together. That's me.'

Evelyn glanced in the direction of the disappearing officer. She would have to hurry.

'Have you thought about a career in nursing, my dear?'

'Now that you mention it, I always wanted to be a nurse when I was a little girl.'

'*It seems a commonly received idea among men and even women themselves that it requires nothing but a disappointment in love, the want of an object, a general disgust, or incapacity for other things, to turn a woman into a good nurse.* Do you know who said that?'

'I'm guessing Florence Nightingale,' said the young woman. 'I've read about her. She was one cool chick.'

'She was indeed. Promise me you'll consider it?'

'I will. Thank you . . . sorry, I don't know your name.'

'Mrs Henry Parker.'

'Henry? Is that short for Henrietta?'

'No, that's my husband's name.'

The birthday girl narrowed her heavily kohled eyes. 'I don't understand. Why call yourself by his name?'

On the dance floor, one of the young ladies was grinding her hips rhythmically against her dance partner's. Another had moved to a dark corner with hers.

'It's difficult to explain. It's just the way things used to be.'

At that moment, Evelyn realised that Henry's name was all she had left of him.

24

Follow the Little Green Man

THERE WAS SOMETHING WRONG WITH THE PILLOW. IT SOUNDED different to normal. Where there should have been soft silence cradling her head, Evelyn heard the distinctive rustle of plastic. Even allowing for the vagaries of her hearing aids, the feathers sounded all wrong.

She lifted her head. The bed was too narrow. Instead of the light blue bedspread that clashed with the hideous gold and burgundy carpet, Evelyn ran her fingers over the waffle weave of a white blanket. Even the door was in the wrong place. She had a feeling she'd been here before. It smelled like a hospital.

Lying back against the plastic pillow in the dimly lit room, Evelyn scanned her body looking for clues as to why she might be in a hospital bed. She could swallow without pain, ruling out both scarlet fever and the tonsillectomy a doctor had threatened her with when she was seven. Under the blanket she was wearing her nightdress. Through the thin cotton fabric Evelyn palpated her own abdomen. Not sore. No dressings or surgical drains. Next she checked her limbs, one at a time. Although she couldn't feel her feet, she could clearly see their outline beneath the blanket, at the bottom of her legs where they were meant to be. Right arm seemed fine. Left arm . . .

Her left shoulder screamed in protest as she waved her arm in front of her face. Pain wasn't the only thing wrong. She barely recognised the cachectic limb attached to her body, with skin like over-rolled pastry and blue, snaking veins. There was a wedding ring hanging loose on her finger, held in place by a bulbous knuckle. It was her ring, but surely not her finger? Her arm? She compared it to the other arm. They were perfect mirror images. To her horror, Evelyn realised she was wearing the body of an old lady.

Frightened and bewildered, she tried to sit up. *Henry.* Where was Henry?

Using the bedclothes for leverage, Evelyn managed to swing her legs over the side of the bed. Once the stars had faded from her vision, she had a clearer view of the room. It was a small and clinical space. Hanging over a chair in the corner of the tiny room was a white dressing-gown, bearing a Golden Cruises logo, and over the seat, Henry's mess jacket. Henry. Was he here too?

The hard floor felt like cottonwool under her feet. She wondered if she was dreaming. Pictures formed in her mind, vignettes of people and conversations, like stills from a movie, each a tableau of a wider scene that she couldn't fully decipher. Music throbbed in her temples in time with her heart. She tasted salt on her lips and felt the wind blow from the ocean through the crack in the door. Inside her eyelids, she saw a bouquet of monstrous carnivorous flowers and her mother lying lifeless against a white sheet.

Shivering, Evelyn put on the dressing-gown. Someone had left their shoes under the chair. Not seeing her navy court shoes anywhere, she put them on and tied the laces. It was tricky on account of the pain in her shoulder, but they fitted perfectly and were surprisingly comfortable. Her handbag was open on the chair. Had someone gone though it? Whoever these people were, they were one step ahead of where she ought to be. They'd strip-searched her and her belongings. They had taken Henry, and now they were trying to get her.

Time was running out. They knew that she knew. The yearning to find Henry drove her like an engine that could not be turned off. But first she had to work out how to escape this place.

Draping Henry's mess jacket around her shoulders, Evelyn crept towards the light and the door.

The alleyway was clear. Venturing out, Evelyn paused to get her bearings. There were doors on both sides of the corridor. None looked like an obvious exit. This was going to be harder than she'd thought. Her fingers found a rectangle of cardboard inside her dressing-gown pocket. It was a map of a ship. Inside, there were a series of blue-black ticks against a number of the public areas. Evelyn wondered if someone had planted it on her, one of *them*. Whoever it was had left a question mark next to the Cellar on deck ten. What did it mean? Was it a clue?

The Cellar.

Was this where they were hiding Henry? She wondered why she hadn't thought of it before. When kidnappers took a hostage, they always locked them up in a cellar. Of course, it all made perfect sense now.

Evelyn's eyes slowly adjusted to the bright lights in the alleyway. A sign with a running man against a green background pointed to the escape. Directly opposite, she could just make out a white-haired man lying in a hospital bed in an exact replica of the room behind her. Next to the bed, a monitor screen counted the man's steady heartbeats. She edged closer, drawn by some invisible and irresistible force.

'Henry?'

At once a memory returned, spreading from her stomach throughout her body like a chill. A déjà vu. The echo of a moment. Henry in a hospital gown.

Creeping towards the bed, Evelyn held her breath. Was it really him?

Evelyn tried to remember her husband's face. She wanted to match it to the unfamiliar features in front of her. Henry's thin nose, his cleft chin and prominent ears. But the man's nose was wide, his chin square and solid, his ears unremarkable. Not Henry.

She backed out of the room. The man didn't stir, soft snores vibrating against his soft palate.

Following the little green escaping man, Evelyn tiptoed towards the exit, her new shoes thankfully silent against the shiny floor. They were the perfect escaping shoes. Perfect for Finding Henry, especially now she knew for sure that he was being held hostage in the cellar.

'Wait! Mrs Parker, where are you going?'

Evelyn froze, her hand poised above the handle of a heavy fire door.

Because he knows, a frightful fiend
Doth close behind him tread.

Neck creaking, she turned to see a young woman dressed in a pair of blue medical pyjamas walking towards her.

'Home,' Evelyn lied, careful not to let on about the cellar.

'It's not safe for you to be wandering around.'

'I am not wandering. I know exactly where I'm going.'

'And where is that, exactly?'

'June 10, 1954.'

'I see,' said the pyjama woman. 'I think you're a bit late for that. How about you come back to bed and I'll make you a lovely hot chocolate?'

The woman herded Evelyn, guiding her firmly by the arm back towards the darkened room. The woman tried to take her handbag. Evelyn snatched it away and held it close to her body. No one was touching her turtles.

When it arrived, Evelyn sipped the hot chocolate cautiously. The woman was watching her. Was it poisoned? Had *they* concealed drugs in the steamy brown liquid?

'It's too hot,' said Evelyn, handing back the foam cup.

'Would you like a biscuit?'

'No thank you.' Evelyn didn't trust *them*.

Evelyn refused to take off her shoes and tugged at the blanket when the woman tried to tuck her in. Tuck. Tug. Tuck. Tug. It ended in a tucking tug-of-war stalemate. The pyjama woman eventually backed down with a sigh.

Propped up against the pillows, Evelyn kept one leg dangling over the edge of the bed, ready to make a swift getaway. She simply had to pick her moment. Luckily, she didn't have to wait long. The woman wearing blue pyjamas – a nurse, according to her name badge – was summoned by a buzzer from another room, leaving her alone again. When Evelyn was sure the coast was clear, she slipped out of bed.

With the utmost stealth, Evelyn crept to the door. A quick left-right-left and she was escaping like the little green man. She heard voices, but they were far away, coming from a room at the other end of the corridor. This time she would escape undetected and find Henry. There wouldn't be much time, once they'd noticed her missing, but in these shoes Evelyn was quietly confident she could outpace anyone half – or even a quarter – her age.

'Mrs Parker! Where are you going?'

'Don't worry, dear. I'll see myself out.'

Evelyn fumbled with the door handle. She had to hurry. The door was stuck, refusing to budge. Behind her, a different woman was striding along the corridor. She was wearing matching medical pyjamas, but this one looked like she meant business.

Evelyn threw her weight into the door. Pain tore through her left shoulder. She felt a hand on her arm.

'Get off me!' she shouted. 'Get off!'

The second pyjama woman put her hands up. 'Okay, okay.' Then she made shushing sounds and spoke in a slow and deliberate voice. 'Mrs Parker, I'm not going to hurt you. I just want you to come back to bed. There's something we need to discuss.'

'Who are you?' Evelyn inspected the second pyjama woman's chest for her name. She had a stethoscope around her neck and introduced herself as Dr Hannah King.

'Where is Dr Johansson? He's my doctor. He's very good.'

'Dr Johansson isn't here.'

Evelyn narrowed her eyes. 'What have you done with him?' Was he locked away in the cellar too? Was it a place to conceal unwanted ship's doctors?

'We discussed this last time, Mrs Parker. And the time before.'

They were back in the room again, the one that wasn't June 10. The woman who claimed to be Dr King held up the bedclothes and indicated that Evelyn should lie down. She did. She needed time to think. This was all moving so fast. Not only had *they* kidnapped Henry, but Dr Johansson too. In his place was an impostor. A ship's doctor who wasn't a real ship's doctor.

'Would you like a hot chocolate?'

'No thank you,' replied Evelyn. She had to keep her wits about her. Not be tricked into taking any drugs. That's how *they* planned to steal her mind. And clearly, *they* were winning. Her thoughts were so muddled, like a radio stuck between two stations. She simply couldn't stay tuned.

'We need to have a little chat about your health.'

'I think you'll find I'm very healthy. For my age.'

'Yes you are, and we want to keep you that way. That's why it's important to be compliant with your medication.'

'What medication?'

'The little white pills, Mrs Parker. They're for your heart.'

'There's nothing wrong with my heart,' said Evelyn. She felt it kick her slightly behind the ribs in protest.

The doctor impostor reached for Evelyn's wrist to take her pulse. 'So, no palpitations?'

'None whatsoever,' said Evelyn. She twisted from the grasp and tucked her arm safely out of reach beneath the waffle blanket.

The 'little chat' turned out to be anything but. It was also rather one-sided with the doctor impostor doing most of the talking. She spoke so quickly, however, that in spite of her encyclopaedic knowledge of medical terminology, Evelyn could only grasp every second or third word.

Fibrillation. Clots. Brain. Infarct. Stroke risk.

The doctor nodded soberly. 'So you can see why I'm concerned.'

Evelyn couldn't.

The door opened and the original pyjama woman entered, carrying a steaming polystyrene cup. 'I've made you more hot chocolate, Mrs Parker. You let the other one go cold.'

She thrust it into Evelyn's hand. Evelyn sniffed it and handed the cup back. 'It's too hot,' she said.

The doctor impostor took a really deep breath. 'Please, Mrs Parker. Will you at least let me run some tests? An ECG and blood tests?'

'Then can I go home? To June 10?'

'Yes, if everything is okay, we'll let you go back to your cabin in the morning.'

Evelyn was satisfied. She knew that the only way to get one over on *them* was to play them at their own game. Pretend to be normal. It was what she did every day, all the while knowing that something was wrong, something dark and ominous she couldn't shake off.

The doctor impostor dragged the chair from the corner to beside the bed. She was at eye level now. They were kind eyes for a professional con artist. Against her better judgement, Evelyn's body softened a fraction.

'It's been quite a night,' said the doctor impostor. She looked tired, Evelyn thought. All doctors did. Henry had looked tired since 1953. 'I'm surprised you're still going.'

'Going where, dear?' Were *they* on to her again? wondered Evelyn.

The doctor impostor had begun to lean, as if she were slowly melting. 'May I call you Evelyn?' She propped her elbow on the bed.

'I'd prefer Mrs Parker if you don't mind.' Evelyn tried to tip the elbow off the bed by pulling the blanket up. Impostor or not, the woman shouldn't be slouching on duty. 'And I don't know what you're talking about.'

'Shall I refresh your memory?' The doctor impostor yawned and stretched her arms above her head.

Indignant, Evelyn replied, 'There is nothing wrong with my memory.' The bits she could remember at least.

'Let's start in the dining room.' The doctor impostor then proceeded to relate a highly improbable tale, beginning in the dining room, or rather not in the dining room, where a couple of passengers named Frank and Nola Fisher had reported their dining companion missing from first sitting. Evelyn had been spotted passing through the atrium at 23.10, followed by a visit to the casino, logged at 23.25. Thereafter, there had been reports of her playing 'Good King Wenceslas' followed by 'Oh Come All Ye Faithful' on the grand piano. After that she'd apparently had a brief encounter with a widower named Gordon Bulstrode, who'd raised his concerns shortly after midnight. The next sighting had been some time later in the disco, where she'd been spotted dancing with a group of young women.

'I find all this very hard to believe,' said Evelyn. 'It doesn't sound like me at all.' She had never gambled in her life, simply couldn't afford to. And as for dancing in the disco . . . well, it was quite preposterous. She wondered if this was one of the techniques *they* used to gain control of her brain, by planting false memories.

'I can assure you there is CCTV footage to prove it. After the disco, you were seen leaving by a side door, following one of the officers into a crew area.'

'Now hold on a moment,' said Evelyn, closing her eyes and concentrating very hard on what was behind them. 'This is ringing a bit of a bell.'

'Which bit?'

'A sign on a door. It said *Crew Only*.'

This was a memory, she was sure now. But a new one or an old one? She'd spent half her life living in crew quarters of some kind, as an officer's wife. A state of limbo in many ways – more than a passenger but not strictly speaking crew since she was never technically employed. Looking back, however, Evelyn saw that she had had a role, had paid her way. Volunteering to lead tour groups, allocating seats on buses and wrangling stray passengers back to the ship on time. She'd bandaged twisted ankles in Pompeii and disinfected monkey bites in Cape Town. And back on board Evelyn had played her part too, organising passenger talent nights, decorating the officers' wardroom for parties and sharing cups of tea with homesick cadets.

Seeing the perplexed expression on Evelyn's face, the doctor impostor continued with her fantastical account of the night's events.

'Do you remember the watertight door?'

'Watertight door?'

'Yes, the big metal doors that separate watertight compartments of the ship on the lower decks?'

'I know perfectly well what a watertight door is.' In fact, Evelyn could bring a perfectly vivid picture to mind, of the giant wall of white, adorned with yellow and black stripes and sinister warning signs. Designed to separate the ship into discrete watertight compartments. To prevent unfortunate sinking. Closed when the ship was at sea and operated from the bridge. A crew member could open one manually, but only in cases of emergency, when his or her life was in danger.

'You passed through one,' said the doctor impostor while rearranging her chaotic hairdo, lassoing it into an untidy bun with an elastic band. In response to a snort from Evelyn, she added, 'Yes, really.'

Evelyn was impressed. 'Well, well,' she said. She was all too familiar with the ill-advised opening of a watertight door. She recalled Henry telling her about one of the ship's butchers who'd mistimed his attempt.

It was during a long crossing. The ship had been at sea for several days. With the watertight doors permanently closed, many crew members were having to take alternative routes to their cabins, often having to climb staircases to higher decks and descending on the other side to avoid the closed door. One night the butcher was returning to his cabin from the crew bar; a little the worse for wear, and clearly irked by the detour, he decided to take a short cut by opening and passing through a watertight door. Unfortunately, although his body made it through before the door closed, his right arm didn't and was severed at the elbow.

'It could have been his bloody neck,' a shaken Henry said when he returned to bed that night. Evelyn suspected this was of little comfort to the poor chap, who had lost not only his arm but his livelihood too. 'He should have known better. He's the one who provides the animal bone to the safety officer to demonstrate the dangers of the doors at crew inductions.'

'Do you know how dangerous these doors are, Mrs Parker? You could have—'

'Lost an arm, or worse. Yes, I'm well aware of their cleaving potential.'

The doctor impostor offered the hot chocolate to Evelyn. It wasn't steaming now. When Evelyn refused, she began to sip the brown liquid absent-mindedly. 'After the watertight door, you were spotted trying to get into the engine control room. Luckily there's a security code required.'

It was all quite baffling. Evelyn had not the slightest interest in the workings of the ship's engines. Now the human body and all its processes, well that was different.

'Did you know I came top of my class in anatomy?'

The doctor impostor shook her head, her expression a blank. 'You've lost me.'

'You know, anatomy, as in the study of the structure of the human body.'

'I'm not with you . . .'

'Bones, muscles, nerves, blood vessels. That sort of thing.' Surely, a real doctor would know this? Hadn't she read *Gray's Anatomy*? At last, here was irrefutable proof that the woman was a fraud. But if she wanted to escape, Evelyn knew she must keep up the pretence and not make the masquerading doctor suspicious. She smiled benignly.

'Look, Mrs Parker,' said the doctor impostor, standing up now and putting her hands on her hips. 'Ships are dangerous places to be wandering in the middle of the night.'

'I couldn't agree more. I could tell you some stories that would make your hair curl.'

'That won't be necessary. I have quite a few of my own, believe me.'

An unruly strand of hair had fallen from her bun, curling like a corkscrew at the side of the woman's face. It must be exhausting for her, all this pretending. Evelyn decided to play along. She would catch her out eventually. 'People don't understand, do they?'

The doctor impostor wasn't following. 'Understand what, Mrs Parker?' Her brow furrowed.

'The sacrifice.'

'Sacrifice?'

'Yes, in devoting your life to the sea. I imagine your shore-based colleagues ask you when you're going to get a proper job, and your family imagine that you're on one long holiday or, worse, they imagine you get paid a fortune to treat seasickness and sunburn.'

The nod suggested the doctor impostor did now understand. 'It's not easy.' She sat down again.

'Being away for months at a time, with little support or back-up. Looking after the population of a small town. Having responsibility for two or three thousand people for days on end in the middle of the ocean. It's not like you can ask a specialist to give a second opinion every time you're unsure about a tricky case. And you can't very well say that you're a bit rusty with dislocated shoulders, or that eyes, ears or teeth aren't really your thing.'

Evelyn noticed the corners of the doctor impostor's mouth flicker into a smile of recognition.

'And you can't very well turn away a waiting room full of passengers because you're feeling a bit seasick yourself,' said the doctor impostor. 'Once, I had to ask the senior nurse to give me an injection just so I wouldn't throw up over the patients.'

'Quite.'

The doctor impostor was more animated now. Evelyn was impressed by her authentic portrayal of a real ship's doctor.

'What people don't realise is that we have to deal with everything and anything on a ship. Most of the time we're too far away from land to just order a helicopter if someone is sick or injured. And the company spends a fortune sending us on all the latest courses: trauma, advanced life support. We're actually very highly trained, and we have a lot of state-of-the-art equipment on board.'

Impostor or not, Evelyn took the doctor's hand and patted it gently. 'I know, dear. I know.' She was suddenly enjoying the conversation. It felt comfortable and familiar. 'Now, how about you do the tests you were talking about, then we can have a nice cup of tea together and swing the lantern some more? There are so many stories I could tell you. Though not all of them are happy ones.'

25

Climbing Jacob's Ladder

IT FELT LIKE AN ETERNITY SINCE THE CREW HAD CLOSED ALL the deadlights over the lower-deck portholes to protect the ship from the rough seas of the North Atlantic. It had only been two days. By then the nausea had passed and I was enjoying the euphoria of an uncomplicated pregnancy, seeing the world through rose-tinted hormones.

The eager anticipation of this particular day had buoyed me through those long hours without daylight. I woke early to the idling of the ship's engines. The excitement of finally opening the deadlights again was met with brief disappointment – the only sight through the porthole was a low bank of grey cloud. There was, however, the relief of placid water.

For me, like the many other passengers on the ship, this was the highlight of the voyage. Today the ship would cross the Americas, passing between two mighty oceans through one of the wonders of the modern world, the Panama Canal.

I dressed quickly and ran a comb through my hair, afraid to miss a single moment. It wasn't the sheer scale of this incredible feat of engineering that entranced me, but as always the human story behind it. More than 20,000 men had died in the early days of construction, from malaria and yellow fever, to save ships the treacherous journey around the tip of South America. Although the mechanics of the project had captivated the imagination of many, including Henry and the chief engineer who discussed such things at length, the cost in human life was simply beyond comprehension.

Outside, the decks were already busy with passengers, cameras at the ready. Even at that early hour the air was thick and humid, and it settled on me like a second skin. The flat Caribbean waters at the entrance to the Gatun Locks reflected the first glimpse of blue sky where soaring frigate birds watched the daily spectacle unfold below. Flocks of noisy green parrots broke the stillness as they rose from the thick jungles like excited children on their way home from school. Leaning over the side of the ship, I watched locals from the nearby San Blas Islands peddling their brightly embroidered *molas* from dug-out canoes.

It was as I watched the pilot board the ship that I felt the first cramping. Gripping the polished handrail, I held my breath until the pain passed. I wasn't too worried at first, thinking I'd leaned out too far over the railings or climbed the stairs from our cabin too quickly. I decided not to mention it to Henry. I didn't want to worry him.

Henry had been called out in the early hours to attend a sick passenger and hadn't returned to the cabin. We'd arranged to meet at our favourite spot at the aft of the ship once he'd finished his short morning clinic. It was a quiet spot, away from the usual crowds, where Henry could avoid opportunistic passengers and their ailments.

I waited and waited, ignoring the worsening cramps, still believing they'd pass, that each one was the last. When Henry didn't show up at the agreed time, I knew he must still be busy with his patient. I was used to our plans being cancelled at no notice. Whenever Henry was late or held up, it was usually for good reason. He would come, once the waiting room was empty and his meticulous notes complete. At sea he was Dr Henry Parker, ship's surgeon first and my husband second.

In the meantime I snapped away with the camera he'd given me as a wedding present. It was a Kodak Signet with a tan leather case, and I had already used up a whole roll of film taking photographs of the extraordinary spectacle unfolding around the ship. The cramps were still bearable. They were nothing out of the ordinary. My womb was getting larger by the day, the size of a pear now, stretching the ligaments as a hot-air balloon tugs at its guy ropes. If anything it was a good sign. The baby was growing.

But as the ship rose through the three compartments that made up the Gatun Locks and, as if by magic, entered the Gatun Lake a whole eighty-five feet above sea level, I knew that something was wrong. Resting on a deckchair to gather myself together, I felt something warm and damp between my legs. When I stood up, I noticed a dark stain on the striped fabric where I had been sitting.

By the time I made it back to the cabin, the pain was much worse, gripping and dragging from my back, through my pelvis and into the tops of my legs. I knew without looking what the slippery wetness on the paper meant, before the ship's vacuum system sucked away the evidence.

Draping a towel across our narrow bed, I lay down and prayed for Henry to return. Through the porthole the solid concrete walls of the Pedro Miguel Locks loomed as the water rushed out into Miraflores Lake, lowering the ship to the next level.

The towel soaked quickly. There was nothing I could do. I had no control over what was happening to me. That moment was the end of hope and the beginning of grief. I couldn't wait for Henry any longer.

The nurse on duty that day was a plain and practical girl. Her name was Miss Winter. These days I might struggle to remember the names of people a second after I meet them, but I will always remember Miss Winter. I will never forget her face when she looked under my skirt and saw the blood.

She was calm and matter-of-fact as she set about washing my legs. It struck me as odd that nurses wore white, given what they were tasked with. I'd never thought to question the stiff white apron and matching hat I'd aspired to as a trainee. White, as a symbol of cleanliness and purity, turned nurses into ministering angels, somehow elevating them to an ethereal state above the dirt and mess of human fragility.

But behind the veneer of white-starched efficiency, I recognised the terror in Miss Winter's eyes. I heard it in the offer of endless cups of tea and the way she wondered out loud how much longer Dr Parker was going to be.

'You mean Henry's not here?'

She looked at me with wide eyes then, as if realising at that moment the full implications. 'No, Mrs Parker, he's ashore. Escorting a patient to hospital.'

'He's not even on board?'

She told me that Henry had left an hour ago, headed for Panama City with his patient. The starched dining-room napkin that passed for her nurse's cap looked farcical as she shook her head. Whoever had thought of such a thing? Was the stiff uniform designed merely to discourage amorous advances by male patients? But with or without that dress, apron and cap, I knew I was powerless against the inevitable. There was nothing that anyone could do. As Florence Nightingale said, *Nature alone heals*. Or takes its course.

Henry later told me about the rickety ambulance, and how whenever the vehicle accelerated and the stretcher with no brakes flew backwards, he was forced to hold the rear doors closed and pray. He told me about leaving the frightened patient in the hands of the mercifully competent local doctors, and racing back via taxi to reach the ship as it exited the last set of locks. How the taxi had been stuck in traffic, and how he'd stood alone on the dockside watching the ship – along with his wife and unborn child – sail out into the Pacific Ocean without him.

'I know there's nothing he can do,' I said, fighting back the tears that pooled in my throat as I lay helpless and scared against the white sheets. 'But I just wish he was here.'

Miss Winter patted my hand and offered me another cup of tea. Bless her kindness and her ridiculous napkin hat, I thought. This woman knew how to be a nurse.

It is however certain that there is nothing yet discovered which is a substitute to the English patient for his cup of tea.

Florence Nightingale was right. By then there was nothing else that could be done besides put the kettle on.

By the time Henry boarded the boat that was speeding out to collect the pilot, the pain had passed. In the minutes it took the pilot boat to catch the ship, for Henry to climb the Jacob's ladder up the corn-coloured hull and in through the gunport door, the bleeding stopped. The message from the officer of the watch was relayed as Henry boarded, and he ran.

But it was too late. He arrived, soaked through with perspiration, his sandy hair almost transparent against his damp scalp. He arrived in time to see Miss Winter wrap our silent baby in a white towel and carry her away. I watched him crumble. No longer Dr Parker, BM BCh, Ship's Surgeon. In that moment he was simply Henry.

As much to give him something to do, I sent Henry back to our cabin to fetch the layette I'd knitted. It had helped to fill the long nauseous hours, and although I'd repeatedly unwound and reknitted my early efforts, I'd finally mastered the art of winding wool around two long metal needles. With the birth still months away, I'd wrapped the white matinee jacket, hat and matching booties in tissue paper and stored them in a small cardboard box on the top shelf in our tiny wardrobe. While Henry was at work I'd lift the box down and lovingly fold and refold the tiny garments. It was the closest thing to handling the baby that was growing unseen inside my body.

Miss Winter duly dressed the baby. For all the weeks that my womb had fed and nurtured our little girl, in the end her body fitted inside a single bootie. I touched her tiny head and then she was gone. I never asked what happened to her. I should have done. That's just the way it was then. If I'd asked, I would have known where to search, where to grieve other than in the cold, grey depths of my nightmares.

26

Has Anyone Seen Nemo?

'HERE WE ARE, MRS P. WE'RE HOME AT LAST.' THE WOMAN had a look of faint triumph. Her round face was difficult to navigate, Evelyn's gaze slipping from one feature to the next like hands round a clock face. And yet she recognised her. This was Nola. Her friend. And this must be Nola's cabin.

Evelyn looked at the number on the cabin door. *June 10.* 'That's the same number as mine,' she said, surprised. Surely the ship wouldn't have duplicated the cabin numbers?

'Here, let me.' Nola pushed a blue and white card into the slot above the door handle and, when a green light flashed, opened the door.

Evelyn walked in with some trepidation. It was as though someone had deliberately placed her belongings around this cabin to confuse her.

'What are my things doing in your cabin?'

'This is *your* cabin.' Nola's soft face came close to a frown.

Evelyn surveyed the scene: the blue bedspread, the books on the shelves, the ornaments. It all felt right. She relaxed a fraction, deciding to trust the brain in her gut over the increasingly unreliable one in her head.

A full circuit convinced Evelyn that this was indeed her cabin. Her home. Nola was inspecting a tiny snow globe of the Eiffel Tower with interest, a kitsch souvenir that Evelyn couldn't recall buying.

'You've seen a lot of the world, Mrs P,' said Nola, studying the Russian dolls that were lined up like the Von Trapp family.

'All the ports at least, and wherever can be reached on a daytrip.'

'Two thirds of the earth is covered by oceans,' said a man who had appeared from nowhere. 'So it's fair to assume you've seen most of it.'

Evelyn's heart stumbled at the sight of a man who wasn't her husband in her cabin, but her gut tried to reassure her. Relax, you know him. He is Nola's current husband.

'You're right, Frank,' replied Evelyn, impressed that her ability to recall names was improving all the time. She'd been worrying over nothing. Her memory was fine.

Evelyn picked up a silver photo frame from the dressing-table-desk and waved it around in front of her eyes until she found the ideal focal length. In the picture, she recognised Henry, looking like a young Alec Guinness, smiling in front of a waterfall. He had his arm around an attractive woman. Evelyn frowned until she recognised that the woman in the photograph was her. 'This was taken at Niagara Falls.'

She handed the photograph to Nola, who made a sighing noise.

'So this is Henry then? Well, well,' said Nola. She handed the photo to her husband.

'Well, well,' he repeated.

Evelyn made her way along the line of framed photographs. Another waterfall. This time a middle-aged Henry. Next to him, Evelyn saw herself, tanned in a bathing suit. A little heavier in the legs, and the first flecks of white at her temples.

'Dunn's River Falls, Jamaica – 1970s, I think.'

'You must have seen a lot of waterfalls in your travels.'

'Niagara, Iguazu, Angel Falls. You're right.'

She loved waterfalls, never tired of watching the turbulent rapids tumble into the arms of the still water below. Serene and majestic when viewed from afar. Up close, a restless, churning wall of water.

'It makes our life on the farm seem a bit dull, eh Nola? Not to mention a bit dry.' Frank's shoulders dropped.

'Don't say that, Frank. We can't have everything in life. We all make sacrifices.' Fizzy Nola fell silent, lost in some private reflection.

'But the way you put your life on hold to look after my mother, after all those years spent bringing up the children, well, I want you to know that I'm grateful. She wasn't the easiest woman . . .'

'You can say that again,' said Nola. 'She'd only live a matter of weeks, they told us, not months or years but weeks. Pity no one told Vera that. I did everything for that woman, washed her, dressed her, fed her, and all she did was complain. I'm sure she only hung around to torture me. Always leaving her tea to go cold, losing her hearing aids, and that bloody bell! The number of times I wanted to shove it . . .' Nola stopped. A strange sound came from her throat and her shoulders heaved. Frank stepped forward and placed a hand on her back. She resurfaced, spluttering through a face full of tears.

'And the thing is, I miss her. I miss the tinkle of her bell and her complaints about the food I cooked. I miss us arguing over which radio station to listen to, and how we'd talk through the night when she couldn't sleep. I miss her stories about Frank and growing up on the farm. It could be so lonely out there in the middle of nowhere, with Frank gone for hours on end. She was company. Good company.'

Frank's eyes welled up too. 'My mother loved you, Nola. I know she had a funny way of showing it, but it's the truth.'

'When she stopped eating, I knew she was coming to the end. But it was so slow. I couldn't bear the thought of her dying alone in some nursing home miles away.'

Nola's face was all wet and puffy. She seemed almost more upset than Frank, who'd lost his mother. But grief was like that. It treated people differently. Some it tore down, leaving them paralysed and incapable of anything. Others marched on, in stoic acceptance, stalked by sorrow that hid in the shadows, only to leap out when least expected. And there were those rendered insensible by loss, who lived in denial. As if not believing a thing could make it less true.

'It's the greatest gift you can give someone,' said Evelyn. 'To look after them like you did, and be with them at the end.'

'She'd have made a good nurse,' said Frank, giving his wife a burly hug.

'*Every woman is a nurse*,' said Evelyn. 'And quite a few men nowadays too,' she corrected. Times had moved on, for both men and women. She wondered what Florence would have made of the modern world. And men on her wards.

Frank replaced the Dunn's River Falls back with the other waterfalls. 'Will you be all right on your own for a while,

Mrs Parker? Only Nola and I are off to see the reef on a glass-bottomed boat. We'll be back in time for afternoon tea.'

Beyond the balcony doors, Evelyn noticed palm trees. She was relieved. The idea of a port day with the ship to herself put her in an unexpectedly good mood. She would find a nice quiet spot on the deck and do some concentrating. There were a number of loose ends hanging, thoughts and worries she needed to tidy up or trim with her mental scissors.

Nola had helped herself to a handful of tissues from a box in the bathroom. Her sniffs and nose blowing echoed around the cabin. 'Right then, Frank,' she said. 'Let's go and find Nemo.'

Evelyn was concerned. Was Nemo missing too?

Nola's face was less moist than before but still puffy. To Evelyn's relief, she'd returned to her usual chatty self. All the tears and talk of dying should have unsettled Evelyn. But ironically, the older she got, the less she worried about dying. It was inevitable at any age. Closer than it was yesterday. Not quite as close as it would be tomorrow. It wasn't death she feared as much as dying alone. She wanted to be like Vera. She wanted a little bell and someone to make her cold cups of tea. She wanted to be with Henry when they finally parted, whichever one of them went first.

'Before we go, Mrs P,' said Nola, 'Dr King told me to remind you not to leave your cabin today. We've arranged for room service to bring you lunch. You need to rest.'

Frank was busy doing something to the cabin door. When he stepped aside, Evelyn saw a handwritten sign fixed to the back of the door, just above the directions to the muster station.

'It was my idea, actually.' Frank stood a little taller. Nola rolled her eyes.

The letters were neatly printed in an old-fashioned hand.

DO NOT LEAVE THE CABIN EXCEPT IN AN EMERGENCY.

FRANK AND NOLA BACK AT TEATIME.

Evelyn read the sign as if the instructions had been shouted into her face. The moment Frank and Nola left, she tore it down. She'd just remembered something important, a tiny scrap of information that she had to write down. It was as fragile as a soap bubble.

Floating.

Hovering.

Evelyn emptied her handbag on the blue bedspread. Unscrewed her fountain pen. Turned the sign over and wrote on the reverse, in scratchy blue-black Quink.

HENRY IS IN THE CELLAR.

~

Evelyn unplugged the television. There was only so many times she could watch the singing-dancing-bingo officer demonstrating the correct way to don a life jacket. There must be other channels, but she'd mislaid the changer-over-upper-downer.

A knock sounded at the door followed by someone shouting, 'Steward.'

She pressed her eye against the peephole. The door opened, shunting Evelyn into the wardrobe.

'Steward,' came the voice again.

Reappearing, Evelyn squared up to the intruder. 'No, I'm Mrs Parker.'

The woman – young, umber-skinned, long-limbed but thick around the middle – was familiar. She smiled nicely.

'Yes I know, ma'am. I came to see how you are feeling.'

The chances of a quiet thinking day were looking frustratingly slim with all these interruptions. Evelyn didn't even try to keep the irritation out of her voice. 'I am very well, thank you.'

She tried to shoo the visitor back out the way she'd come. The woman touched the gold name badge on her chest, drawing Evelyn's attention to it. Grace. *Tuesday's child.*

'Would you like me to come back later and service your stateroom?'

'That won't be necessary, I'm going out for a while.' Evelyn glanced down at her dressing-gown and Finding Henry shoes. 'Once I'm dressed.'

'Would you like me to help you? I'm not supposed to, but it's no trouble.'

'Go on then,' conceded Evelyn, more to get rid of the woman. 'Blue dress.'

'The one you wore to the farewell drinks? That's my favourite, ma'am. You look lovely in blue.'

'Colour of the ocean.'

'And the sky, ma'am.'

The woman had removed the hanger and was holding the dress against her body, waiting.

'The colour would look perfect on you, dear. I have so many dresses. I'd like you to have it.'

'No, I couldn't. It's an expensive dress.'

'You could always take the sleeves off and there's plenty of spare fabric in the bodice if you wanted to let it out. Go on, please try it.'

Grace froze, dropping the dress. 'No, ma'am, I couldn't.' She backed away, feeling for the door behind her, and was gone.

Alone, Evelyn bent over to pick the dress up off the floor. Straightening again triggered a series of aches and pains, her private rollcall of decrepitude. The dress was a little old-fashioned, but the fabric was excellent quality and the seams were still sound. Evelyn tried not to be offended. It would have made a wonderful frock for a christening.

27

The Wisdom of the Cloth Rabbit

I ALWAYS WAITED FOR HENRY TO LEAVE THE CABIN BEFORE I soaked the pillowcase with tears. The Panama Canal was now way behind us and we had taken to endless discussions about the weather to fill the raw silences. It was almost a relief when Henry left each morning to his clinic and I could pick my emotional scab in private.

'This will do you no good at all,' Florence Nightingale said to me that morning. I heard her voice so clearly that I was afraid to open my eyes.

'What's the point of getting out of bed? There's nothing to get up for.'

'*Nature alone cures.*'

'I don't want to be *cured*. I want to know what I did wrong, why I lost her.'

'I will not give you false cheer, my dear. She had not properly formed and would not have survived to term. It is nature's way.

And let me tell you that lying in bed will not make you feel better. Look what happened to your mother. You have lost a child and you will always carry that grief.'

'What would you know? You never married, never had a child of your own.' I opened my eyes but kept them focused on the damp weave of the white cotton pillowcase.

'One does not need to experience everything first-hand to understand. It is a nurse's job to observe and have empathy. I would go so far as to say, *if you cannot get the habit of observation one way or other, you had better give up being a nurse, for it is not your calling.*'

I gripped the pillow, wiped the last of my tears. 'I know,' I said, 'I've read your book and filed it away, chapter by chapter, inside my brain, but it's just words. And words can't bring my baby back.'

'And neither will lying in bed. Up! You need light, fresh air and a cup of beef tea.'

The sun was bright after so many days spent in the ship's dingy interior and it took several minutes for my eyes to put the colour back into the bleached scene. At first I couldn't look at the ocean, imagining the cold waves dragging her down.

My body showed no outward sign that I had carried a child, if only for a few weeks. It had ruthlessly returned to its normal shape, and my monthlies had resumed. I felt betrayed.

My muscles began to loosen in the warm air and I was relieved to be moving once more rather than curled up in self-pity. I'd completed almost an entire lap of the promenade deck when I saw Henry in the distance. I recognised him immediately on account of his ears which, although his tawny hair had grown, still protruded under his officer's cap. My heart sped up, as though my blood was carrying more love than oxygen, and I realised that having lost my child, I couldn't risk losing my husband too.

He was sitting on one heel, arms resting on his other knee, talking to a small boy. They were laughing at something, and as I approached I saw Henry holding a tatty cloth rabbit. He danced the rabbit on his knee like a ventriloquist with a dummy, his squeaky rabbit voice raising a steady stream of giggles from the boy. I paused a few feet away, not wanting to disturb the show. Henry's face was animated, and I realised it was the first time I'd seen him smile since Panama.

Henry rarely mentioned his own father. He had been, I gathered, a distant man who had tried to balance the smothering affections of Henry's mother with cool detachment. Henry had barely had time to imagine himself as a father, but in that moment I glimpsed the kind of devotion our child would have had with him as a parent. And even with Henry working away on ships for eight months of the year, they could still have enjoyed a meaningful father–daughter relationship. But alas, it wasn't to be.

I wondered what Henry had been like before I knew him, a toddler taking unsteady steps, a schoolboy in an immaculate uniform, a gangly teenager limping battered and bruised from the rugby pitch, the young man graduating with honours. Before I could find comfort in those images, they were gone again, evaporating like a sea mist before my eyes.

I realised that we had been carrying the burden of each other's unspoken grief. Our misery and sadness had been doubled rather than halved by sharing. Henry handed back the boy's rabbit and shook his hand. The lad skipped away, back to his parents, and when Henry rose to his feet again, it was into my waiting arms.

28

The Other Mr Coleridge

EVELYN WAS SURPRISED TO FIND THE CELLAR LOCATED ON deck eleven. She'd expected it to be hidden away somewhere in the bowels of the ship. According to her increasingly ragged pocket map, it was sandwiched between duty free and the cinema. Neither of these was a place she frequented as a rule, the former due to her uncertain finances, the latter on account of a film called *Sirens*, which to her disappointment had had nothing to do with Greek mythology.

It felt good to have a sense of purpose again, after being cooped up in her cabin for what seemed like days but could conceivably have only been hours. With the three bulkheads and sliding balcony door of her cabin closing in on her, Evelyn had decided to go for a walk. Henry was still missing, but someone had left a clue. In blue-black fountain pen, an unknown person had written *HENRY IS IN THE CELLAR*. It looked too scratchy and wobbly to be her handwriting, yet not quite as indecipherable as Henry's doctor scrawl.

So far her mission was going according to plan. No one had stopped her or tried to return her to her cabin. It was testament to her skill in disguise. In order to travel around the ship incognito, she'd tried to emulate the standard cruise ship camouflage with slacks, a pastel blouse which she entered head first on account of the already fastened buttons, and her Finding Henry shoes. She'd never worn slacks before, and indeed couldn't recall ever buying a pair. With hindsight, the slacks seemed an odd shape, rather loose around the waist and fitted over the bottom. They would have been a better shape for Henry.

She had to pause on exiting the lift to roll up the bottoms, which made for a smoother progress now she wasn't tripping over the leg fabric. But they were remarkably comfortable as a garment and, with her legs unfettered by the hem of a skirt, Evelyn was able to stride out, overtaking several dawdling passengers.

All but invisible to the other passengers, Evelyn had, however, noted a number of crew watching her as she passed by. Like those of the Mona Lisa, eyes followed her wherever she went. Once or twice she'd sensed *they* were even following her, only to turn around and see a crew member reading a notice or polishing a handrail.

Evelyn took a detour through the duty-free shop to throw the hounds off the scent of the fox. She sprayed herself with a series of perfume tester bottles. But just as the mixing of many different-coloured paints as a child had created a disappointing sludge-brown, so the spraying of as many varied perfumes created a rather unpleasant odour. She heard Florence Nightingale pass judgement with a click of her tongue.

In disease where everything given off from the body is highly noxious and dangerous ... plenty of ventilation to carry off the effluvia.

In her hurry to escape the effluvia in duty free, Evelyn almost ran into four stripes. It was the eating-drinking-and-sleeping officer. Luckily he was intercepted by a disgruntled passenger, and Evelyn was able to sidestep into the photo gallery.

The taking-photos person was busy and didn't notice Evelyn skulking. This was another place she didn't usually frequent. To her relief, the ship's photographers had long since stopped trying to snap her portrait. But Evelyn was fascinated by the hundreds of smiling faces beaming down from the walls of the gallery. If these pictures were to be believed, ships were happy places.

Evelyn wondered if she might find a picture of her friends, Frank and Nola. It was only a matter of days until they disembarked at the end of their holiday, and she at the end of her life's journey. On the far left wall were the embarkation photographs, snapped as the passengers boarded, pale and work- or travel-weary, trailing small suitcases on wheels and forcing smiles through gritted teeth. On the next wall, the same passengers looked a little more relaxed, their smiles less strained as they shook hands with the captain against a faux *Titanic* backdrop. By the far right-hand wall, most passengers looked tanned and relaxed, their grins as wide as their waistlines as they huddled in around their dining tables with new-found friends.

Just as she was about to abandon her search for Frank and Nola, she noticed something. There, amongst the dozens of other huddled dining groups, was a threesome. A rosy-cheeked woman with happy teeth sitting next to a serious-looking warty-headed man, and between them a white-haired woman with a face like a scrunched-up paper bag. Wearing a tiara.

Checking first that the taking-photos person was still busy, Evelyn removed the photograph from the wall and slipped it into her handbag. It was a squeeze to close the fastening, and she had to rearrange a set of Russian dolls and the wooden turtles to make room.

Out of the corner of her eye, Evelyn saw the taking-photos person look up from his busy thing but she was gone before he could say anything, the combination of her Finding Henry shoes and her new Borrowing Photos slacks allowing her a clean getaway.

Outside the cinema entrance, Evelyn turned full circle trying to orientate herself. She rotated the map upside down, cocked her head to one side and squinted. According to the pocket map, she had arrived. This was the place: a small, dimly lit area consisting of half-a-dozen tall tables and bar-type stools. Rows of bottles lined the walls behind locked glass doors, and when Evelyn looked closer, she saw that the tables were made from upended wine barrels, adorned with bunches of plastic grapes.

She struggled to contain her disappointment. The place was deserted apart from a kyphotic old man balancing precariously on a bar stool against the far wall. He had his curved back to her and she couldn't see his face. Above his head, Evelyn noticed a sign that brought everything crashing back down to earth.

Welcome to the Cellar.

How could she have been so foolish? All her built-up hopes crumbled into the starboard-side carpet beneath her cottonwool no-good-for-Finding Henry feet. This was her last chance, the final unticked place on the map. If Henry wasn't here, in the cellar, she would have no choice but to conclude that he simply wasn't on board *Golden Sunset*. He had disappeared into thin air, or joined their daughter in the depths of the infinite ocean. At least they were together now, swimming with the dolphins. Life had been careless with those she loved. With the end she'd feared right in front of her, Evelyn could see no reason not to join them.

Crushed by her stupidity, Evelyn turned to leave, but not before taking a second look at the man sitting at the far end of the Cellar bar. There was something about the shape of his head and the pattern of his sparse greying hair that made Evelyn's skin tingle. She felt the blood surge through her body, starting inside her Finding Henry shoes, all the way up the legs of her Borrowing Photos slacks and into the blouse she now noticed was buttoned up all wrong.

'Henry?' she said, her voice quivering on her thin breath. 'Is it you?'

She inched towards him, willing him but at the same time not wanting him to turn around. It was important to hold on to this moment, having let so many others slip away before it.

He turned at the sound of her voice. Adjusted his hearing aid. Smiled.

'Did you say something?' said the man-who-wasn't-Henry.

'Sorry, I thought you were someone different.'

'Different? How ironic.' He laughed.

'I don't understand,' said Evelyn, inching closer to hear his frail voice. She noticed a walking frame, the type that old people pushed about, parked behind the man who wasn't her husband. 'Did I say something to offend you?'

The man put a photograph down on top of the wine-barrel table and sighed. 'Not at all, in fact you're absolutely right. I always knew I was different. But times were different then.

Being different, well, it's different today.' His eyes moved to his lap.

Evelyn inched closer, wondering if she'd misheard. 'So you're saying that being different would have been different in a different time?'

'That's exactly what I'm saying. It's so refreshing to find someone who understands.'

None the wiser, Evelyn followed his gaze to the sepia photograph on the wine-barrel table. A young version of the different man-who-wasn't-Henry smiled back at the camera. He was lithe and muscular, his shapely calves shown off below a pair of baggy shorts that had once been the fashion. Next to him, a bespectacled young man was standing in a self-conscious position, as if he didn't know what to do with his body. They stood apart, their hands almost touching as they leaned back against a sea wall. There was a small dog at their feet.

'I mistook you for my husband.'

Something moved across his face, amusement perhaps. His eyes were gentle, thought Evelyn, the type that sloped down at the edges, making him look both kind and sad.

'Care to join me?' The man pulled out a bar stool for Evelyn. 'I'm afraid the cellar door is closed whilst we are in port, but I can offer you an excellent coffee. Or tea? I have the eye of the bartender over there.' He waved and said bartender arrived as if by magic.

'What can I get you, ma'am?' said the bartender, pen poised above his notepad.

Not sure whether it was morning or afternoon, Evelyn decided against coffee. She had enough trouble sleeping without the palpitating effects of caffeine to add to her insomnia. 'I'll have a tea, please.'

'English breakfast, Irish breakfast, Australian afternoon, orange pekoe, lapsang souchong, peppermint, chamomile or lemon and ginger?'

Evelyn considered the options. 'Do you have any beef tea?'

'No, ma'am,' replied the waiter, frowning.

'Hot chocolate then,' said Evelyn.

The bartender hurried off to prepare her drink and another cappuccino for the man with the grey hair.

'I'm a beef tea man myself,' said the man. 'I suppose it's gone out of fashion, like everything else I enjoy.'

Evelyn harrumphed. 'I know, things just aren't the same anymore. They used to do the most wonderful braised tongue in aspic.'

'It sounds delicious. Now you're lucky if your meat isn't still bleeding.'

'Or your fish is even cooked.'

The man chuckled. 'It's a funny old world.'

The drinks arrived. The hot chocolate was too hot and Evelyn pushed it aside while the man brought his cup to his lips with shaking hands.

'Is this you?' said Evelyn. She squinted at the photograph, pretending not to notice the puddle of coffee forming in the man's saucer. The corners of the photo were frayed and creased as though it had been handled more than was usual for a casual snapshot.

The man nodded. 'It was. In a different life.'

Evelyn wondered how many lives the man had had. Was he about to tell her he was also the reincarnation of a thirteenth-century Tibetan monk, or an animal of some kind? Luckily the man continued before Evelyn could get too confused.

'I've been many people in my lifetime,' he said, 'played many roles to try to fit in. I've tried to please everyone else in my life except myself.'

Something about this rang true for Evelyn. 'I think we all do, don't we?'

The man-who-wasn't-Henry laughed and shook his head. 'Not nowadays. People are much freer to be themselves, to do what pleases them.'

Evelyn wasn't sure what this had to do with the photograph. It sounded like the beginning of a generic conversation between two antiquated strangers who'd found themselves united in their mutual bafflement over another generation. Everything and everyone was so impatient these days, so intolerant of old people and their slowness. It was as though time itself was impatient. Even nostalgia wasn't what it used to be.

'Who is this?' she asked, pointing to the other figure in the photograph.

'His name is David. I knew him before I met my wife. He wrote to me a little while ago telling me he was dying of cancer. He sent me this photograph.'

'That's nice,' said Evelyn. 'About the photograph, that is,' she added quickly.

'And do you know the first words he wrote in his letter?'

'Dear . . . ?'

'You probably don't remember me.'

'I'm sorry,' said Evelyn. 'Your face is certainly familiar but I'm not very good with names.'

'That's what he wrote. *You probably don't remember me . . .*'

'Oh, I see. Did you?'

'Remember him?' The man pulled a fake grape away from its bunch and began to roll the purple plastic between his fingers. 'The irony is that I spent fifty years trying to forget David. I tried not to think about him every single day of my life. I became a husband and a father of three, built a successful business and even wrote a novel. All so I wouldn't remember our brief time together.'

'Why is it so hard to remember some things and even harder to forget others?'

'And therein lies the conundrum.'

'It's like my brain has stopped making new memories,' said Evelyn. 'I sometimes wonder if I've simply filled it up, like a cupboard with too many things crammed in.' The handbag burst open on her lap. She wondered how the plastic grapes had found their way in there.

'Like pouring water into a bucket that's already full?'

'Yes, that's it! I remember things that happened fifty years ago as if they were yesterday.'

'And forget what you did five minutes ago?'

They bonded in the silence of their shared bewilderment.

'I've been diagnosed with Alzheimer's disease,' the man said, turning to face her.

Evelyn did a double-take. 'Are you sure?'

'I'm afraid so,' he replied. 'My doctor told me that as my condition progresses, there may be entire periods of my life that I forget, even the happiest times. And people too. One day I won't recognise my own family. That's what frightens me the most.'

The man had finished his coffee. The hot chocolate was still too hot. Evelyn listened as the man talked. At last, here was someone, a complete stranger, who understood her. He was the only person on the entire ship who didn't treat her like a child, using a special voice or speaking extra slowly. He was frightened too.

'Do you know that I can still recite all one hundred and forty-three verses of *The Rime of the Ancient Mariner* from memory?' said Evelyn. 'But sometimes I forget what I'm doing while I'm doing it.'

They laughed.

'I'm sorry, I don't know your name.'

'Mrs Henry Parker. Please call me Evelyn.'

'Lovely to meet you, Evelyn. I'm Bill. Bill Coleridge.'

Evelyn sat back on her stool. Surely he was having a little intellectual joke at her expense. 'Coleridge? As in Samuel Taylor Coleridge?'

'No relation, I'm afraid. Now that you mention it, I'm told his remains turned up recently, in a church in north London. In the wine cellar of all places.'

Evelyn remembered why she was here. 'I've lost my husband.'

'I'm so sorry to hear that, my dear,' said the Mr Coleridge who was very much alive in this wine cellar.

'Not half as sorry as I am. I've searched the ship from top to bottom and still haven't found him.'

Evelyn rummaged under the handbag grapes for the pocket map and smoothed it out on top of the wine-barrel table. The diagram of the ship was covered in blue-black question marks, each crossed out. With one exception. The cellar had been her last hope.

By some miracle Evelyn's fountain pen had also risen to the surface of her handbag. She used it to turn her final question mark into a cross. She ticked COLERIDGE off too. She'd found Henry's favourite poet, but not Henry.

Mr Coleridge understood. He sat pensively for a moment before saying, 'I'm moving to an aged care facility soon on account of my dementia. It's early stages and I manage. Just.

But I worry about what's ahead. I never want to be a burden to my family. My wife married someone else a long time ago, though we're still good friends. My children are too busy with their own lives to look after me.'

Evelyn searched his wise, kind face for clues. He looked like every second person aboard this ship, his devastating diagnosis invisible to a casual observer.

'*And till my ghastly tale is told . . .*' she began.

'*. . . this heart within me burns,*' Mr Coleridge finished.

On the wine barrel in front of them, Evelyn's hot chocolate had gone cold. Was this what was happening to her? Did she have Alzheimer's too? As her brain gradually ran out of steam, would the time come when she stopped eating and drinking as her brain forgot how to keep her body alive? Would there be a time when she forgot Henry altogether, a time when she simply stopped looking for him?

'I hope that if something has happened to my Henry, he's in a better place.' Suddenly Evelyn was afraid of remembering. What if some terrible truth returned to her that she couldn't forget?

Mr Coleridge placed his big warm hand over Evelyn's. It felt secure, comforting, and for a few moments all was well.

'Would you care for a walk, Mrs Henry Parker?'

'I'd like that, Mr Coleridge.'

He invited Evelyn to steady herself against him as he pushed his walking frame. She threaded her arm through his as if closing the link of a chain. She wondered why it was that some people felt like old friends the very first time you met them.

Leaning on Mr Coleridge who was leaning on his walking-thing-with-wheels was the steadiest Evelyn had felt in a long while. She wondered whether it was time to get herself one. It was like a shopping trolley she could sit on if she needed a rest. At the very least, the metal basket at the front would give her somewhere to put all her things. Her handbag was growing heavier by the day.

'Did you know that my husband was a ship's doctor?' said Evelyn as they strolled arm-in-arm-on-walker.

'How very interesting. I've always been fascinated by the sea. If I had my own way, I'd spend the rest of my days living aboard a ship like this. It would work out a damn sight cheaper than a nursing home. What with waiter service at every meal, delicious food, live entertainment every night and twenty-four-hour medical care on board, it makes perfect sense.'

'Well, it's funny you should say that, Mr Coleridge ...'

29

For Those in Peril on the Sea

TWO WORDS, MULTIPLE SYLLABLES. EVELYN'S FINGER TRACED the spines of the faded textbooks on her shelf. One of them must hold the answer, the reason her feet were both numb and painful. As a child she'd suffered with chilblains, and in the harsh winter of 1947, when the ice had formed on the inside of her bedroom windows in London, she'd fallen asleep with her feet on a hot water bottle. This felt exactly the same. It began with a P. She could see the words in the distance but couldn't get quite close enough to read them.

If anything, removing her Finding Henry shoes had made the whole thing much worse. She put them back on again. Besides, it was important to be ready and receptive to any potential new leads. The trail had gone cold, but Evelyn wouldn't give up until she found Henry. In the meantime, her mouth was dry and she needed a mint.

The side seam of her handbag had begun to gape, Evelyn noticed as she searched for her packet of mints. Things simply weren't built to last anymore. Twenty years was nothing for a handbag.

Evelyn returned the turtle and the Russian dolls to the shelf, and found the plastic grapes a new home in her fruit bowl, making a mental note in capital letters: *DO NOT EAT*. She smiled at her new friends before placing the borrowed photograph of Frank and Nola in pride of place on the bookshelf. The pile of unopened envelopes taunted her from the dressing-table-desk. The need to deal with all this correspondence was like walking with a stone in her shoe. Or perhaps a different annoying thing, given the circumstances with her feet.

The next item out of her handbag, crumpled and pebble-dashed with mysterious golden crumbs, was the pocket map. Evelyn's gnarled fingers tore the flimsy cardboard and dropped the shreds into the wastepaper bin. The armchair welcomed her with a sigh. She popped a mint into her mouth and tried not to chew it.

Through the balcony windows, Evelyn watched an island retreat towards the horizon, chased by a thick blanket of grey cloud. A fork of white lightning split the sky three ways, the thunder too far away to be heard above the wheeze of the ship's air conditioning. Evelyn loved a good storm.

The second flash of lightning was followed two-Mississippis later by a knock at the cabin door. Evelyn levered herself out of the chair and shuffled across the cabin.

'Can I help you?' she said through the thinnest of door cracks.

Her new friends smiled their best borrowed-photograph smiles. 'We've come to take you to dinner.'

Dinner? Had she even had lunch? Evelyn began to wonder if she might actually starve to death without friends.

'Do come in,' she said, hoping they wouldn't notice the state of her cabin. The bed was unmade and the dressing-table-desk was piled high with paper and mint wrappers.

'Are you ready to go?' Nola's eyes darted from surface to surface, doing a mental tidy-up.

'Go where?'

'To the restaurant. For dinner. First sitting is in five minutes,' said Frank as the bathroom door swung open and hit him in the back.

'Bit of weather tonight, Mrs P,' said Nola. 'We'd better hurry if we want to line our stomachs. I'm already feeling a bit peaky.'

She didn't look seasick, thought Evelyn, noticing Nola's even rosier than usual cheeks and sunburnt nose.

As if reading her thoughts, Frank added, 'Glass-bottomed boat. Can you believe it? And us both farmers. You'd think we'd have been more careful.'

'Still, it was worth it for the fish, wasn't it, hun?' replied Nola. 'You'll be pleased to hear we found Nemo. He's alive and well and reunited with his father.' She chuckled.

'That *is* a relief,' said Evelyn. It seemed like the right thing to say. She was thinking about fish. Salmon. Bears catching salmon. *Alaska.* 'Did I ever tell you about Alaska?'

Frank and Nola exchanged glances.

'Why don't you tell us on the way?' said Nola. She gestured towards Evelyn's shoes. 'I think we should do up these laces, don't you? Frank, why don't you see if you can find Mrs P's cabin steward – Grace, I think her name is, and tell her we're going out. It doesn't look like this cabin has been serviced today.'

'Good idea,' said Frank, looking relieved to be delegated a task while Nola kneeled to tie Evelyn's Finding Henry laces in a double bow.

'Your feet are looking a bit puffy, Mrs P.' Nola had also started to look a bit puffy as she tried to stand up again. 'Have you been resting and elevating your feet like the doctor told you?'

'Absolutely,' said Evelyn without a pause. 'All day.'

Frank returned. 'No sign of her,' he said. 'No one's seen her since this morning.'

'But Virgilio is my steward,' said Evelyn. 'He's very good with fruit. And necklaces.'

Nola was busily inspecting the fruit bowl. She tutted and rolled her eyes. 'Look at this lovely mango. It's gone all mushy. You really should eat it while it's fresh. And this banana's all brown.'

'Banana? Get rid of it, quickly! It all makes perfect sense now.' The child whistling, the Friday departure from Le Havre, and now the banana in the fruit bowl. No wonder Henry had gone missing! Evelyn grasped Nola by the arms. 'Tell me,' she pleaded, 'which foot did you step ashore with?'

Bemused but apparently game to go along with Evelyn's derailed thought process, Nola replied, 'Now let me see . . . It was a tender port today. The harbour was too shallow for the ship to go alongside. But I distinctly remember stepping out of the tender with my right foot. I know because I've had that knee replaced and it doesn't bend as far as it should in spite of all the exercises. I know ninety degrees was a bit optimistic, but I'd have settled for a hundred and ten.'

'Thank goodness.' Reassured, Evelyn allowed Nola to guide her towards the door. She liked it when Nola talked, even if she couldn't make sense of the words. Silence, she decided, was far more frightening. It only made her worries and fears easier to hear.

Outside her cabin, parked between the burgundy and gold tramlines of the carpet, was a tray. On the tray, a club sandwich and French fries sat untouched. What a waste of good food, thought Evelyn. 'I'm starving,' she said.

To leave the patient's untasted food by his side, from meal to meal, in hopes that he will eat it in the interval is simply to prevent him from taking any food at all.

Nola's hand rushed to her mouth as the smell of the cold food wafted.

'Not me,' said Nola, who was now clutching her ample stomach. 'Looking on the bright side, though, I could be back to a size eight by tomorrow morning.'

Frank reappeared in time to chuckle at this. 'Don't you go changing now, Nola. I love you just the way you are.'

Evelyn came to an abrupt halt. Something was wrong. 'Wait,' she said.

'What is it?' said Nola.

'I think I should wait for Henry.'

Evelyn saw Frank and Nola look at each other and mouth some words she couldn't hear.

'Mrs P,' said Nola, 'Frank and I have something important to tell you. It's about Henry.'

'Let's wait until we get to the dining room,' added Frank. 'It's probably best you're sitting down.'

~

There was a buzz of excitement and apprehension in the over-breathed air of the elevator. Predictably, the topic of conversation was the weather and the captain's warning to take care when moving around the ship in the coming hours.

'One hand for yourself and one hand for your ship.'

Evelyn was no stranger to the elements and the way sudden shifts in pressure and wind direction could play havoc with carefully planned itineraries. She also knew a thinly veiled storm warning when she heard one, and what it meant, both for a ship and the tender stomachs of the passengers clinging to it.

'It's cyclone season,' she announced, killing the lively pre-dinner chatter inside the elevator. The deathly silence was broken only by the *ping* of the doors as they arrived at the restaurant.

'Come along, Mrs P, we don't want to miss Italian night.' Nola bustled towards dinner.

Frank lurched to the left as he stepped out of the elevator, the ship taking an unexpected roll against a wave. 'Oopsie,' he said, correcting his balance.

'Don't worry. Everyone looks drunk on a ship,' said Evelyn as Nola did a quickstep to starboard when the ship righted itself.

A waiter wearing a red, white and green striped waistcoat squirted their hands with clear jelly from a bottle and waved them on into the restaurant. Evelyn headed towards her usual table but was intercepted by a deft manoeuvre from Frank and redirected towards a table set for three in the centre of the room.

'Here we are,' announced Nola.

A waiter scooped Evelyn skilfully into a chair and pushed her towards the table, then flicked open a starched white napkin and draped it over her lap. He was about to hand her a menu when he suddenly disappeared from view, reappearing several seconds later from the floor at her feet.

'Sorry, ma'am,' he said, brushing himself off.

'It's a bit sporty tonight, isn't it?' Frank said, turning the three wineglasses upside down to lower their centre of gravity as they slid across the tablecloth. 'You don't get this on a tractor.'

'I bet you've sailed through some storms in your time, Mrs P.'

'Henry and I have weathered our fair share.' An undercurrent of anxiety tugged at Evelyn. It wasn't the storm. *Henry*. She wrapped the napkin around her hands, tighter and tighter. Her eyes found Nola's.

Nola reached for Evelyn's hands under the table in the tangle of starched linen. 'About Henry . . .'

Henry was left dangling as the table took on a sudden and dramatic lean, sending Frank's bread roll lurching to port. Tumbling from his side plate, it bounced once on his knee and made a dash for freedom under a neighbouring table. At the exact moment a red, white and green waiter went to retrieve it, the whole dining room pitched then yawed. Glass smashed. A woman screamed.

'Goodness,' said Frank, grasping the sides of the table to steady himself.

Nola, looking suddenly less fizzy, followed suit. When the ship hit another wave, she groaned and laid her head down on the tablecloth. Around the dining room anxious passengers looked to see how others were reacting, waiting for their cue to start panicking. To their credit, the tricolour waiters soldiered on, balancing bread baskets and water jugs whilst trying to stay on their feet.

There was a crash against the window and a wall of grey water climbed the side of the ship. More screams followed. Shouts of 'Hold on!' A child crying. Another wave, then another threatening to engulf *Golden Sunset*.

Feeling peckish, Evelyn tore a corner from her bread roll and smeared it with butter. She'd survived worse. Swallowing the morsel, she took a sip of water from a glass that she hoped was hers on the chaotic table arrangement, cleared her throat and began to sing.

'*Eternal Father, strong to save,*
Whose arm hath bound the restless wave . . .'

Not-so-fizzy Nola watched her warily from the tablecloth.

'*Who bidd'st the mighty ocean deep*
Its own appointed limits keep.'

The only man-made sound in the dining room was Evelyn's tremulous tones rising above the crash of crockery and cutlery, her voice growing stronger and clearer. She'd lived through the Blitz in 1940 and remembered how important it was to keep spirits up in the air-raid shelter.

She continued, her breath finding its strength with each line of the seafarers' hymn.

'*Oh, hear us when we cry to Thee,*
For those in peril on the sea!'

A portly man on the next table stood up and, grasping a nearby pillar for support, belted out the next verse.

'*O Christ! Whose voice the waters heard*
And hushed their raging at Thy word . . .'

Next to him, a woman with a stiff hairdo stood and added her falsetto. '*Who walkedst on the foaming deep . . .*'

'Holy moly. She sounds like she's found a goldfish in her knickers,' groaned Nola, her face now the same colour as the tablecloth.

'*Oh, hear us when we cry to Thee,*
For those in peril on the sea!'

Around the restaurant, the passengers joined in one by one. The waiters battled valiantly with their carbonaras and linguines, juggling *insalata mistas* and *farfalle alla genoveses* while the busboys wielded dustpans and brushes.

'*Thus evermore shall rise to Thee*
Glad hymns of praise from land and sea.'

The final refrain was accompanied by a thunderous round of applause, followed by an almighty clap of real thunder.

With spirits – if not appetites – restored, first sitting dinner drew to a close. Several passengers stopped to thank Evelyn on their way out, one of whom miscalculated the roll of the ship and nearly came to rest sitting in her lap.

'A splendid evening!' announced the gentleman of the second verse as he and his wife staggered past Evelyn's table. She sensed they might have liked a longer conversation, but the ship had other plans and tossed them prematurely towards the exit.

Evelyn turned triumphantly to her fellow table guests. 'Henry will be so sorry he missed this. It's his favourite hymn. He made me promise we'd sing it at his funeral.'

A fizzless Nola looked wary, as if she was sitting on something very uncomfortable. 'I need to talk to you about Henry,' she said. 'I think it's only fair that you know the truth.'

'The truth?' Evelyn swayed, trying to counteract the movement of the ship.

'Best she hears it from you, Nola.'

Nola swallowed. 'Henry is . . .' she started but trailed off, eyes suddenly glazing over. Before Evelyn could learn the truth about her husband, Nola turned green and was gone, sprinting towards the exit with a napkin across her mouth.

30

Worse Things Happen at Sea

DAYBREAK LIT THE CABIN IN EERIE MONOCHROME. HER EYES were open but the rest of her body was not ready to wake. Evelyn turned her head to Henry's side of the bed. The pillow bore a dent where his head should have been. A single grey hair lay curled up like a sleeping cat on the white cotton pillowcase.

'Henry?'

There was no reply. Evelyn had heard him stumbling around the cabin during the night. He'd have disturbed her less if he'd turned on all the lights and simply gone about his business. Typical Henry. Whatever antics he'd got up to in the dark, however, this morning he was gone.

Evelyn levered herself up on one elbow, her vision slowly adjusting to the dim light. A shadow moved – a figure sitting in the armchair in the corner of the cabin.

Her breath hitched. Heart skittered.

'Is that you, Henry?'

A woman rose from the chair. Thin, frail. As the light hit her face, Evelyn recognised her.

'You should have listened to me.'

'Mother?'

'I told you to keep an eye on him.'

'What are you doing here?'

'You lost your baby and now you've lost your husband. Exactly as I predicted.'

Evelyn rubbed her eyes, trying to un-see her mother. She felt unusually light and agile in her body as she swung her legs out of bed. The carpet was soft beneath her feet.

'How could you be so cruel? I never stopped searching for her. I've spent my whole life at sea, just to be near my child.'

Her mother sneered. 'And Henry? Where is he?'

Evelyn didn't answer. She heard a noise through the bathroom door. A thump. A moan. A ribbon of light escaped beneath the door. There was someone inside.

With one tremulous knuckle, Evelyn knocked. 'Henry? Are you in there?' When there was no reply, she knocked again, louder this time.

Evelyn tried the door, the handle as cool as a weapon in her hand. She pushed, meeting resistance at first. She pushed again. Something shifted behind the door before it swung open.

There, lying crumpled on the bathroom floor in a dark halo of blood, was Henry. Her heart paused, the seconds from the last beat stretching out until her vision turned gauzy.

She'd found him.

~

It took a while to rise through the layers of sleep and register that she'd been dreaming. Evelyn's body was hot with adrenaline, her breaths shallow.

She waited for her mother to reappear, smelling of Chanel and Gitanes. But the chair in the corner of the cabin was empty. Outside, it was still dark.

Evelyn's heart stumbled as the terrifying images of Henry replayed. They were too vivid to be a dream, too terrible to be real.

She threw back the bedclothes and in one movement was standing, stars bursting across her vision. She waited for them to clear and headed for the bathroom in the dark.

One hand poised to stifle a scream, Evelyn opened the door and turned on the light. A white hand towel in the shape of an elephant sat goofily on the vanity but otherwise the bathroom was empty.

A sound had woken her, she was sure of it. There was someone outside the cabin.

There it was again. A faint noise at the door.

Tap, tap.

The door opened. A young girl's voice, apologising. Coming into the cabin.

The wind whined through a tiny gap in the balcony window. The ship bucked and kicked through the storm. Had there been a storm blowing when she went to bed? She couldn't remember. There'd been so many ships, so many storms.

'Sorry to disturb you, ma'am,' said the girl who wasn't Virgilio. *Tuesday's child. Grace.* She grasped the doorframe, her eyes wide with terror, her forehead seeded with tiny diamonds of sweat.

'Come in, dear. What's wrong? What time is it?'

The undulating floor tossed the two women simultaneously across the cabin. Grace grabbed the dressing-table-desk for support. The wad of envelopes slid from the horizontal surface onto the floor, followed by the Russian dolls and the mother-and-baby turtle. On a deck above, there was an ominous crash.

'Ma'am. I'm sorry.' Before she could explain further, a spasm engulfed the girl, and she bent in half and groaned.

Beyond the swaying curtains at the balcony window, a bright fork lit up the broiling sea, and was gone again. Evelyn fumbled for the light switch and turned the night into an electrical day.

There was something very wrong with the girl, her face contorted with pain and fear.

Evelyn laid the girl down on the bed. 'Where does it hurt, my dear?'

'Belly . . .' The girl's words sounded harsh through her clenched teeth.

Inside Evelyn's freewheeling mind, the cogs suddenly caught and her thoughts changed to a new gear, clear and concise. Evelyn lifted the burgundy polo shirt that matched the hideous carpet and was too small, warmed her hands with her breath and placed them either side of the domed belly. She felt the skin harden beneath her fingertips. The girl's body was wracked with agony, tightening, clenching against the contraction. Her throat made a strangled sound as she fought with every muscle in her body to suppress it. Evelyn saw the struggle in the tense sinews of the girl's arms, her blanched fingers gripping the bedspread.

'You need a doctor,' said Evelyn. 'Now, as luck would have it . . .'

'No, ma'am. Please.' The pain passed and the girl relaxed. Her eyes remained wary. 'Please, Mrs Parker. If they know I'm sick, they'll send me home. My fiancé and my family are relying on me. I have to finish my contract. You have to help me.'

'Me? I'm not a doctor.'

'Please. You're a nurse. I've seen all the books on your shelf. Sometimes I look through them when I'm cleaning the cabin.'

'I haven't practised for a long time, although I did come top of my bandaging class in 1951.'

It was little comfort for either of them. This wasn't something that could be remedied with a figure of eight or pressure immobilisation.

The girl made a high-pitched sound of surprise as a gush of rusty fluid saturated her pale shorts, forming a dark puddle before soaking into the bedspread.

'Am I going to die?' she gasped.

'Don't be silly, dear. You're not going to die. You're going to have a baby.'

A new kind of noise came from the girl then. More of disbelief than pain. She began to sob and shake her head. 'No, no, no,' she repeated.

'Yes, yes, yes,' Evelyn confirmed.

'But I'm not married! I can't have a baby!'

Evelyn didn't really have time to debate the whys and where-fores. It was a bit late for the whole birds-and-bees conversation. However strong the powers of denial, a human brain could only keep up the pretence for so long.

A baby was on its way. And two people who loved each other, who'd planned a life together, would become parents before they were married. Worse things happened at sea.

The girl's sobbing turned into a deep guttural noise that rumbled in her chest. She clutched her abdomen and tried to struggle up. Evelyn helped remove her shorts and underwear. She rubbed the girl's back as she rocked backwards and forwards on hands and knees as if in a trance.

Between the girl's legs, Evelyn saw a dark ellipse form at the perineum.

'I can see the baby's head.'

'No!' The girl hissed the protest through her teeth. 'No, it's not possible.'

Evelyn began to hum. *Eternal father strong to save . . .*

There was a thing she was meant to do in a situation like this. What would Florence Nightingale do?

But how can I obtain this medical knowledge? I am not a doctor. I must leave this to doctors.

The idea chafed. This was childbirth. It was what women's bodies did. Surely it made no difference whose hands caught the newborn baby, hers or Henry's.

A chill passed through the cabin. She smelled sulphur and kerosene. Evelyn shivered. There was someone standing behind her, looking over her shoulder. A woman in a long dark dress with a white apron.

Evelyn didn't need to see the woman's face to know who it was. Her body stiffened under the silent scrutiny of her heroine. Unfolding her legs, Evelyn tried to stand, grasping the bed like a toddler preparing for its first steps.

There was something she had to use at a time like this. It began with T.

Telepathy? Television? Tele-something.

'Don't leave me, Mrs Parker,' puffed the girl.

'I won't. I just need to send a telegram.'

Evelyn lifted the thing made out of bent plastic. It was attached by a tail of coiled wire to a box with numbers.

'Hello,' she said into it. The thing-with-a-tail didn't reply. Stupid contraption. She shouted, 'Hello?' Silence. 'Hello?' More silence.

Evelyn put the thing-with-a-tail back into its place then picked it up quickly, as if to take it by surprise. This time the silence was buzzing.

In front of her eyes, a list of numbers. Front desk, room service, the spa, dining room. None of these seemed to fit the bill. This was more of a situation. An urgent situation. One could almost class it as an . . .

Emergency.

Evelyn pressed 000 and waited. Almost immediately a voice came on the end of the phone.

'I'm looking for Henry,' said Evelyn. 'He's the ship's doctor.'

There was a pause and possibly a sigh on the other end of the line. 'Mrs Parker, is that you?'

'Yes, yes. Can you tell Henry to come straight away?'

'Mrs Parker, Henry isn't here. This is the nurse. You've come through to the emergency line. It's the middle of the night.'

'What a bother,' said Evelyn, irritated. 'Could you send Dr Johansson instead?'

'Dr Johansson went home ages ago. What's the matter? Are you having palpitations?'

'No, there's nothing wrong with me. It's the baby.'

A pause. Then softly, 'Mrs Parker, the baby died a long time ago. I'm so sorry.'

'But it's not dead, it's about to be born.'

There was another sigh, and perhaps a yawn on the line. 'How about I arrange for Dr King to do a cabin visit in the morning?'

In the morning? It would be too late by then. Evelyn tried to arrange the right words, but the harder she tried, the less sense she made, even to herself. She let the thing-with-a-tail clatter against the bedside table, where it lay dangling, defeated.

The girl looked up, her face full of terror, before returning to swaying backwards and forwards on her hands and knees.

Evelyn could see the textbook as clearly as if it was open in front of her. She could do this. It was a straightforward cephalic presentation, young primip but strong and healthy, with no obvious complications in spite of the lack of antenatal care. Steadying herself against the bulkheads, Evelyn hurried to the bathroom and turned on the hot tap. Florence was already there, waiting behind the shower curtain.

Compare the dirtiness of the water in which you have washed when it is cold without soap, cold with soap, hot with soap. You will find the first has hardly removed any dirt at all, the second a little more, the third a great deal more.

Evelyn watched the suds form as she scrubbed the soap bar between her palms. Clean, cleaner, cleanest. Florence gave a nod of approval. Sacrificing the elephant, Evelyn dried her hands on its ear. Still humming Henry's favourite hymn, the one she would sing – or perhaps already had sung – at his funeral, Evelyn returned to the girl carrying an armful of fresh towels.

Not even Florence could bring Henry back to her now. He was gone. A new life was about to enter the world he had left a better place. And Evelyn was ready.

Evelyn laid a towel across the bed under the girl's knees and draped another over her shoulder, like a chef waiting to serve mains. With some difficulty, she bent her fossilised legs in two and crouched down behind the rocking, groaning girl.

'Excellent, my dear. I can see the baby's head quite clearly now,' said Evelyn, angling her head. 'It's crowning.'

For all the reading she'd done in preparation for her interview at King George V, the textbooks she'd devoured and stages of labour she'd memorised, it had all been for nothing. She'd written and cancelled as soon as *Orcades* docked. All that theoretical knowledge she'd so carefully committed to memory was nothing compared to delivering a real baby.

'I need to push!' The girl's legs began to shake, her skin glistening. And then her body did the most natural thing in the world and began to expel a new life.

The ellipse became a circle of dark hair, then a dome, the surrounding skin thinning and yielding with each push. Evelyn placed her fingers over the baby's head, finding beneath the bloodstained hair the divots of the fontanelle that separated the soft bones of the baby's skull.

'I can't do this!' High-pitched, the girl's protests echoed around the cabin.

Evelyn hummed. *Oh, hear us when we cry to Thee* . . .

The girl quietened, panted.

'Now then, my lovely,' said Evelyn, finding deep within her an elusive calm, 'you *can* do this and you *will* do this. Wait for the next pain then I want a big push.'

They waited, the minutes between the contractions stretching out like an elastic band. Evelyn heard her heart rushing in her ears, accelerating with each beat. Faster, skipping, stumbling. *Thud-thud* . . . *thud* . . . *thud-thud*. Her breath quickened, trying to keep up.

The sound of the pain started low, growing inside the girl until there was no room for the fetus. The head emerged, slimy and blood-streaked.

For those in peril on the sea.

Instinctively, Evelyn's fingers found a meaty rope wrapped around the base of the baby's neck. She hooked it and gently released the cord over the head.

It was as though Evelyn was seeing the textbooks in three dimensions, animations of the diagrams playing in full Technicolor like a movie. Vivid and familiar.

She was at peace. She could stop looking now. Henry was gone. Their daughter was gone. And soon she would join them.

Evelyn watched the head rotate. She moved the girl's fingers to her almost-born baby, and together they guided the head, releasing the first tiny grey shoulder. A little push and the baby slipped out with a gush of pink liquor. Still trailing the cord inside its mother, the baby lay on the towel, dusky and still.

Beyond the balcony doors, the wind held its breath in the first blush of daybreak. Evelyn scooped up the baby into a clean towel and lifted it onto her lap. It was a healthy size – seven pounds at least. She rubbed the towel up and down the little grey body.

A girl.

The baby's limp and damp body soon began to lose heat in its new air-conditioned world. Evelyn tossed away the first wet towel and rubbed with a white fluffy bath towel. It was important to warm the baby and stimulate it to breathe. Warm it and it will breathe. The baby will come to life. All she had to do was rub and warm, and warm and rub. After all that time in the icy depths, Evelyn needed to bring the baby back to life. It wasn't too late. It was never too late to put things right.

A grimace appeared on the baby's face. Then she took a breath. Let it out in a feeble cry. The next breath was deeper, the cry stronger.

The baby cried. And breathed. And cried. The oxygen molecules turned the baby's skin from grey to pink, the colour spreading like a drop of Quink ink in water. Ten tiny fingers and ten tiny toes. Feet and fists thrashed the air at the indignity of being born into a cold bright world.

Tuesday's child, full of Grace turned to look at her newborn baby, now screaming and squirming in the towel. She took the bundle from Evelyn's arms and held her, marvelling at the child her mind had convinced her body she wasn't carrying.

'Congratulations,' said Evelyn. 'The cord was round her neck, but she looks very healthy.'

Healthy, and very alive.

The baby was saved but Evelyn knew her job wasn't over until the placenta was delivered. She waited for the umbilical cord to lengthen, followed by a tiny gush of blood. She caught the dark fleshy disc in her spare hand and lowered it to the soaked towel on the floor.

The carpet would be ruined. But Evelyn had never liked it. A new pattern wouldn't go amiss, one that matched the bedspread at least. She'd mention it to the eating-drinking-sleeping-and-carpets officer next time she saw him. Naturally the company would have to change all the other carpets to match.

Florence was still there but she was resting in the armchair, reading a book. She was an old lady now, her hair grey but still parted in the centre beneath a white lace headscarf knotted under her chin. She looked peaceful and contented, a thick shawl draped around her sloping shoulders. Ready to go off duty after a long, long shift.

Evelyn hadn't heard the cabin door open and was surprised to see two women in blue pyjamas standing beside her.

'What on earth . . . ?'

She was just about to apologise for waking them and insist they return to bed when she noticed one had a stethoscope looped around her neck. Like Henry used to carry. The other was carrying a big green bag with reflective strips down the side and a red cross symbol. Red for blood.

'It's a baby!'

'Where did that come from?'

Evelyn wondered what they taught in nursing or medical school nowadays. Goodness knows what might have happened if she hadn't been on hand.

'Let me help you up, Mrs Parker.'

'No dear, I can manage.' But Evelyn was stuck with her knees locked under her haunches refusing to unfold. *Stubborn old body.* Her heart began to flutter like a bird trapped inside her thorax. Suddenly she was tumbling through space, her limbs unhinging. She was losing her grip. She couldn't hold on any longer.

The next moment was a blur of arms, legs, bodies and bloodstained towels. Then she was lying on a bed. And noise, all around. She didn't need her hearing aids to recognise the cry of a newborn baby.

'Are you all right, Mrs Parker?'

Evelyn watched faces float across her field of vision. She tried to touch one but her arms were too heavy, one shoulder sore and bruised. She let them go.

'You gave us a bit of a fright there. Lie still for a moment.'

The faces became voices.

Evelyn tried to sit up, to get to the baby. Her baby. Her little girl was crying. Cold and hungry. This time she wouldn't let them take her away wrapped in a single knitted bootie.

'Don't get up yet.'

'My baby . . .'

She heard voices talking over the top of one another. Evelyn's pulse banged in her ears, an off-beat *thud-thud . . . thud . . . thud-thud-thud*. She felt her chest contract, squeezing the breath from her lungs. The strength faded from her body and she succumbed to the same hands that had taken her baby.

31

Lying In

EVELYN COULDN'T UNDERSTAND WHY SHE WAS WEARING spaghetti. She vaguely recalled the tricolour waistcoats of Italian night, but she tried to avoid overcomplicated food on account of the dry-cleaning bills it inevitably caused. The individual pasta strands trailed from a beeping television screen beside the bed. Each was attached to her chest wall with a sticky pad that made an annoying sound when she attempted to peel it off.

There was also a clear plastic tube attached to her forearm that stung when she tried to pick away the white sticky rectangle holding it in place. She remembered her mother ripping band-aids from her scraped knees and the hollow reassurance that it would hurt less if she simply got on with it. After loosening one sticky corner with her nail, Evelyn did as her mother suggested and yanked the entire contraption away with a single tug. It hurt, as she suspected it would, and left a trail of blood trickling from her forearm onto the hard floor.

Was it any wonder she couldn't sleep with the cacophony of beeps and voices and crying babies? New mothers needed their rest. The endless cycle of feeding and changing was exhausting and fell on the shoulders of the mothers of her generation, along with endless washing, wringing and ironing, cooking and cleaning. Evelyn had a vision of a woman in front of a stove in a Hygena kitchen, a small child clinging to her leg. The woman wore an apron and navy court shoes but the image was gone again as quickly as it had appeared.

Matron would have her guts for garters when she returned from tea. There was blood everywhere. Evelyn dabbed at the gushing hole in her vein with the corner of the bedclothes. She tried elevating her arm above her head, but this merely sprayed the blood further, like an elephant blowing water from its trunk.

A messy-haired woman wearing medical pyjamas and a stethoscope around her neck ran into the room, shouting.

'Do keep your voice down, dear,' said Evelyn, holding a blood-soaked finger to her lips. 'You'll wake the baby.'

'Look at all this blood everywhere!' The woman attacked Evelyn with a square of gauze, pressing down firmly enough to be uncomfortable. 'You should be resting.'

'I know, but I think the baby will need feeding soon.'

Above the sound of beeps and feet and assorted distant voices, Evelyn could hear the unmistakable sound of a hungry infant.

'Hold still,' said someone else who'd appeared beside the bed. 'You've pulled your cannula out and the heart monitor is going ballistic with all this moving about.' She tutted and reattached the spaghetti either side of Evelyn's breastbone. It was easy to tell which was the nurse.

They were attacking her from all angles now. Stabbing her tender skin with sharp things, tying up her arms with bandages, strangling her with spaghetti.

'Stop, you're hurting me.' Evelyn was too weak to put up much of a fight. 'Help! Help!' she screamed instead, secretly impressed with her own volume.

'Calm down, Mrs Parker, no one is trying to hurt you. You're in the hospital,' said the one with the stethoscope. 'I'm Dr King and this is Nurse O'Reilly, and we're trying to help you.'

'Where is Miss Winter? Don't let her take the baby away. She mustn't throw her overboard. She's alive!'

'Very much alive,' said the nurse, managing to smile and look puzzled simultaneously. 'Thanks to you, Mrs Parker.'

'Yes, you did an amazing job last night.'

Evelyn relaxed a fraction. She and Henry had waited a long time for this baby. To hear her tiny lungs full of air instead of sea water had made it worth the wait. She could relax now. It had been such a long journey to get here, but it had all been worthwhile in the end.

A ship was no place for a baby and Evelyn knew that this meant disembarking at the next port. In her mind's eye she saw vivid images of a pram under a tree, a child on a swing, chubby fingers licking batter from a mixing bowl, and a crayoned *Mummy* on a birthday card. It was like a brochure for motherhood, and she flicked through the glossy pictures with her heartbeat quickening at each one.

The nurse changed the sheet and blanket, rolling the blood-stained linen into a bundle and throwing it into a yellow bag in a pedal bin.

'There we are, all nice and clean.'

'Corners,' snapped Evelyn, demonstrating the looseness of the covers with her foot. She tutted and rolled her eyes as she'd seen her friend Nola doing. Florence Nightingale would have been a world-class eye-roller too.

'Would you like your favourite, Mrs Parker?'

Her favourite what? Evelyn wondered. Was the nurse referring to a dress, given that she was lying here in her nightdress? She could hardly take the baby home looking like this.

'Blue, with the three-quarter sleeves and full skirt.' It was the kind of outfit the Royal family dressed their new mothers in.

The nurse paused and smiled. 'I was thinking more along the lines of a cup of tea, actually.'

'Beef tea?' said Evelyn.

'I'm afraid we're all out of beef tea, Mrs Parker, but I make a mean hot chocolate.'

~

Evelyn pushed the hot chocolate aside. It was too hot. She'd noticed that in order to stop the beeping machine from beeping, all she had to do was lie very still and not touch her spaghetti. This, she supposed, was what they called 'lying in', when a new mother simply lay and rested after the birth of her child, for anything up to a couple of months. If Evelyn were back in London, she'd be at the General Lying-In Hospital, under the watchful eye of Florence Nightingale, across the road at St Thomas'. But she'd only been here a matter of hours and she was already bored.

The bossy one poked her head around the door and said in a cheery voice, 'Visitors!'

Already? The baby was only hours old and Evelyn was still weary and sore from the delivery. She didn't remember many details, but the outcome had been a happy one, and that was the way Mother Nature worked. Editing the whole horrific ordeal was key to survival of the species, thought Evelyn. She closed the gaping neckline of her nightdress, ashamed of her diminished breasts. How on earth was she meant to feed the baby?

Evelyn prepared for her mother and father to enter the room bearing a fruit basket and perhaps a small knitted gift for their first grandchild. Instead, a sunburnt couple stood grinning in the doorway.

'Congratulations,' said Fizzy Cola, Nola. 'A girl! She's a gorgeous little thing, isn't she, Frank?'

'Yes, dear, a gorgeous little thing.'

They'd seen her already? It was so cruel for the staff to keep Evelyn from her own baby. Bonding was so important. Right now, for all Evelyn knew, her little girl could be imprinting on the wrong person entirely.

'What does she look like?' In her eagerness to sit up and hear the details, Evelyn dislodged a strand of spaghetti. The nurse appeared briefly to silence the machine and was gone again, in the direction of the baby Evelyn still hadn't laid eyes on.

Frank and Nola looked at each other.

'Well,' said Frank, clearing his throat. 'I'd say she looks just like her mother.'

This was reassuring news. Her energy was returning by the minute and she was itching to get home. She'd had enough of lying-in.

'And here she is,' said Nola, moving aside.

Standing in a long white hospital gown at the end of the bed was Tuesday's child. And in her arms, an actual child. Evelyn could hear the snuffles from inside the swaddle of blankets.

'Pass her over,' said Evelyn, leaning forward as far as the spaghetti would allow. 'Let me see her.'

Evelyn's heart swelled at the sight of the dark hair protruding from the baby bundle. Such dark hair! Considering how fair both she and Henry were, it was most unusual. The beeping television beside the bed registered her surprise in a series of noisy electronic squiggles and spikes.

'Are you feeling okay?' The one with the stethoscope appeared from thin air and checked her pulse. Evidently satisfied that Evelyn was still alive, she ushered the bundle to the bedside.

Grace pulled the blanket open. The little girl's eyes were huge and bright, moving unfocused from one face to another. Tiny fists opened and closed, while a tiny mouth gurned for a nipple.

Evelyn replayed the words that now made painful sense. 'She looks just like her mother.' The same bright enquiring eyes. The same burnished skin the colour of umber.

He went like one that hath been stunned,
And is of sense forlorn:
A sadder and a wiser man,
He rose the morrow morn.

This was not her baby. Painful truths flooded back, breaking like waves on a rising tide. She was old and frail, and her own baby long gone. Her life was already lived, and most of her future was now her past.

Quite a crowd had gathered in the room. Her faithful friends Frank and Nola, the nurse and the one-with-the-stethoscope-who-wasn't-Dr Johansson. An assortment of stripes had assembled at the back: the head driving-the-ship officer, and the eating-drinking-and-sleeping officer. Smiling from the far corner was an old man with a walker, who wasn't Henry.

And here, holding her baby, was Grace. Her bedroom steward who never was, and never would be, Virgilio. A mother now with a beautiful daughter.

'I have to thank you, for everything you did for me. You saved this little one's life,' said Grace. There was a collective nod of heads around the bed.

'How are you feeling, my dear?'

'It was a shock at first, but now I've had time to get used to the idea, it feels like the most wonderful gift from God. I'm looking forward to taking her home to meet my family.'

'Every baby is a gift. Enjoy motherhood, my dear.'

'I will, Mrs Parker. I spoke to my fiancé on the satellite phone. He was very surprised but he's overjoyed to be a father. The company are flying him out to meet me in Sydney. Everyone in the village is so excited too. My grandmother especially. She loves babies. In fact she was the island's only midwife when she was younger. Not properly trained, of course, she never had the opportunity, but she learned through experience, like every generation before her.'

Fizzy Nola stepped forward. 'Tell her, Grace. Tell her what you told me.'

Grace beamed. 'I have named my baby Eve, after you.'

A ripple of applause erupted in the quite crowded room.

'Cord around the baby's neck, Mrs Parker,' said the one-with-the-stethoscope. 'Well spotted. We were lucky to have you on board. I don't think I remember much of my obstetrics training, and it's not as if there's a baby born on a ship every day.'

'I always wanted to be a midwife,' said Evelyn wistfully. She was filled with conflict, pride and regret colliding like the meeting of two mighty oceans.

'It was certainly a night to remember,' said the one-with-the-stethoscope.

'A cruise to remember,' added Nola.

Frank clasped his wife's hand and kissed it.

The baby was revving up to a full cry with restless snuffles and whimpers. The stripes took this to be the perfect time to exit. Everyone left apart from Frank and Nola.

'I think *they* might be hiding something from me,' said Evelyn, trying to contain the words in a whisper.

'Whatever do you mean, Mrs P?' Nola's whispered pretence was easy to see through.

'Have I got cancer?'

'No, no. Nothing like that. The doctor told me she needs to monitor your heart for another few hours. Something about an arrhythmia. She's worried you've been having TIAs. Apparently they're like tiny strokes. It can cause demen—' Frank coughed forcefully into his fist. Nola continued cautiously. 'Trouble remembering things.'

Evelyn was relieved she didn't have cancer.

'There's something else . . .' said Frank, inviting Nola with a glance to finish his sentence.

Nola exhaled. 'This is a bit tricky. I'm not sure I'm the right person to be telling you this. It's about what we were discussing last night on the way to dinner, about Henry . . .'

'Tell me what?' *Henry.* She'd forgotten about him.

Nola fidgeted. She was uncharacteristically lost for words. It was ironic, thought Evelyn, that for once she could keep up with what her friend was saying, but it was nothing more than a meaningless stream of 'um's and 'aah's.

Evelyn's heart trembled. The machine made a series of high-pitched noises that jump-started Nola back on track. 'Oh, Mrs P, I don't know how to say this.'

'Say what?'

'Alaska,' Frank interrupted, frowning at the wavy line on the beeping television.

Nola swallowed. 'Yes, that's right. You were going to tell us about Alaska. Frank and I have always wanted to go to Alaska. Haven't we, Frank?'

'Yes, dear. We've always wanted to go to Alaska.'

Evelyn sank into the starched sheets and shivered.

32

Wastrels of the Sea

No matter how thick the clouds in the overcast sky, there was something about the light that made the colours here more vivid, almost unworldly. I had long ago given up trying to re-create the ethereal blue of the ice from my man-made paint pigments. Like healing, there were some things that were best left to nature. No matter how many times I'd sailed into Glacier Bay, I was always in awe of its majesty.

There was no sign of Henry. The white top of his officer's hat should have been easy to spot in the crowd, his dark-coloured bridge coat less so. A man walked past wearing shorts. Others hunched forward in their windcheaters, like some strange hooded order of Gore-Tex–clad monks.

The ship edged further into the bay with hushed engines. Only two hundred and fifty years ago, I marvelled, all this had been ice. I loved to watch the other passengers' faces change as they tried to take it all in: the towering mountains topped with purest snow, mirrored in the green ice-rubble water below. Most looked through binoculars or the viewfinders of automatic cameras. I wondered how many would recall this place in years to come, their only memories locked away in dusty albums, long forgotten.

Henry would be along soon, after finishing his morning clinic. He would have to be quick. His tea was cooling rapidly in the frozen Alaskan air. I blew across the top of mine simply to watch the last of the steam rise and condense, then took a sip.

Was this the last time we would see the glaciers first-hand? Would we too come to rely on fading photographs to revisit this place in the future? We hadn't really talked about what lay ahead, but at our age, with Henry fast approaching seventy, we couldn't hide the fact that we were collecting more last times than first times.

I saw a flash of white cap amidst the waterproofed hoods. Henry appeared a second later and pecked my frozen cheek. Something was troubling him. I handed him a mug.

'Sorry I'm late,' he said.

'Busy clinic?'

Henry sipped his tea and turned up his collar while he gathered his thoughts. It always took him a while to leave one world – his work and his patients – and enter the other, the one where he was a husband and not a doctor.

'If only.'

I searched his face, trying to decipher him. His hair was almost white beneath his cap, his head a size too small, as if his skull had shrunk with age. His jowls were loose under his chin and the softened bones of his spine beginning to bow under the weight of his overactive brain. He looked as though he could do with putting his feet up after a seventy-year day.

It was hardly surprising. He was the oldest doctor in the fleet by far, the others all robust South Africans or assured young Brits looking for adventure. The new doctors and nurses were beginning to treat him like some relic of a bygone era, trusting their algorithms and didactic protocols over Henry's wisdom and experience.

'I'm listening,' I said. It's what I did best, helping Henry to find his own solutions.

His coat suddenly looked too heavy for his shoulders. 'An old couple, in their eighties. Multiple medical problems,' he began. 'Usual thing – family put them on a cruise, knowing that there's round-the-clock medical cover, and expect us to perform miracles.'

'You can only do so much, Henry. You're only their doctor for a fortnight.'

'It's just frustrating to think that I can't help them. They're clinging to each other, their lives only holding together by the thinnest of threads. It's as if they're both about to fall over the edge at the same time, one dragging the other.'

'Oh, Henry,' I said. I found one chilly hand and gave it a squeeze.

'The worst thing is, they told me this was their last holiday. As if they'd decided this was it, that they were finished. They seemed so resigned to it.'

I watched the words steam from Henry's lips. Sometimes I wondered if he regretted becoming a ship's doctor, whether he craved the continuity of family practice where he could really get to know his patients. On our very first meeting I'd asked if he'd ever considered a career as a 'proper doctor'. I wondered if he'd ever forgotten.

I glanced sideways at him, trying to connect his anxious dots. The tip of his nose was red now and the mist had condensed on the dark woollen fabric of his bridge coat. His glasses were starting to fog.

'We do need to make some decisions,' he said. 'About what's next. We've only got another four cruises until I retire. We haven't really talked about where we'll go after that.'

Four cruises. Was that all that remained of our lives at sea? There had been many contracts when I'd eagerly counted down the days until Henry and I could walk down the gangway together. Even life aboard a luxury liner could be exhausting. But invariably, after basking in those first few leisurely lie-ins, the days began to stretch out into meaningless hours and we'd begin to talk about the next contract, the next ship and exciting new itineraries. On land, Henry was like a fish, gasping to return to sea. And for me too the sea was home, and where I felt closest to our daughter.

'I haven't given it much thought,' I lied, turning away from Henry and balancing my tea on the mahogany railing. I took a deep breath of cool misty air and tried not to imagine us in a retirement villa or, later, a nursing home.

'*But we, the gypsies of the East*—' Henry gripped the handrail, his purple-tinged fingers almost touching mine.

'*Waifs of the land and wastrels of the sea?*' I was one step ahead as usual.

With his trimmed hair and immaculate uniform, a cup of English breakfast tea in his hand, I imagine Rudyard Kipling would have considered Henry looked more of a chinless wonder than a gypsy or a wastrel, but I didn't say so.

We were interrupted by a tremendous roar. I looked up just in time to watch a huge sheet of ice calve from the glacier. A cloud of white ice rose from the water and a wave travelled towards us across its mirrored surface. The old, making way for the new as fresh snow and ice pushed the glacier ever onward towards the ocean. Henry breathed it in and stood taller.

I began to recite more of Henry's favourite words, this time from the tiny book he'd once given me, my most precious possession.

'*And now there came both mist and snow,*
And it grew wondrous cold:
And ice, mast-high, came floating by,
As green as emerald.'

Henry's lips were warm as he kissed me on the cheek, though his nose was cold and wet.

'You have the most extraordinary memory, Mrs Parker,' he said. 'I've tried for more than fifty years to memorise that poem. And listen to you. You can remember it word for word.'

He was right. I did know the Ancient Mariner. I'd been married to him for long enough.

'It's just one of my many talents, Dr Parker.'

Henry laughed. I liked it when he laughed. His lined face had become more expressive with age, as though the years had deliberately punctuated every emotion.

'There's nothing for you to worry about, Evelyn,' he said, face serious again. 'You know I'll make provision for you, don't you?'

'What are you talking about?'

'For when I'm gone. Everything is already taken care of.'

'I don't understand.'

'I'm lucky to have found you, Evelyn, but we have to face facts, I won't be around forever.'

'Don't be daft.' With my hand on the polished rail, I felt no different to the bilious young woman who'd first met Dr Henry Parker on the deck of *Orcades*. It was hard to accept that time had aged us both. I wasn't ready to face mortality, neither mine nor Henry's.

'Evelyn, my darling . . .' He waited for a noisy family group to pass. 'We have had the most wonderful lives together, but it doesn't change the fact that we're both getting older.'

'We're still fit and healthy though.'

Although he hadn't suffered one in years, Henry pinched the bridge of his nose in anticipation of a migraine.

'But we won't always be. In the not-too-distant future we won't be able to look after ourselves anymore. We'll need help.'

He was right. Old age had snuck up on us as slowly as the glacier, a few centimetres a day, over a lifetime. One day we'd been perfect snowflakes, the next dirty lumps of ice ready to calve.

'So what do we do?'

Live-in carer? Nursing home? Neither of us had stopped to consider the options beyond the ship and the sea that was our home.

'Money isn't the issue here,' said Henry. His eyes drifted from mine and reached deep into his own thoughts.

'And the apartment has been a good investment.'

'An excellent investment,' he agreed. I sensed Henry had found my trail of breadcrumbs.

'So if we released the capital . . .'

There comes a time when married couples speak in incomplete sentences, when they hear each other's thoughts as their own.

'We could afford it, as long as we were careful.'

'Careful,' I said, nodding.

'Not too extravagant.'

My nodding became shaking then nodding again.

I saw my grin reflected in Henry's eyes. 'Are you thinking what I'm thinking, Mrs Parker?'

'It would work out cheaper than living ashore. As long as we agree not to live too long.'

We did the calculation simultaneously in our heads. Not so much a round-the-world cruise to celebrate retirement, but a round-and-round-and-round-the-world voyage that would take the rest of our lives to complete.

'And at the very end? What happens if one of us dies before the other?'

'If I die first,' said Henry, unbuttoning his increasingly tatty bridge coat and drawing me into his warm body, 'I want to be buried at sea.'

33

An Upgrade

EVELYN ARRIVED BACK HOME TO FIND JESUS STANDING IN the doorway. It was actually pronounced 'Hay-zoos', the young man informed her as he backed the heavy industrial carpet cleaner out of the cabin.

'Where's Virgilio . . . Tuesday's child?'

Jesus shrugged, then apologised for not being Virgilio, and for being born on the wrong day.

'Grace had a baby, remember?'

When Evelyn turned to see whose words she'd heard, she saw her friend Nola had been pushing the deckchair-with-wheels. Her other friend Frank was there too, like a wingman.

'Baby Eve, such a gorgeous little thing,' he chuckled.

'That's right, Frank. Baby Eve. A gorgeous little thing.'

'I like my parrots,' said Evelyn. She felt safe with Frank and Nola. She loved how they always gave her two chances to understand things. When they were with her, more things made sense than when they weren't.

The cabin was swarming with eating-drinking-sleeping-and-carpets stripes. One of them, on seeing Evelyn, apologised for the intrusion and reassured her they wouldn't be much longer.

'What is going on?' said Evelyn, trying to stand up but getting her feet tangled in the footrests.

'Mrs Parker,' said four-stripe eating-drinking-sleeping-and-carpets officer. 'I really am most terribly sorry. We were hoping to have all this done before you got back from the medical centre.' Evelyn noticed him exchange glances with Frank-and-Nola. 'But I see the doctor has discharged you a little ahead of schedule. I—'

The screech of packaging tape across the flaps of a cardboard box cut his next words short. When Evelyn looked closer, she saw boxes of all sizes, some lying on the floor, others covering the bed and dressing-table-desk. Her belongings were being wrapped in tissue paper and packed, precious item after precious item, into the boxes.

'My things! What are they doing with my things? Am I being burgled?'

'Nothing for you to worry about.' Nola rested a soothing hand on Evelyn's shoulder. 'They're just packing, ready for the move.'

'Am I being upgraded?' A tiny seed of hope germinated. She'd always fancied a suite. Even a mini-suite would be an improvement. This cabin had been her home for a long, long time, but there was barely room to swing a towelling elephant. Evelyn rubbed her hands together excitedly. With the extra hanging space, she could even do some shopping.

Nola creaked to a squatting position, her apple-rosy face level with Evelyn's. Frank folded himself in half until his face was there too.

'Mrs P,' began Nola.

'There's something we need to tell you,' said Frank. 'You're not being upgraded.'

'This is your last day on *Golden Sunset*.'

Evelyn felt dizzy, looking from one face to the other and back as her friends spoke in stereo.

'Tomorrow morning, when we arrive in port . . .'

'. . . you'll be leaving the ship . . .'

'. . . and going to your new home.'

'New home.'

Evelyn rummaged through the untidy drawer where her thoughts and memories lay tangled in bits of old string, paperclips and spare batteries. She simply couldn't find what she was looking for, the words skimming across the surface of her comprehension.

'I don't understand,' she said. '*This* is my home.'

Nola chewed the next words as if to soften them. 'You're going to a lovely *new* home, Mrs P.'

'A lovely *new* home,' Frank added to clarify things.

'What kind of home?' Evelyn was suspicious now.

'You're going to love it, Mrs P. It's a special home where you'll meet lots of other people just like you. You'll all have so much in common. So much to talk about.'

'Aha,' said Evelyn, suddenly catching on. She'd thought they were referring to a *nursing* home. Heaven forbid. Now she realised they were talking about moving her to a *nurses'* home. Like the one back at St Thomas'.

'There'll be so many activities for you to get involved in.'

'Like bandaging, you mean?'

'Yes, bandaging! I'm sure there'll be bandaging.'

'Splint padding?'

'Possibly.' Nola looked less sure.

'I can make an excellent many-tailed binder, you know.' Evelyn was excited. For the first time in a very long time, she felt her life was on the up. She had something to look forward to and a sense of purpose. She'd neglected her career for far too long. It was time to go back and start again. All the way to the moon and back was a good age, but not too old to fulfil her dream.

Evelyn intercepted a tissue-wrapped parcel on its way into one of the boxes. Unwrapping it and letting the paper fall to her feet, she saw a photograph of three young women in nurses' uniforms inside a simple wooden frame. They were linking arms and smiling into the camera, black lace-up shoes firmly planted on a patch of grass. Their hairstyles were similar: short waves arranged around identical white nursing caps. Each wore a starched white apron, the vertical creases standing to attention. A memory stirred. The one in the middle was familiar, the other two less so.

Evelyn kicked away the footrests and wriggled out of the uncomfortable deckchair. It felt good to stretch her legs, to take the weight off her sitting bones. There was no time to lose. Matron wouldn't take kindly to her turning up late tomorrow.

The books were next. Mustn't forget the books. Evelyn dismissed the one-striper who was supervising a no-striper in transferring the dusty textbooks to the packing box. This was a job she must do herself. It wasn't to be trusted to an underling.

I attribute my success to this: I never gave or took an excuse.

Florence Nightingale was first into the box, her words paving the way for the other nurses. Next came a rather musty-smelling *Practical Nursing, Fourteenth edition.* Evelyn opened the stiff cover and read the frontispiece. *Printed in 1944 by William Blackwood & Sons Ltd, Edinburgh and London.*

'By W. T. *Gordon Pugh FRCS. Consultant Surgeon,*' she read out loud, as if seeing the words for the very first time. '*Assisted by Alice M. Pugh, SRN.* That doesn't seem right.'

Frank donned his spectacles and read the words out loud. 'That's what it says.'

'Why was this nursing textbook written by a surgeon?' she said. 'He was *assisted* by Alice Pugh SRN. Was that his wife, do you think?'

Nola took the book from Evelyn's hands for a closer look. 'I don't know. It says here she was Matron. It's possible, I suppose.'

'But why didn't *she* write the book? I imagine she was just as capable as him, in fact I dare say there were many things she knew that he didn't, and things she could do that he couldn't.'

'Times have changed, Mrs P, we all know that. It was different when we were young. I expect it'd be just as likely to be the other way round nowadays – you know, female surgeon, male nurse. Just look at that young Dr Hannah King. Very impressive.'

'Very impressive,' Frank agreed.

Evelyn couldn't bring Dr King to mind. She pictured a stethoscope and a Viking helmet, hiking poles. None of the usual tricks worked. That name was a blank.

'Dr Johansson is my doctor,' she said eventually, trying to deflect the conversation away from what she didn't know. 'Yes, such an excellent doctor. I've been married to him for sixty years, you know.'

A crash from the wardrobe turned everyone's heads. A no-striper emerged carrying a small cardboard box in one hand and its dust-covered lid in the other, his fingerprints like footprints in snow. He tilted the box towards Evelyn.

'What would you like me to do with this?'

'Let me see,' said Evelyn, taking the box. Her stomach fluttered with the wings of a dozen sooty moths. There, nestled on a bed of scrunched tissue paper, was a single knitted woollen bootie. It was discoloured by age, but the wool was still soft between Evelyn's fingers as she plucked the bootie from its resting place and brought it to her cheek. Her mind conjured the metallic tang of blood and heard the deafening silence of a tiny motionless heart.

Her own heart stopped, paid respects, then started to beat once more.

She delved into the remaining tissue paper, searching. She pictured her fingers winding the wool around the cool grey needles, the knitting growing row by row into her lap. The matinee jacket with the threaded ribbon around the neck, and the hat – where were they? They were odd items for someone to steal or hide. Why leave the single bootie in the box? Before anyone noticed, Evelyn secreted the lonely bootie away in her handbag for safekeeping and tossed the empty box towards the overflowing wastepaper bin. Some things in her head were so bewildering she couldn't even turn them into questions. Would the day come when she'd have answers to all her questions? Or was she destined to return full circle to childish thinking in which, to save her from hurt, adults would willingly lie to her rather than shatter her trust?

'What shall I do with this?' Another person speaking. Another question. More not knowing.

'Chequebook, Mrs P,' Nola interpreted.

The four-stripe eating-drinking-sleeping-carpets-and-cheque-book officer stepped forward. 'I will take care of anything official,' he said. 'It can all stay in the safe overnight, along with the money.'

Evelyn's ears pricked. 'Money? What money?'

'I'm referring to the incident in the casino the other night. We're talking about a significant sum of money. Sunset Cruises simply can't be held responsible.'

Had she developed a serious gambling problem without even realising it? wondered Evelyn. She couldn't afford to accumulate a debt at her age. What sort of figure had she racked up in her fugue? How many fewer years would she have to live in order to match one evening of recklessness?

'How much money?'

The four-striper ran his fingers through his hair and sucked air through his teeth. 'Sixty-something,' he said.

'Sixty dollars?' That *was* a lot of money.

'No,' said the four-striper, shaking his head. 'A little higher.'

'Sixty-one dollars?'

'Higher.'

'Sixty-two?'

'Nope.'

This was getting tedious. Evelyn's thoughts hurt. Any higher and she'd have to already be dead to afford it. No wonder they were evicting her from the ship and sending her back to work. 'How long do I have left to live?'

The four-striper's eyes gleamed. 'Sixty-five thousand!'

'Days?' That was longer than Evelyn had anticipated. She didn't know whether to be relieved or not.

'Dollars, Mrs Parker. Sixty-five thousand dollars. You're the first passenger on *Golden Sunset* to win the jackpot!'

Win? She was more confused than ever. 'You mean you owe *me?*'

'Yes! It's *your* money, Mrs Parker.'

'Holy moly,' said Nola. 'That is a lot of money. What are you going to do with it?'

Evelyn thought about it for a moment.

'I think I might go on a cruise,' she said.

34

A Shore Excursion

RED BORDER, YELLOW SWIRLS. STARBOARD.

Evelyn felt queasy. She was accustomed to seeing the pattern on the carpet from the height of a standing body rather than a sitting one. And whoever was pushing the deckchair-on-wheels was doing it all wrong. Indignant, she gripped the bulging handbag in her lap. Seeing a mint poking from the side pocket, she unwrapped it and put it quickly into her mouth. It was her last one. This time she wasn't sharing.

'Slow down,' she said, moving the mint to one cheek with the tip of her tongue. 'Whatever is the rush?'

She heard a woman's voice behind her. 'Sorry, Mrs P, we have to get a move on. Only, there's somebody waiting for you at the gangway.'

'Gangway? What are you talking about? Who is waiting?' Evelyn swivelled on her uncomfortable bottom. A breathless woman with rosy cheeks was pushing the deckchair-on-wheels. Evelyn relaxed. It was Nola. She liked Nola. Frank was walking a couple of paces behind, pulling a miniature suitcase on wheels. Evelyn liked Frank too.

The leaving-the-ship area was crowded. Sun-tanned passengers milled around, with patient end-of-holiday expressions on their faces. Some guarded overstuffed luggage, others chatted in small groups. There was a buzz of excitement and lots of laughter. A breathless woman with grey hair chased three little girls as they ran excitedly between the bodies.

Evelyn usually avoided the crowds on turnaround day, trusting the efficiency of the crew to empty and refill the ship like a well-oiled machine. She watched the faces of the disembarking passengers as they squinted in the bright outside sun and headed for the gangway and their old lives. A mixture of diesel and fresh paint wafted in through the big hole in the side of the ship and into Evelyn's nostrils. It was all so familiar but her stomach shrivelled with apprehension. Something different was about to happen.

The deckchair-on-wheels came to a stop a few metres from the gangway. On seeing Evelyn, a security guard in a white uniform spoke into a black object in his hand. It spoke back, a crackling, distorted voice. The security guard smiled and waved a grey-haired man on board. He was wearing an open-necked shirt, and some sort of identification badge hung around his neck on one of those lantern-halyard-*lanyard* things. He surveyed the atrium as if to get his bearings. The security guard pointed in Evelyn's direction. The open-necked-shirt-man smiled and waved. Evelyn looked over her shoulder to see if anyone was standing behind, but saw only the backs of other passengers as they queued for the gangway.

To her surprise, the man walked straight towards her, leaned down and kissed her on the cheek.

'Hello,' he said. Taken aback, Evelyn recoiled. 'Sorry I'm late,' he continued. 'Couldn't find a spot.'

Perhaps he was a visiting dermatologist. 'Try a magnifying glass. I might have one in here somewhere . . .'

Evelyn began to empty the things out of her bag, attempting to be helpful. She gave up when she ran out of lap. Before her helpful could become useful.

After shaking hands, the open-necked-shirt-man began talking to Frank and Nola. Evelyn didn't catch his name but she was rather put out. They were her special people and she didn't like sharing them.

Evelyn made a noise in her nose as the talking between the shirt and her special people continued. As usual, she couldn't follow what they were saying. Nowadays people spoke so quickly. The 1950s were much better for conversation. Every now and again she caught a snippet. There was thanking – lots of thanking. Something about kindness. A pleasure. Somebody had done the least they could. A weight had been lifted from somebody's shoulders. Evelyn soon lost her foothold in the nonsensical exchange. She pouted and folded her arms.

A four-stripe eating-drinking-sleeping-carpets-and-cheque-book officer arrived flanked by a young woman with blood stripes. She was carrying a large white envelope like the kind that usually held those large black and white photographs of broken bones. The others acknowledged her briefly before the whole tedious exchange started all over again: the handshaking introductions, the thanks, the kindness and the pleasurable weightlifting.

Evelyn yawned. For once she considered having a little snooze but the deckchair-on-wheels was very uncomfortable.

Then she heard some interesting-sounding words that caught her attention.

Casino. Winnings. Fortune. Worthy causes. Something about an island. A scholarship in Evelyn's name. Apparently it had been her idea, though Evelyn couldn't remember having it. The scholarship, they all agreed, was a fitting tribute. The perfect legacy.

Evelyn was soon bored again. She wasn't used to being ignored. People were much ruder than they used to be. If there was one thing she hated more than being spoken about, it was being spoken over. Flicking aside the foot-resting plates of the deckchair-on-wheels, Evelyn stood up and straightened her blouse. There was a button missing from the front and the cuffs were frayed. The waistband of her skirt hung around her hips and there was a stain just above the hem. She'd worn the same clothes to the moon and back. And it showed.

A group of passengers parted, revealing the ship's boutique. Seizing a gap in the human traffic, Evelyn headed for the brightly coloured display of dresses and shirts. No one gave her a second glance as she weaved through the crowd. When politeness proved inefficient, she resorted to lowering one shoulder – the second one, the first hurting quite a bit when she tried it – and barging. But to Evelyn's disappointment, when she reached the boutique it was closed, a metal grille down over the entrance. How silly of her. All the shops were shut when the ship was in port. She'd have to come back once they'd set sail.

When she turned around, Evelyn faced a wall of people. A human motorway. She didn't know which way to go. Suddenly she couldn't think where she was or what she was meant to be doing. Stifling her panic, she noticed a young woman in uniform striding purposefully. Following this woman was the sensible thing to do. At least she seemed to know where she was going.

Evelyn arrived at the woman's destination – the shore excursion office in the corner of the atrium – a fraction after she did. And what a fascinating place it turned out to be.

On the wall behind the desk were screens that showed moving pictures of all the places it was possible to go. She wondered why she hadn't gone to more of them while it was still possible. Time was running out for Evelyn to do all the things she had left to do and to go to all the places she still had left to go. Suddenly the white sandy beaches with palm trees in the posters looked tame next to the movies of overly happy people doing the most extraordinary things. Flying behind a fast boat. Breathing underwater. Driving through sand dunes on miniature tractors.

One movie in particular caught Evelyn's eye, and imagination. She stood mesmerised as two people climbed inside a gigantic plastic ball. A man threw several buckets of water inside, then sealed the hole with a big plastic bung before pushing them off the top of a steep hill. Evelyn watched agog as the ball gained speed, rolling and bouncing down the grassy embankment. At the bottom, the two occupants emerged laughing and squealing with delight. She'd never seen anything like it.

'Are you thinking of booking an excursion?' asked the young woman behind the counter.

'I'd like to go on that one, please,' replied Evelyn, pointing to the television and the giant plastic ball now rolling down the hill a second time. The entire thing only lasted a few seconds. She could definitely fit it in before she died.

'You mean zorbing?'

'Yes, *zorbing*,' said Evelyn, moving the word around her mouth as if it was a mint.

The woman appeared to be a little flustered. She produced a brochure and invited Evelyn to take a closer look. 'It says here . . . blah, blah, blah.'

Evelyn transferred her gaze from the brochure to the woman's face expectantly. 'Yes?'

'There's a height restriction of a hundred and ten centimetres, but there's nothing here about an age limit.'

'Well then,' said Evelyn. 'Where do I sign up?'

The potential for fun ended with the arrival of some people. The four-stripe eating-drinking-sleeping-and-other-things officer, the red-for-blood officer, the open-necked-shirt-man and her special people. Nola looked less fizzy than before and Frank a great deal more earnest.

'We thought we'd lost you,' said Nola.

The shirt-man said, 'You're hard to keep up with, young lady.'

The shore excursion lady appeared relieved at the arrival of reinforcements but let Evelyn keep the zorbing brochure.

'It's time to go now,' said the eating-drinking-sleeping-and-leaving officer, indicating for Evelyn to sit in the deckchair-on-wheels once more.

'Goodbye,' said Evelyn. 'Thank you for coming and have a safe trip home.' She waved at the officer.

Nola placed a hand on Evelyn's shoulder. 'No, Mrs P,' she said. 'It's time for *you* to go. This lovely gentleman is taking you home.'

'Which gentleman?'

Looks were exchanged and nobody seemed to know what to say next. Then the shirt-man put his arm around Evelyn, which she thought quite forward of him. There were tears in his eyes, poor love, and she felt her heart quiver. She looked more closely at the man. Bits of him were familiar but she couldn't assemble them into anyone she knew.

'Me,' he said. 'I'm taking you home. Do you know who I am?'

Evelyn searched his face for clues. There was something about the way his features were arranged that made her feel warm inside.

'I'm terribly sorry,' she said. 'I know we've probably met before but I am simply appalling at names. Always have been.'

The man's face was a mixture of smiling and crying. He was in his late fifties or early sixties, Evelyn guessed, judging by his white temples and the spread above his waistband. He looked kind and Evelyn felt unusually at ease with him, as though she'd known him a long, long time.

The man tried again. 'I'm Michael.'

'Michael? I've always liked that name.' Then it hit her. She did know this man. It was like looking in the mirror and seeing the wrong reflection. 'You're my chauffeur, aren't you?' How embarrassing that she hadn't recognised him.

'No.' A new wrinkle appeared on the man's forehead. 'I'm your son.'

His voice was barely a whisper but the words echoed in Evelyn's head. The floor tilted, as if the ship were climbing a giant wave. Hands grasped her flimsy limbs and scooped her into the deckchair-on-wheels before her bones dissolved.

Her *son*? What cruel joke was this? Was this all part of some elaborate scheme to get *their* hands on her money? This man must be an impostor, like all the others, albeit a very convincing one. If she had ever had a son, this was what he might look like: the ice-and-fire eyes, the protruding ears, the weight of the world bowing his shoulders. There was a thread of truth dangling just beyond her reach. It was all so confusing.

Suddenly her heart hammered behind her ribs. Evelyn felt a heavy weight crushing her chest, forcing the breath from her body.

'But I had a daughter.'

'And a son. After the baby you lost. Remember? I'm Michael. I'm married to Susan and we have two children, Sarah and Hugo. Sarah's a surgical registrar at Prince of Wales Hospital. Your grandson Hugo is a lawyer. He works at Dobbs & Co in the city. He takes care of all your finances and correspondence. I take you to see him every turnaround day.'

Evelyn couldn't fit the pieces of the puzzle together in any meaningful way. She felt like a stranger in her own life. Perhaps it was best to stop trying so hard and just accept. Her chest untightened. There was room to breathe again.

It was starting to come back to her. Snippets of reality. Little details. A shortbread finger. Something about socks. 'Does he like toucans?' she said.

'I'm not sure about that,' laughed the man-who-was-her-son. *Michael.* 'You can ask him next time you see him.'

Evelyn was more confused than ever, but it seemed to be a nice sort of confusion. Things were turning out better than she'd feared, and each time she learned a new truth, it was a good one. She had a son and daughter-in-law and two grandchildren, and the only thing she knew about them was that she loved them. Long after her head had forgotten how to love, her heart still remembered.

A baby's cry broke the awkwardness. Distant at first, the sound grew louder and stronger. Evelyn's heart swelled in her chest. Coming towards her in an identical deckchair-on-wheels was a young woman holding a white blanket bundle against her chest.

'Tuesday's child is full of grace,' said Evelyn, reaching her loose-skinned arms towards the noise. 'Let me see her.'

Grace handed across the bundle.

'We wanted to say goodbye, Mrs Parker, and thank you again. For everything. I can't wait to tell my grandmother about you and your extraordinary generosity.'

Evelyn folded back the corner of the white blanket. The baby's face was screwed up and her little mouth shivered with the force of her screams.

'Well, well,' said Evelyn. 'Who's a gorgeous girl? And such a big noise for such a tiny pair of lungs.'

Resting the bundle on her lap, Evelyn unwrapped the blankets and circled the baby's chest with her hands. She held her up until they were eye to eye, and at that moment something passed between them. The baby stopped crying with a sigh and seemed content to dangle from Evelyn's clutch, regarding her with a wisdom that was beyond her tender age. An old soul. Evelyn brought the baby's head to her nose and inhaled the memory of motherhood.

'I'd say you've got the magic touch, Mrs P,' said Nola.

'Magic touch,' repeated Frank, smiling.

'Mum has always had a way with babies.' It was Michael-who-was-her-son talking again. 'And she will soon be a great-grandmother. Sarah, that's my daughter who's training to be a surgeon, is expecting her first baby in the spring. You remember Sarah, Mum?'

Evelyn tried. Tried to remember the granddaughter who was about to make her a great-grandmother. She searched the images that lay like scraps of film on the cutting-room floor and tried to rearrange them into her family. A crib with a musical mobile. A bucket and spade. Sewing buttons on a school blazer. A graduation ceremony. The crib again, in a different room.

Evelyn drew the infant into her body, laying her carefully and skilfully in the crook of her arm.

There is no better society than babies and sick people for one another. Florence Nightingale never had any children and yet she recognised the healing power of new life and hope. And for that reason, Evelyn felt sure that whatever it was she'd lost would turn up eventually.

35

Situation Vacant

HENRY DIDN'T APPEAR ON THAT LAST MORNING, AS *ORCADES* changed course and slipped almost silently past the Heads towards Sydney Harbour. After four weeks at sea, leaving behind London and the ghosts of war, the ship was finally stable in the placid waters of Port Jackson, and yet I felt strangely off balance again. My ears had adjusted to the movement of the ship as Dr Parker had predicted, and I'd fallen asleep on that last night to the contented murmurs of the bulkheads.

It was impossible to see past the crowds lining the decks, eager for a first glimpse of their new lives in Australia. All the years that had come before, and the adventure of a whole month at sea cast aside, discarded. Ahead of the travel-weary passengers, their new lives awaited, as welcoming as freshly laundered sheets on a turned-down bed.

There was no sign of Henry at the quiet aft end where we'd accidentally bumped into each other almost every morning of the voyage. He was a busy man and I imagined him hunched over his desk preparing his voyage report to send back to head office in London, or counting pills, or whatever doctors did when they approached the final port. As the harbour came into view, insecurity took the place of the excitement and optimism that had been building during the long journey from London.

I remembered Dr Parker's comments that had haunted me since the night of my twenty-first birthday. I felt foolish. I, a naïve young woman, had been little more than a distraction, amusement for the male crew to relieve the tedium of a long journey. Pleasant as our time together had been, the ship would soon be heading back to England, and a new crop of passengers would fill the cabins and entertain the single officers. And the chief officer and the ship's doctor would once again compete for the prettiest girl and her best friend.

The first glimpse of the Sydney Harbour Bridge off the starboard side sent the crowds rushing for a better view. Instead of elation, my stomach became tighter and smaller, mirroring the shrinking moments of the voyage. Here was Sydney and the life I'd dreamed of. Away from the smog and ration-strangled England, Australia was a bright and vibrant country full of hope and opportunity. And yet I willed the ship to slow, willed the voyage to continue.

There were twelve thousand miles between the girl who'd run away and the woman soon to arrive. Time had stood still long enough for me to catch up. I'd come of age on this journey. I'd finally found myself in the sea.

'Quite beautiful.' I heard a man's voice. I knew without turning who was standing behind me. 'No matter how many times I see her, she always takes my breath away,' he said.

'I take it you're referring to the Harbour Bridge, Dr Parker?' My heart quickened before I gave it permission to.

'Naturally.'

'How strange to refer to such a feat of solid mechanical engineering as *she*.'

I sensed Dr Parker move closer, picturing him in his uniform and cap, imagining his warm breath mixing with the sea breezes that whipped along the decks and down the back of my neck.

'Sailors, for all their uncouthness, have always appreciated beauty, Miss Des Roches. Take the elegance of a ship in full sail. How could something so magnificent not be thought of in the same way as a woman?'

'Is that why ships are always referred to as *she*?'

Dr Parker brushed aside a strand of hair from the nape of my neck. I wanted him to kiss me there, to feel his lips like the beat of butterfly wings against my skin. Twenty-one and never been kissed.

'I would say so, but sailors are by nature a superstitious bunch and many have looked to their ship to nurture and protect them against the sea and the elements, like a mother. The sea is strong and beautiful but can turn and drown a man in a breath.'

'I have read that women are considered bad luck on a ship.'

'Once upon a time, perhaps. Less enlightened sailors feared a woman on board would anger the sea gods and cause bad weather and rough seas.'

'In your experience, do they still believe that?'

We were facing each other now. I studied the extraordinary colour of his eyes, the angle of his jaw, a small red mark where he'd cut himself shaving, one lock of rusty fringe touching his eyebrow. The harbour must have slipped by, one landmark at a time – Bradleys Head, Garden Island and Fort Macquarie Tram Depot – yet I saw nothing but the flare of amber around Dr Parker's irises.

'I think most sailors welcome a benevolent feminine spirit to bring a ship good luck.'

'Is that why ships have a godmother?'

'Quite so, and why we launch a ship by breaking a bottle of champagne over the bow.'

'It seems a waste of good champagne, Dr Parker.'

'It is an offering to the gods of the sea, like Poseidon. A bit like offering a bride.'

A bride? I was taken aback. I knew very little about Greek mythology, but recognised Poseidon as a first-rate cad who'd had more than his fair share of consorts. Hadn't he even assumed the shape of a stallion to seduce Demeter, the goddess of mares? My hackles rose.

'Is that how you view women, Dr Parker? As some sort of lucky charm or talisman for a safe sea crossing?'

I was piqued. I'd allowed myself to be seduced by the idea of Dr Parker as an educated modern man who read Coleridge and Kipling and complimented me on my sketches, when in reality he was entirely typical of his generation and countless generations before. Clearly he saw a woman as purely decorative and her rightful place in the kitchen, the perfect housewife with a choice between Suntone Yellow or Corinth Pink formica units. Women had come so far, first in winning the vote and then in capably taking over jobs in factories and on the land while the men were away fighting in two world wars. And for what? To find ourselves back where we started, dreaming of a new refrigerator or vacuum cleaner?

'You underestimate me, Miss Des Roches. I am a man of the sea but for me a bride would be a partner, not a commodity. I happen to believe in marriage as a lifetime union, but one that should only be entered into with a full understanding of the risks and benefits.'

'Risks and benefits? You make it sound like a hernia repair.'

'I'd say it is more akin to a career.'

'A career? You see marriage in terms of a job contract?'

'Quite so. In fact, I happen to know that there is currently a vacancy for such a post aboard this very ship.'

'The ship's assistant surgeon is looking for a wife?'

'Quite so, Miss Des Roches.'

The ship was rapidly approaching the Harbour Bridge. I could sense the looming girders that spanned between the sandstone pillars, just as I'd pictured. That mass of riveted steel signified the end of one journey and the beginning of a completely different one.

Dr Henry Parker continued. 'The successful candidate would have a very different life to the one she had planned. It would mean giving up her own career, whatever that might be. She would need to be resilient and resourceful, adaptable and independent. She would be the rudder that keeps me on course. It would mean months away from home. A life in a tiny cabin with next to no wardrobe space, living in close proximity to two thousand other people. There'd be bad weather and seasickness, homesickness and never a place to escape. I would be called away at all hours, at the beck and call of the other crew and passengers. She would have to put up with attractive women throwing themselves at my uniform, and most of all she'd have to put up with me, every day.'

I took a deep breath. 'That's quite a job proposal, Dr Parker.'

'And when we had children, she would need to cope single-handed while I was away.'

'What makes you think I'd want to apply?' I already had a job lined up, a new life waiting for me, one I could almost see approaching on the near horizon. It was one I'd had my heart set on since I was a little girl, a life of independence, where my opinion counted. Was I really considering a life in a gilded cage like my mother?

Dr Henry Parker regarded me from behind his salt-encrusted lenses. 'Nothing,' he said. 'I was just hoping, that's all.'

Overhead, the sky turned to steel and the eerie silence to gasps of human awe as *Orcades* slipped under the Harbour Bridge, her pale grey smoke reaching up to touch its suspended metal beams. Two feats of human engineering, each bowing to the other. Henry's words echoed with the snap of hundreds of camera shutters. I ducked as the funnel cleared the bridge with room to spare. And we both laughed. When Dr Henry Parker took my hand, I no longer felt the teak deck beneath my feet. My body was air.

In a few moments the bridge was retreating over the stern and the impossible blue of the sky appeared once more overhead. Past Luna Park, *Orcades* sailed on towards the wharf at Pyrmont, the shore approaching so fast after the indolence of the past four weeks.

Two plucky black-bottomed tugs pulled the twenty-eight thousand tons of hull and steam turbines towards the edge of the young country. It wasn't too late to change course and head back out to sea. Unconstrained by rails or tracks, a ship was free to make her own unhurried way, at one with the wind and the waves. Free to make her own choices.

36

Mal de Debarquement

With her lucky right foot, Evelyn stepped off the deck of *Golden Sunset* and onto the gangway. She conceded to Nola's arm for support, but with the gangway too narrow for three abreast, Frank followed in close procession, then a man in an open-necked shirt pushing the deckchair-on-wheels.

Crew lined the promenade deck, all waving and shouting farewells over the railings. Every colour of skin and uniform, every number of stripes, all clapping and cheering. Evelyn waved back demurely. It was an extraordinary send-off, considering she would return in a few hours. Off to see young Dobbs in the city, then back in time for a quick cup of tea before lifeboat drill. She had a good feeling about today. Her shoes were more comfortable than usual and Evelyn had the idea she could keep walking, as far as was necessary.

The chauffeur trotted off to collect his car, leaving Evelyn with Frank and Nola on the kerbside. Nola was chattering, her words wrapping around Evelyn like a warm blanket. Frank stared wistfully over her head. Evelyn concentrated very hard on staying upright, the ground rocking beneath her walking-as-far-as-necessary shoes. The ship stood regally alongside the dock behind them, and yet Evelyn still felt the movement of the ocean beneath the concrete. A sudden squall of nausea blew in, as it had when she'd set foot on *Orcades* on her very first voyage, and she waited for her sea legs to become land legs once more.

Several minutes passed before a long black car pulled up next to them.

'Is this my hearse?' said Evelyn, flinching from her pale reflection in the shiny windows.

At that, Nola burst into tears. 'Oh, Mrs P,' she said, wiping her nose across one wrist. 'I'm going to miss you.'

'I'll be back in time for tea,' said Evelyn, not sure what all the fuss was about.

Frank had brimming eyes too. He sniffed a couple of times before grasping Evelyn by the shoulders and kissing her on one cheek. 'Nola's right. We're going to miss you,' he said.

Nola moved in for a kiss too, wetting the other cheek. Evelyn wiped away the moistness discreetly with the monogrammed handkerchief she found lodged beneath the wristband of her watch.

'This has been a truly memorable holiday,' said Nola. 'I can't thank you enough for making it so special for us, for all your wonderful stories . . .'

'For teaching us so much about ships . . .'

'And seasickness, let's not forget the *mal de mer*, Frank.'

'Samuel Coleridge and Florence Nightingale.'

'Don't forget Sister Pugh.'

'And Grace and little Eve.'

Evelyn was relieved when the chauffeur interrupted the rollcall. She couldn't remember his name, but he seemed nice enough. He reminded her of someone she'd once known. He loaded Evelyn's miniature-suitcase-on-wheels into the car and opened the passenger door for her.

'There's something else I need to thank you for,' said Nola, now almost strangling Evelyn with her arms in an embrace. 'Remember I told you that Frank and I have always wanted to go to Alaska?'

'Always wanted to go to Alaska,' parroted Frank over her shoulder.

'Well,' continued Nola, 'Frank used the last of our internet credit on board and booked us a cruise to Alaska! And next year, we're off to see the Panama Canal.'

'Did I tell you about the time—' Evelyn was interrupted by a sob into her left ear.

'And Mrs P, it's all down to you.'

'All down to you,' said Frank into Evelyn's right ear.

'Yes, you showed me that there is plenty of life left to live. I lost my purpose after we lost Vera. I thought that was it, that life was heading the same way for me and Frank. I saw us fading away, spending the rest of our days watching television and letting our tea go cold. But that's before I discovered mindful colouring-in, and before you opened our eyes to cruising.'

Evelyn wasn't sure who Vera was, or whether Frank-and-Nola had ever found her. She wished them well on their search.

'Travel safely, Mrs P.'

'Bon voyage, Mrs Parker.'

They were still waving when the chauffeur closed the passenger door and pulled away from the kerb with a toot. Soon they were out into the sunshine and heading through the maze of city streets. Evelyn tried to stay alert, to concentrate on where they were going. The endless stop-start of traffic lights and junctions and diversions hindered their progress. The traffic soon snarled and the car idled in a gridlock. The connections in Evelyn's brain had come grinding to a halt too. It was time to switch off her engine.

The leather seats of the hearse were soft and cushiony against Evelyn's spine, and though she didn't know where they were going, she felt safe. Safer than she had felt in a long time. Safe enough to close her eyes as the car rode the waves of an invisible ocean.

'Mother,' said a voice. 'We're here.'

There was a crick in Evelyn's neck when she woke and her chin was damp with saliva. It took a moment to work out she was inside a car.

A man smiled at her from the driver's seat. Evelyn wondered if they had met somewhere before.

'Where am I?'

'*Home.* You're home.'

37

The Ancient Mariner

THE FIRST BUTTON LOWERED THE CAR WINDOW; THE SECOND blasted Evelyn with cold air. The quick-release handle sent her knees crashing into the dashboard. A watertight door was easier to escape through than a car door.

The chauffeur was vaguely familiar. He opened the passenger door from the outside but Evelyn brushed away his attempts to help her out of the hearse. She wasn't dead yet.

'I can manage,' she snapped. On seeing his face crumple, she added, 'But you can help me with this.' Evelyn passed him her handbag. It was quite heavy and for some reason it wouldn't close properly. She couldn't imagine how she'd managed to accumulate so many essentials.

They'd parked under the sprawling limbs of a Moreton Bay fig and the air was surprisingly cool in the giant tree's shade. Evelyn shivered. To her right, a carpet of velvet lawn reached towards what looked like a cliff edge. Beyond, a wedge of ocean sparkled between the trees. To her left, overlooking the water, stood a handsome house, its large sandstone façade blushing in the morning sun.

A well-groomed middle-aged woman appeared next to the vaguely-familiar-chauffeur. She wore a uniform but no epaulettes or stripes.

'Are you the travel agent?' Evelyn asked, looking her up and down.

'I'm Wendy Jenkins, the director of nursing.' She extended her hand.

'Mrs Henry Parker,' replied Evelyn, shaking the damp hand then wiping her palm down her skirt. *Director of nursing*. At a country house hotel? Whatever next?

'Would you like us to call you Evelyn or Mrs Parker?'

'Neither,' replied Evelyn, sniffing. 'I'm not staying. The ship sails at five.'

Evelyn set off across the grass towards the ocean, stopping at the edge of what turned out to be a sweeping lawn rather than a cliff face. A pair of seagulls circled overhead. They weren't the noisy boisterous herring gulls that had farewelled the *Orcades* at Tilbury docks, but more serene birds who seemed content to glide on the thermals enjoying the view.

'Is this where you put people in the big bubble and push them off?' said Evelyn, eyeing the slope.

'Only if they misbehave.'

Evelyn studied the woman's face, and decided that she wore a wry smile rather than any real malevolence.

'Only I brought my bathing suit,' Evelyn said, peering over the edge, her heart quickening at the thought of the ride down the hill in the giant plastic ball.

'Why don't you come inside and have a cup of tea first, then we can talk about the activities.' The woman turned to the hearse driver. 'I'll send the porter for the luggage.'

Evelyn snatched back her handbag. She didn't want a strange man touching her essentials.

The woman-who-wasn't-the-travel-agent after all led the way across the crunchy gravel towards the hotel. Evelyn heard but couldn't feel what was beneath her feet. There was something wrong with them, something that made the sharp little stones feel like cottonwool under her soles. It had a name, this condition. It would come to her.

'A cup of tea would be lovely, and perhaps a sandwich,' said Evelyn as she climbed the smooth stone steps at the front of the hotel. There was a ramp adjacent with a grippy rubber surface. It was nice to see they catered for old people too.

'We have three acres of gardens and, as you can see, the most amazing ocean views.' The woman seemed genuinely impressed with her view. Evelyn was less so. It was rather disappointing after being on a ship, on the actual ocean. But she didn't want to be rude.

'Amazing,' said Evelyn, unamazed.

She followed the woman into the entrance hall of the hotel. It took a few moments for her eyes to adjust to the light and take in the tall ceilings and sweeping Edwardian staircase. Dozens of paintings adorned the walls, ships of all sizes and ages, from old steamships and transatlantic liners to cruise ships and modern bulk carriers. It must be some sort of themed hotel, thought Evelyn. Sunset Cruises were obviously trying it out and she must be their secret shopper.

The chauffeur had followed them. He stood expectantly, looking at Evelyn. 'Well?' he said.

Embarrassed, Evelyn began to rummage in her handbag. She'd never had to carry cash before, a little like the Queen.

'I'm most terribly sorry,' she said, handing him the carved wooden turtles. 'I don't think they're awfully valuable but they might cover the fare. I'll have to owe you the difference.'

The vaguely-familiar-chauffeur looked sad and handed back the turtles. Evelyn was worried the hearse had cost more than she'd anticipated.

'What do you think?' he said. 'Is it what you expected?'

'It depends. I'll withhold my opinion until I've tasted the sandwiches.'

The woman-who-wasn't-the-travel-agent thought this very funny. The chauffeur looked as if he'd just read how to put on a brave face in the instruction manual.

'I'm sure you're going to be very happy here, Mother,' he said.

Evelyn was about to chastise his impudent familiarity when she noticed something on the wall behind the reception desk. She inched closer. Even without the glasses she didn't need, she could read the brass letters on the wooden plaque.

The Dreadnought Home for Retired Seafarers.

Evelyn's knees unlocked. She was a marionette and someone had snipped her strings.

A deckchair appeared from behind and the next thing she knew she was being wheeled along a narrow passageway. Evelyn tried to focus on the paintings and decorative memorabilia displayed on mahogany tables, but the effort of keeping up with the passing scenery made her feel nauseated. Like counting telegraph poles on a train. The same feeling she had experienced when *Orcades* hit the Bay of Biscay.

Evelyn's head spun. She tried to steady it with her hands. What was this place and what was she doing here? She was lost inside a vast and featureless place that used to be her brain. She was all at sea.

'Here we are, Mrs Parker. This is your room.' The woman knocked softly then entered the room, holding the door open for the deckchair-on-wheels.

The light blinded Evelyn and she had to shield her eyes from the glare of the sun reflecting off the ocean beyond the big bay windows. As her eyeballs began to relax, she sensed a familiarity, not with the place but with some of the objects in the room. She couldn't settle on each individually but the sum of the parts added up to a sense of unexpected intimacy.

She felt a hand on her shoulder. It was the vaguely-familiar-chauffeur. Evelyn followed his gaze across the room to a tall-backed armchair positioned to make the best of the view. She could just make out the top of a white head over the top of the studded leather chair.

'I'm terribly sorry,' said Evelyn, 'I think there's been some sort of mistake.'

The vaguely-familiar-chauffeur was crying again. Perhaps the fare had been more than she thought.

Then a scent hit her nostrils and travelled around her body until it settled in her chest, urging her heartbeat to quicken, transporting Evelyn to another time and another place.

Citrus, spice, wood and leather. And the ocean.

She flicked the deckchair's resting-feet-plates aside with her finding-something-important shoes and pushed herself up with shaking arms. Evelyn couldn't feel the carpet beneath her feet as she approached the armchair. She was floating above it.

His face was melted down one side, as if the man had been left by the fire too long but had tried to disguise it with a wispy beard. He raised one wobbly arm in greeting.

'E . . . Evelyn.'

Hot tears ran down the ravine at the side of Evelyn's nose. She knew this man. She'd been away from him for so long.

'Father?' she said, her voice barely more than a whisper. 'Is it really you?'

Evelyn tried to recall her father's face but saw only a middle-aged face, the first silver creeping into his hair. This wasn't the clean-shaven father she remembered. He was dead. The smog had stolen the air from his lungs a long time ago.

The man beckoned. 'Evelyn,' he said again, tears in his rheumy eyes. 'It's me.'

Evelyn began to recite the words she'd committed to memory over sixty years ago. They were as fresh and sharp as a newly minted page of text.

The Mariner, whose eye is bright,
Whose beard with age is hoar.

'Henry,' she said. 'I've found you at last.'

38

Swimming with the Turtles

YET AGAIN, THERE WAS A MAN IN EVELYN'S BED. IT WASN'T the first time she'd woken up next to a complete stranger – in fact, it had become such a regular occurrence over the past weeks or possibly months that she refrained from screaming and instead lay studying the sleeping man.

He didn't look like an axe murderer or rapist, more like a senescent Santa Claus. One side of his face was corrugated with wrinkles and creases, the other strangely smooth, as though they belonged to two different people. Evelyn reached over and touched his cheek with a curly finger, tracing the whiskers that sprouted from his jaw.

The man opened his eyes, the muscles around his amber-flecked irises constricting like a camera lens to bring her into focus.

'Good morning,' he said as though he'd woken up next to her every day of his life.

Evelyn tried to stay calm. His breath was sour but his voice was as warm and familiar as slippers.

'Who are you?'

'Clark Gable,' the man answered.

'What a lucky girl I am,' said Evelyn, feeling a smile form on her lips.

'I'm the lucky one,' said Clark Gable. He brushed the side of Evelyn's face with a knotty thumb. 'Still as beautiful as ever.'

Evelyn mock-shooed him. 'Be off with you.'

The tide returned with her memories, and Henry. She stroked his beard.

'Do you like it?' Henry jutted his chin, lifting his head a fraction off the pillow.

'No,' Evelyn replied. 'It makes you look old.'

'I *am* old. Don't you think it makes me look distinguished?'

'You look like the wreck of the Hesperus! Besides, it's terribly unhygienic.'

Henry feigned outrage before his lopsided face softened once more. 'Michael bought me a new razor, but I vowed I wouldn't shave until you joined me here.'

'What are you talking about? Your razor is on the shelf in the bathroom where you left it. You're just getting lazy in your old age.'

Henry squeezed her hand beneath the bedclothes. Chilly fingers around chilly fingers. 'I'm sorry you had to go through all that, finding me after I collapsed in the bathroom. It must have given you such a fright. And if it hadn't been for young Dr Johansson acting so swiftly, arranging the medivac from the ship, well . . .'

A tear spilled from Henry's eye and soaked into the pillow-case. Evelyn searched the lined face that was like an ordnance survey map of his life's travels, and tried to be patient. He often talked gibberish, making up all sorts of stories. About how he'd suddenly lost consciousness and hit his head. Apparently it had been touch and go, and everyone had prepared for the worst. How he'd spent weeks in hospital and then rehab where she'd reportedly visited every turnaround day, sitting at his bedside, reciting passages from Coleridge. He'd written letters to her, he said, explaining that they were on the waiting list for a double room at the Dreadnought Home for Retired Seafarers. One, he'd insisted, that had an ocean view. In the letters Henry had reassured her that it wouldn't be long until they were reunited for good, that it was best she stayed on *Golden Sunset* – at home – until all the arrangements were finalised.

Evelyn felt as though she'd listened to the same story over and over again. Henry was getting repetitive in his old age. She'd read somewhere that people with dementia often made up stories to plug the gaps in their memories. It had a name. Confabulation. Yes, that was it. She'd tried to correct him but in the end she let it go. Whatever the truth, wherever he'd been, all that mattered was that they were together again.

Evelyn reached for the handkerchief under her wristband and mopped his tear-streaked cheek. 'I've been meaning to return this,' she said. She refolded it and pushed the white cotton square beneath Henry's pillow.

A sudden burst of sunlight made them both squint. Evelyn levered herself up on one elbow to see a woman in uniform throwing back the heavy curtains at the bay window.

'Good morning,' said the woman breezily. 'It's a beautiful day.'

Evelyn tried to recall if she'd left the *Do Not Disturb* sign on the cabin door last night. 'Where's Virgilio?' she said.

The breezy woman ignored her. 'Breakfast will be along any minute,' she said.

'Did we order room service?' Evelyn looked at Henry.

'It's all included,' he said. 'Every morning. What a treat.'

Evelyn wasn't sure she appreciated the intrusion. She preferred the cabin stewards to be more discreet, on hand when she needed and otherwise invisible. She snorted her derision.

The breezy woman hummed as she opened the largest of the windows. 'There you go. Nothing like a bit of fresh air.'

When a cool breeze reached Evelyn, she shivered in her thin nightdress and pulled the bedclothes up to her chin. 'Would you mind closing that porthole?'

'Now, now, Mrs Parker, doors are for closing, windows are for opening.'

'I think you'll find Florence Nightingale's exact quote is: *Windows are made to open; doors are made to shut – a truth which seems extremely difficult of apprehension.*'

Henry chortled beside her and said, 'You are really the most extraordinary woman, Mrs Parker.'

The breezy woman appeared on Henry's side of the bed with an enormous mechanical contraption that looked like a cross between a crane and one of those exercise machines from the gymnasium. With a skilled and practised motion, he was out of bed and airborne, transferred to the reclining armchair overlooking the bay window. He looked frail in his striped pyjamas, his shrivelled arm and clawed hand at odds with Evelyn's mental picture of her husband in his uniform. The one she always saw in her memories.

Evelyn swung her own legs out of bed, her feet finding a pair of rubber-soled shoes with laces on the carpet. It was quite a nice carpet. In blue. It matched the bedspread perfectly. Evelyn was pleased the ship had had such a tasteful refit this time. She pulled on her *Golden Sunset* waffle dressing-gown and shuffled to join Henry in an identical armchair facing the window.

Evelyn leaned back and lifted her feet in the air for a closer look. She couldn't remember buying the strange white shoes and they weren't her usual style.

'Do you like the shoes? I hope I chose the right size.'

'They're exceedingly comfortable,' she conceded. 'They're perfect for my peripheral neuropathy,' she said, the name of the thing with her feet slipping off her tongue without the slightest hesitation.

'Now listen to you,' said the breezy lady as she plumped the pillows on the bed. 'You sound like a medical textbook, Mrs Parker.' Her cheeks were unusually red in an odd pattern that spread across the bridge of her nose.

When she'd gone, Henry said, 'Were you thinking what I was thinking? I spy with my little eye a diagnosis beginning with L.'

'The classic butterfly rash of lupus.'

'Spot on, Sister Parker. I'll have a discreet word and suggest she discusses it with her doctor.'

They sat in silence, basking drowsily in the warmth of the early morning sun. A line of photographs on the windowsill told the story of their extraordinary lives, one freeze-frame moment at a time. On beaches and in ancient cities, smiling on glaciers and beside lakes. Then Kodachrome snaps of a baby wearing a knitted matinee jacket growing into a small boy then a young man who looked like the vaguely-familiar-chauffeur who often visited. And Evelyn, a young woman growing into an old lady flanked by a rosy-cheeked woman with happy teeth and a serious but kind-looking man with sunspots. In some of them, Henry. In all of them, smiles.

'Who is this?' Evelyn picked up a loose colour photograph that was leaning against one of the frames. Peering through the magnifying glass that she'd found lying between the frames, she studied the vivid colours that had caught her eye beside the fading shots of her past.

It was a photograph of a single-storey brick building with a pitched roof. The grass and low trees surrounding the building were lush and green, red hibiscus flowers dotting the low canopy. Standing in front of the building was a young woman in a white nurse's uniform, grinning at the camera. She had almond-shaped eyes and skin the colour of burnt umber. A chubby-thighed baby, face framed by a mop-head of dark curls, sat astride her hip. She was flanked by several other women in uniform, all squinting in the bright sun at the photographer.

'That's Grace and baby Eve,' said Henry, with a patience that hinted at an old and well-trodden story. 'Remember?'

Evelyn looked to Henry for more words of explanation. She couldn't think why this woman and her child were special, but she knew they were.

'How do I know them?'

'You delivered Grace's baby on the ship. Now she's training to be a midwife. She's the first recipient of the Evelyn Parker Midwifery Scholarship.'

'I always wanted to be a midwife,' said Evelyn. She searched for mental images of handing slippery infants to their mothers, of washing and drying and weighing newborn babies, of snapping photographs of beaming parents, but found only a wafer-thin memory of holding a wrinkled baby to her own breast and smiling for a camera. With Henry.

Henry reached for one of the many photo frames arranged on the table. Three young nurses, their arms linked. He handed it to Evelyn. 'This was taken in 1958, on the day you graduated from King George V Hospital. As a midwife, Evelyn. You were a midwife. Then Michael came along a year later, and with a husband away at sea you had to choose between your career and motherhood.'

In her dressing-gown pocket, Evelyn found a small knitted bootie. Just as she was slowly letting go of the present, the past was slipping away too. Her memories were little more than distorted echoes of events long ago. She couldn't choose which to hold on to and which to let go. Today, like ancient snowflakes packed together to make the celestial blue of the glacier; tomorrow, gone, calved back into the ocean.

The sea was calm outside, although Evelyn still felt the rocking motion. She'd adapt eventually. In the meantime, the sun was already promising a scorcher, and she and Henry had the whole day to themselves.

After breakfast, they would walk a brick, a soldier, a button and a marble around the promenade deck, stopping at their usual spot for a cup of tea and a game of *I Spy a Diagnosis*.

When the sun went down, they'd dress for dinner. Wearing her mother's tiara, Evelyn would straighten Henry's bow tie while he patted his cheeks with Acqua di Parma and fastened her zip. If they were lucky, they would watch the sun set over the starboard horizon and come home to find a heart-shaped chocolate waiting on each pillow. Weary, they'd close their eyes and let the ocean rock them to sleep, side by side.

And in her dreams Evelyn would always return to a pristine white beach where the sand felt soft between her toes and Henry's hand was warm in hers.

Acknowledgements

First and foremost, my sincere thanks to the talented and enthusiastic publishing team at Hachette Australia, namely Alex Craig, Rebecca Saunders, Fiona Hazard, Alana Kelly and Sarah Holmes, and to Kimberley Atkins, Thorne Ryan and her team at Hodder & Stoughton in the UK.

Thank you to Karen Ward, Julia Stiles and Kate Goldsworthy for keeping track of Mrs Henry Parker's wandering mind and reining in mine. I always feel I'm in safe hands with such skilled editors.

Heartfelt thanks go to my agent, Haylee Nash, and mentor, Valerie Parv, who encouraged me to trust my instincts and tell this story from the heart.

To my writing group: Pamela Cook, Michelle Barraclough, Penelope Janu, Rae Cairns, Laura Boon Russell, Terri Green and Angella Whitton, thank you for your collective wisdom, encouragement and friendship.

I am extremely grateful to the various professionals who fielded random queries about everything from nautical terminology and officers' uniforms to the history of women at sea. To Tony Draper, Matthew Nell, Jo Stanley, and Rob McLaren from Miller Rayner: I truly appreciate your time and expertise. To Linda Moffatt at the Vaughan Evans Library, thank you for unearthing just the right books and untangling my microfiche.

The following books proved an invaluable resource during the writing of this book: *From Cabin 'Boys' to Captains: 250 Years of Women at Sea* by Doctor Jo Stanley, published by The History Press, and *Seafaring Lore & Legend* by Peter D. Jeans, published by McGraw-Hill.

I would like to acknowledge the use of lines from *The Rime of The Ancient Mariner* by Samuel Taylor Coleridge (1772–1834) and 'The Exiles' Line' by Rudyard Kipling (1865–1936). The traditional seafarers' hymn 'Eternal Father, Strong to Save' was written in 1860 by William Whiting, inspired by Psalm 107. Furthermore, I acknowledge the use of passages from Florence Nightingale's seminal work *Notes on Nursing, What It Is and What It Is Not*, published in 1859. Widely accepted as the founder of modern nursing, Florence Nightingale inspired the young Evelyn and countless others to pursue a career in nursing, and her teachings have doubtless saved the lives of millions.

This book is dedicated to Stretch, the handsome Second Engineer officer who swept me off my feet aboard MV *Royal Princess* all those years ago. Thank you for your love, laughter and support (and for your attention to detail in all things technical). Our voyage together continues.

To my children: William, I am so proud that you are following in Dad's footsteps and look forward to seeing you wearing your mending-the-engine stripes one day. Charlotte, thank you for your patience, your sense of humour and for not rolling your eyes too often.

In essence, this book is a tribute to all ships' doctors and nurses, the unsung heroes and heroines who treat everything from seasickness to life-threatening medical emergencies, often in the most challenging of situations, with skill and dedication. This story was inspired by the adventures and camaraderie that made my own brief years at sea among the most memorable of my career, and for that opportunity I have to thank Dr Jason Reddy.

Finally, to my alleged Spanish Armada ancestors who survived their shipwreck in 1588: I'm so relieved the swimming lessons paid off.

When one book ends, another begins...

Bookends is a vibrant new reading community to help you ensure you're never without a good book.

You'll find exclusive previews of the brilliant new books from your favourite authors as well as exciting debuts and past classics. Read our blog, check out our recommendations for your reading group, enter great competitions and much more!

Visit our website to see which great books we're recommending this month.

Join the Bookends community:
www.welcometobookends.co.uk

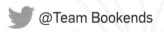 @Team Bookends 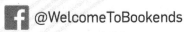 @WelcomeToBookends